AS SURE AS THE SUN

AN ACCIDENTAL ROOTS NOVEL

ELLE KEATON

DIRTY DOG PRESS

Dirty Dog Press
Seattle, WA 98118

As Sure As The Sun (Accidental Roots 4)
Copyright 2017 by Elle Keaton
Edited by Alicia Z. Ramos

Cover design: Cate Ashwood

❀ Created with Vellum

ACKNOWLEDGMENTS

Thank you, *everyone*.

To my children, Zoë and Harper who have been incredibly patient, and encouraging, through this endeavor, as well as being my most enthusiastic cheerleaders. I love you so much.

To my friends who both vocally and silently support me.

To Erik who is amazing.

To my editor, Alicia Ramos, who edited the heck out of this manuscript, checked facts and made certain I didn't stray too far. Any errors are mine alone. Alicia probably tried to talk me out of them, yet I insisted. Again and again.

Lastly and most importantly, thank you readers for actually *wanting* to read things I make up.

The town of Skagit exists *only* in my imagination as well as the wonderful people who inhabit it, any similarity to real people or places is coincidental.

This book is a work of fiction and should be treated as such. I certainly exerted my creative license with some details regarding the timeline of the Bosnia war, a few other things only exist in my imagination; the court house in Winthrop, the sanatorium and assisted living facility in Wenatchee.

ONE

"Bolic."

Sacha glanced in the direction Rick was pointing. Their target slipped out from between some loose pieces of plywood covering the doorway, gesturing with his free hand while he talked on a cell phone. The man saw Sacha, and his eyes widened for an instant before he turned and bolted in the opposite direction.

Sacha took off after the government's prize witness against the US boss of the Molejevic crime family, keeping his prey's flashy red parka in view. He heard Rick shout something but couldn't quite make out the words. As he ran, he gave thanks that Jacobsen looked like a Ross Dress for Less clearance rack had thrown up on him. He and Rick had spent two days freezing their asses off waiting for Jacobsen to show. No way was Sacha going to lose him now. His knee twinged, threatening retribution as he pushed himself faster; he ignored it.

Jacobsen was no Usain Bolt but he knew the neighborhood better than Rick or Sacha, plus the streets were slick from intermittent rain showers and Sacha had to avoid slipping on metal sewer and electric access points as well as litter and unidentifiables. The rain started spattering down again. In moments, Sacha's hair was plastered to his head and rivulets of rain ran down his face made it hard to see. Still, he had almost gained enough ground to grab the back of Jacobsen's jacket when the man took a sharp left into a tiny alley.

The stench of past-due trash rose up around Sacha. He forced down a reflexive gag as he sped down the dark, narrow space between two brick buildings. It was dank and barely wide enough for two men to walk side by side. Sacha was big enough to feel claustrophobic as he pounded after Jacobsen, losing a little ground because a trash container loomed from the shadows, forcing him to slow down. Jacobsen glanced over his shoulder at Sacha and grinned. Putting on a burst of speed, their uncooperative witness leapt to catch the bottom rung of a sketchy-looking fire escape and began to clamber up it with familiarity.

Using the brick wall to push off, Sacha leapt for the fire escape, barely grabbing hold of the grimy metal bar. Praying to any possible saints of US Marshals, he hoisted himself upward, hoping the flimsy, weathered metal would support his weight. Sacha's prayer held for a few seconds into the climb when two things happened. The first was an ominous creaking that echoed up and down the alley, along with the earsplitting shriek of metal on metal. The second was the silhouette of a large-caliber handgun appearing from a window several stories above him. Fingers flexed on the trigger as Sacha lunged to his right, leaping off the fire escape... except that it followed him, peeling away from the brick wall it had formerly been attached to.

This was going to hurt.

His stomach lurched, and for the briefest moment he was weightless before gravity came calling. All the air left his lungs when he hit the top of the old recycling container. He sort of bounced and, unfortunately, rolled off onto the concrete underneath the now-defunct fire escape. Flakes of rust, pelting rain, and litter that until that moment had been lodged for God knew how long in the metal grating of the fire escape showered down around him, on him. In a kind of slow motion he had only read about, the fire escape creaked to the right and smashed into the brick wall opposite. More rusty flakes showered down, along with pieces of the old metal structure itself.

Sacha lay where he'd fallen, trying to suck a few molecules of oxygen into his lungs, thanking fuck for the fire escape collapsing under his weight. If it hadn't chosen that moment to disintegrate, rather than reconsidering his life and most especially his career choices, Sacha would be a dead man with a hole in his head the size of a fist. The weighty mass of the forty-caliber bullet displacing the atmosphere alongside his ear was as close as Sacha wanted to get to death today.

Groaning, he rolled over and craned his head toward the window Jacobsen had disappeared into. There had only been the single gunshot. Sacha didn't know if the guy had actually been trying to kill him or was simply trying to get him to stop following. Regardless, whoever it had been was going to be extremely sorry he opened fire on an officer of the law.

His partner, who hadn't been right behind him, came panting around the corner. Rick's searching gaze landed on Sacha where he lay in the stinking trash and dog... or possibly human... shit behind the derelict building their perp had disappeared into. Sacha thought even Sig Jacobsen should have had better taste than this place. Fuck, rats had better taste.

"Fucking hell." Sacha rolled onto his hands and knees, pushing himself to his feet. Every one of his thirty-nine years was making itself known. By some kind of miracle he'd merely had the wind knocked out of him and would have some impressive bruises tomorrow from hitting the trash container, but nothing felt broken. His knee throbbed, threatening imminent collapse, but after a second he was able to ignore it. Rick, the prissy asshole, didn't bother to offer a hand, and when he got close enough he wrinkled his nose.

"Where the fuck were you?" Sacha brushed at unnamable bits stuck to his jacket and jeans without much result. Giving up, he unzipped his jacket, took it off, and dropped it to the ground beside him. Sacha didn't care that he was shivering in the forty-degree weather and getting wetter by the minute as the rain increased in intensity.

"I was a little behind you. I tried cutting through to the other side when he turned." Rick brushed nonexistent grime off his suit jacket.

"You know, to head him off. But the other end was blocked. I had to turn around and come back." Sacha forced aside the urge to grab Rick by the neck and throttle him. They had been after Jacobsen for weeks, and now the guy had vanished into thin air. "Oh, wow, Bolic, you landed in—"

"I know what I fucking landed in," Sacha ground out. "I could have been fucking killed. Did you see the shooter?"

Rick looked around, like he was going to see the shooter waving for his attention from a nearby window. Sacha had been lying in non-metaphorical shit for several minutes, checking all his parts to make sure they worked properly. The shooter was long gone, and Sacha was going to be hellishly sore for a few days. "You know what? Never fucking mind."

They walked back to their car in stony silence, abandoning Sacha's jacket in the alley. Rick knew better than to try and talk to Sacha when he was in a shit mood. Which was most of the time.

When Sacha had returned to regular service after two brutal years undercover, he'd hoped the transition would be easier than going under. Not so far. He took a deep breath, immediately regretting it when his side hitched, searching for patience he wasn't known for. It wouldn't help his case if he ripped Rick a new one... in public, anyway.

Since returning to duty in February, Sacha had been assigned three partners. The first lasted a single retrieval before demanding a change, claiming *insurmountable personality differences*. What the fuck ever. The second lasted three weeks before digging up a reason not to work with Sacha ever again. The kid had been witless. Sacha tried to get him to understand that there were capital-R rules, and then there were guidelines. Not every fucking guideline had to be followed with unerring rigidity. Sacha hadn't survived twelve years in the Marshals service because he followed every guideline like it was God's word.

Unfortunately, their current vehicle had not been stolen, vandalized, or towed away. The early-2000s Subaru Forester was so boring no one, not even taggers, took a second look at it. It sat where they'd left it, three blocks up from the alley.

"I'm driving." Sacha held his hand out for the keys.

"Sacha…" Rick whined.

"I've had enough close calls for one day; I'm driving."

"Fine." Rick slammed the keys into Sacha's palm before opening the passenger door and getting in.

Sacha slid into the driver's seat. "What's your problem? I'm the one who was almost killed. Once by you and once by Jacobsen."

"Whatever."

Fuck's sake. Sacha took a deep breath in through his nose. Ignoring Rick's passive-aggressive bullshit, he started the engine. Talk radio blared out of the car's speakers, making conversation unnecessary. Neither one of them moved to turn it down.

Partner number three, for the past two months, had been Rick Lancer, prick extraordinaire, who was smarter than he acted. But this was the third time (or fourth if Sacha counted nearly being T-boned the other day when Rick was fucking talking while driving and not watching the road) Sacha had nearly been killed since he'd been back on active duty. Maybe the universe was trying to tell him something. Maybe it was time he listened.

The lure of *something different* flitted along the edge of his thoughts. Maybe he needed real change, not merely a new partner. A career change. He'd had the thought before, but the onus of *duty* had always stopped him from leaving the service. When he left the army and joined the Marshals, his drive had been to bring down as much scum as he could. He'd made a promise to his foster sister Mae-Lin, and to himself, that as long as he walked this earth he would work to rid it of human traffickers.

His heart wasn't in the fight anymore. Not with the same fire that'd led him down this path so many years before. Maybe he needed to find a different way to fight. He didn't see himself giving up, but he needed something else, something intangible and indefinable. He was tired of trying to explain himself when no one listened. His body wasn't bouncing back from back-alley tackles—or falls from fire escapes—quite the way it had when he was twenty-five. Change was in the air.

TWO

Sacha took the next few days off. His knee was aching, and he needed to think without Rick's constant, irritating presence. He never made hasty decisions, but he felt itchy, like the time was now; if he didn't change course soon he might never get the chance again. A bullet, a back alley, a car accident, any of those things and he would never get the chance to live a different kind of life. One he barely allowed himself to dream.

Spending his time off in his apartment was its own special torture. Home had never meant the same thing for him as it did for most of his colleagues. He didn't have a wife and kids; he didn't even have any house plants, had never been in one place long enough to have a pet. Most of his possessions fit inside a few boxes. A half-formed idea had been bouncing around in his head for several months, ever since he had returned from the west coast. A place that felt like it *could* be home, more than any of the other choices in front of him. It wasn't Baltimore, Miami, or Kansas City.

Skagit was a small town in western Washington, and it didn't so much beckon Sacha as lure him. It was a place he could start again, make different choices. Ones that wouldn't mean he lived his life alone. There were people there he could almost consider friends, or they would be if he made any sort of effort at all.

He spent the first night off flipping through channels, trying to get interested in the spring baseball stats. Baseball was the single sport he remotely enjoyed, and it didn't hold his interest. The second night, after spending the day cleaning and at the gym, he drove out to a club he'd been to before.

Contrary to popular opinion, there were plenty of gay bars in Kansas City. Sacha preferred the quiet ones. Less chance of seeing anyone he knew, or anyone seeing him. He was too old for disco balls, flashing lights, and twinks wearing jeans so tight they needed a can opener to get them off. And explaining to anyone he worked or associated with that he had always been gay, just never out was... beyond his bandwidth. His stomach twisted painfully contemplating his colleagues discussing his personal life behind his back.

He sat at the bar nursing a drink, watching the small crowd of young, and seemingly carefree, men dance and flirt. Sometimes there was a soul brave enough to approach him. Mostly they left him alone.

"Another?" The bartender, tall, with well-defined muscles and heavily tattooed forearms, interrupted Sacha's wandering thoughts.

"Yeah." He pushed his empty glass across the bar. "Make it a double."

The bartender smirked, grabbed the bottle off the back bar, and poured a hefty couple of fingers into Sacha's glass. "That what you need?" Light-blue eyes lingered on Sacha for a beat longer than necessary, sending a delicious shiver down his spine.

"It's a start."

"Long day?"

"Day, week, last couple of years, yeah." Sacha downed most of the contents of the glass in a single gulp this time. The burn felt good going down his throat. He was still alive, still had choices. He hadn't left his place with the intention of getting drunk, and he wasn't, really, but the liquor did make his tongue looser than normal.

The bartender wandered off toward the other end of the bar. Sacha watched him walk away, enjoying the confident swagger... and the view of his ass as well. He was probably in his late twenties or early thirties, dark hair clipped close to his skull. Not something Sacha normally liked, but it worked for this guy, accentuating his sharp cheekbones and deep-set eyes.

Sacha stared into space, sipping his drink and listening to the pop-country-whatever music playing in the background, his attention again caught by the couples dancing fearlessly together. Soon enough the bartender was back in his line of vision.

"I'm Derek." He leaned against the wooden bartop. His tattoos were colorful and intricate, swirling up his arms before disappearing underneath the tight sleeves of his shirt.

"Sacha."

"I'm off in an hour." Derek waggled his eyebrows and winked.

An hour was almost too long. An hour gave Sacha time to reminisce, nearly drowning his desire. An hour gave him time to replay lessons taught to him as a youth. Brutal teachings about what it meant to be a man and what it meant to be slaughtered because of who a person slept with or loved. He hunched closer to the bar, allowing the alcohol he'd consumed to subdue, for now, most of those memories. Only anticipation of another man's skin and hard body against his own kept him there.

A glittering liquor bottle appeared in his line of sight, and Derek raised his eyebrows in question. "One for the road?"

Sacha tipped his glass slightly. "One more. Thanks."

EVERYTHING WAS EASIER in the dark. Easier to pretend he was someone else, someone who was out, comfortable with his sexuality. Easier to let himself grab Derek's ass and pull his hips closer so their erections brushed against each other.

Derek was close to his own height, which turned him on, and not shy about what he was hungry for. Their mouths came together in a bruising kiss; they'd hardly gotten Derek's front door shut behind them before he pushed Sacha against the entryway wall and rubbed against him, hot hands groping under his T-shirt and skimming his chest and abs. Soon enough they were both naked and making their way to Derek's bedroom, where a king-sized bed waited.

Long after Derek faded off to sleep, murmuring something along the lines of "S'okay if you stay, man, s'late," Sacha lay in the dark thinking about his life. About how he would like to wake up next to someone he cared about. It wasn't going to be a hot bartender, because he couldn't stay in Kansas City. Any change he forced onto his life would not happen in the city he had tentatively called home for a decade. Rolling over, Sacha felt around on the floor for his jeans and T-shirt and dragged them on over his tired body. He found his shoes in the living room, looked around to make sure he hadn't left anything behind, and quietly let himself out the front door.

The next morning dawned painfully bright, the sun shining cheerfully through his bedroom windows. Sacha squeezed his eyes shut against the glare before dragging a pillow over his face. Forgetting to draw his curtains was a rookie move. The bedsheets were tangled around his waist; pushing them further away so he could sit up, he swung his legs out of bed. The mattress shifted under his weight. His bad knee twinged when he stood, reminding him, again, how old he felt. How old he was.

His mind was made up. He was retiring. Taking the first steps toward change. Shuffling over to his closet, he searched for the perfect outfit to hand in his resignation.

"I CAN'T CHANGE YOUR MIND?" The question was half-hearted. Sacha and Ted Tracy had a tumultuous relationship at best, and it hadn't been improved by Sacha's inability to keep a partner. Sacha's old friend and boss Johnny Vallez had retired and moved to Miami while Sacha was on loan to the FBI. Johnny would have tried harder to change Sacha's mind.

"Nope." His lips made a popping sound. He didn't owe Tracy any explanation. Tossing his badge and service weapon on the desk gave him a sharp stab of regret. But that was for the past, not his future. Sacha was tired of regrets.

Tracy leaned back, resting his clasped hands across his belly. "Well, it's tough to see you go. Good men are hard to find."

What a complete douche. Mindful of listening ears out in the bullpen, Sacha managed to keep his mouth shut. Instead, he smiled. From Tracy's reaction, his attempt must have looked more like a grimace. That was that. Sacha quickly emptied his desk into a small cardboard box and took the elevator to the lobby, walking out of the building into the Kansas City morning sunshine.

THREE

SACHA: MID-JUNE, SKAGIT.

Minute particles of plaster dust poured down: a shower, a rainstorm. Sacha lay where he'd fallen, individual motes spilling from the hole in the ceiling, first quickly and then more sedately, before floating down to where he lay, covering him like snow. Or a shroud. Fucking ladders.

Curiosity overcoming the pain radiating from his hip and lower back, Sacha carefully rolled over. Groaning, he pulled himself up to hands and knees, and then stood. Brushing at the dust on his clothing, he gingerly made his way back up the ladder, his body complaining each step of the way. There was a jumbo-size container of pain reliever in his future if he had any plans to sleep tonight... or move in the morning. His nearly-forty-year-old body was not meant for this.

When he regained the topmost step of the ladder, he braced himself and stretched as high as he could before sticking his hand into the dark opening above his head. His fingertips barely brushed the ceiling, but sure enough, he felt the cold answer of metal against them. *Yes.* There was a tin ceiling hidden behind the 1970s plaster cover job. Holy fuck. Maybe, *just maybe*, this wouldn't turn out to be the worst decision he'd ever made.

The worst decision he had *recently* made was choosing to camp out in his newly purchased property instead of finding somewhere decent to stay. A place with amenities, like a shower and a kitchen. A person could only warm so much on a hot plate, and a hand-washing sink didn't replace a shower. A commercial building built more than a hundred years ago did not have such niceties.

Since regardless of what his bank balance looked like, Sacha chose to live like he was down to his last penny, he'd tossed a sleeping bag and air mattress down, calling it good. The box the air mattress had arrived in displayed a well-rested blonde woman in a variety of positions on the mattress, but Sacha was not well rested. Each morning he'd woken miserable and aching on top of a flat plastic sack instead of a bed. A week in, he was ready to surrender.

Staying in the vacant building was a matter of pride as much as money. If his battered body could get up every day... he really didn't know what he thought he was proving. That he was a stubborn bastard, he supposed. But he'd been a bastard all his life; it wasn't going to change anytime soon.

The building was meant to be an investment. It was an investment. He was going to restore it, put it back on the market, and buy another one. Buyers were into the retro look, and Skagit had a lot of old buildings waiting to be brought back to life. The century-old Warrick Building had drawn him from the first. Located in the close-to-being-gentrified-but-not-quite business neighborhood north of downtown Skagit, the building screamed potential.

He hoped to restore it to its original glory as closely as possible. Fixtures and everything. Never mind that he had never done much of this kind of work before, or ever. That was what the internet was for, right? There was no doubt in his mind that the structure harbored secrets—at some point a gorgeous granite exterior had been masked behind a plaster-and-wood façade to make it appear modern. The lure of the building's hidden history had brought him this far. The tin ceiling was icing on the cake.

Today he'd woken after no more than six miserable hours of semi-sleep, again, and he was feeling... worn down, weary. The promise he'd seen, the hidden beauty of the old bank building built in 1899 from local white granite, had faded somewhat, replaced by a dull throb behind his right eye. Tin ceiling or no tin ceiling.

Coffee. He needed real coffee. He eyed the tiny single-serve machine he'd bought. It was not going to be enough to get him to noon, much less through the day. Sacha needed, like some kind of junkie, a huge iced coffee with several shots of espresso added to it. And sugar, lots of sugar. The cheap beans he'd purchased and the single eight-ounce cups his machine sputtered out left a lot to be desired.

Climbing back down the ladder, Sacha got a whiff of himself. Fuck, he needed a shower too, but coffee came first. A trip to the gym's shower room was the sole way he would achieve true cleanliness, but no one in Skagit would mind if he was a little dusty. He brushed off as much of the plaster as he could before heading out the front door.

Sacha got a couple funny looks as he locked the door behind him. Neighbors weren't used to seeing anyone come in or out of the building. The realtor had told him it had stood empty for years: the original bank had gone out of business during the 1940s, and a bookstore had occupied the first floor at some point during the 1970s. The time between was a mystery. After the bookstore closed, the place had been used for storage for over thirty years before falling vacant.

The morning sun bounced off the windows of the brick-and-stone buildings on the opposite side of the street and into Sacha's eyes. Squinting against it, he wished for his sunglasses, but he wasn't turning back now. The need for caffeine was too great.

By the time the closest coffee shop, cleverly named the Coffee Place, came into view he felt better, his sore muscles warmed up and his head clearer. The lack of sleep was taking its toll, Sacha admitted. Staring middle age right in the face and trying not to flinch.

The door of the shop swung open. Another early-morning patron slid out, a huge to-go cup in one hand. The man's eyes widened, and he gasped. "Sir, are you okay? Has there been an accident?" Putting his coffee down on an outside table, the stranger carefully took Sacha's arm and pulled him away from the entrance.

Sir? He wasn't *that* old.

"Sit here. I'll get help."

"Wait. No. What are you talking about? I'm fine," Sacha sputtered. He stopped mid-protest, taking in the stranger who had accosted him.

The man was, by anyone's standards—although Sacha had a lifetime of practice at not overtly noticing that kind of thing—*gorgeous*. A flicker of attraction sparked inside his chest, catching Sacha off guard. Forget spark, Sacha practically caught on fire.

Nearly as tall as Sacha, the man was slim and graceful where Sacha was a lumbering bear. The stranger's most striking features, though, were his kind, caramel-colored eyes filled with concern and a dash of humor. Not many people found Sacha amusing, so it caught him off guard.

He was familiar with fear or wariness, sometimes loathing, but never amusement. Sacha was ensnared by the inner light in the man's eyes, or some bullshit thing he had no words for. He needed to do something to keep them focused on him. Instead he was standing and staring like a village idiot.

"Have you looked in the mirror? Because what I am seeing is not fine." The man made a "Take a look for yourself" gesture toward the plate-glass window of the coffee shop, unfazed by Sacha's larger size and snippy attitude.

It took Sacha a moment to recognize the ghostly figure reflected in the window. A dried trickle of blood lay along the side of his temple, and he was covered from head to toe with a fine layer of plaster dust... which explained the odd looks on his walk here.

Laughter took him by surprise. He doubled over, using his knees for support. Now that he knew it was there, the plaster itched like crazy against his skin, and the throb behind his right eye was a fucking headache from when he fell off the ladder and banged his head against the hardwood. He looked like a fucking zombie.

He kept trying to catch his breath to explain, but the sight of himself looking like he was a cast member from *The Walking Dead* would set him off again. He was wheezing; every time he tried to say something, anything, he could only squeak. After a few moments of this, the stranger went inside, returning moments later.

"Drink this," he commanded, shoving a glass of water under Sacha's nose. Their fingers touched briefly, and Sacha could swear he felt an electric shock pass between them.

The glass, cold in his hand and wet with condensation, helped ground him. He gulped the water down, feeling it soothe his dry throat. Out of the corner of his eye, he watched the stranger watching him.

"Who *are* you?" Sacha asked.

"Seth Culver. You?"

"A—uh, Sacha, Bolic." Good fucking lord, he even sounded like an accident victim.

"Well, A-uh-Sacha, what in the hell did you do to yourself?"

Sacha looked pointedly at his coffee cup. "I need one of those." He was not going to be dissuaded from his mission. "Please, I can't go in there like this."

Seth rolled his eyes but stood, waving off the cash Sacha tried to shove in his hand. He went back inside, returning with a large cup of drip coffee that matched his own. Sacha accepted the gift, cupping it with both hands and sucking in the heady aroma of roasted coffee beans. His laughing fit had passed, but he still felt odd. He'd probably hyperventilated.

They sat at one of the outdoor tables arranged along the sidewalk. Sacha took a fortifying sip of caffeine before starting his tale, the hot coffee a pleasant distraction.

"I probably hit my head when I fell off a ladder earlier." Seth's eyes widened, and Sacha saw a possible trip to the ER in his future. "Let me finish. I bought a building, and I'm renovating it. I was up on the ladder, and I fell... actually it was more of a slide. Obviously, I'm fine."

A dark eyebrow raised mockingly. "Yeah, *obviously*. Is there a reason you didn't shower or change your clothes?"

Sacha looked down at himself. "There's no shower in the building?"

"You can't go around town like that. I don't know you, but I do know you can't go out, more out, in public. Like that." Seth pinned Sacha with an assessing stare. "You're not a serial killer or a mob boss or anything, are you? My brother will kill me if I accidentally bring one of those home."

Sacha shook his head. Explaining that he had pretended to be both a killer *and* a mob boss for a few years would be too much for a first meeting.

"How about we head back to your building, grab some fresh clothes, and you clean up at my place?"

The head injury must have been affecting him because, instead of doing the smart thing and declining, Sacha agreed to go to a random stranger's house and take a shower. A stranger he found very attractive. Muttering and shaking his head, he gulped the rest of his coffee, needing the distraction of the burn as it slid down his throat.

Seth cocked his head. "What was that?"

"'Bila ne bila.' It's a Russian saying: 'Whatever happens, happens.'"

"I'm not the one who looks like I crawled out of a ditch. Or a fresh grave." Seth remarked.

Sacha laughed again.

FOUR

SETH

What was he doing, offering a hulking, dark-haired stranger covered with plaster dust and blood, a shower at his place? Seth had woken that morning with the intention of getting some chores done and placing some flyers around town looking for homeowners needing landscape work done, not bringing home a stray human. Admittedly he had a soft spot for strays, and he suspected the guy was hot under that layer of muck. Hot as in sexy as fuck. The spark between them had been real and scorching. Seth had seen Sacha's eyes flicker with awareness before he'd quickly looked away.

So… three minutes after meeting Sacha Bolic, Seth was offering to help him out. It was basic human kindness to offer a shower, right? Seth couldn't let him wander around Skagit like that. And Seth didn't sense any weirdness, or threat, from him.

The first seven-and-a-half years of his life, Seth had lived on the streets with his con-artist, drifter mother. He had learned early to read people. His gut told him when to run, when to hide, and it had never let him down. Right now his gut was telling him this man would not harm him, and he was going to trust it.

Seth's life had changed when his mother, Jaqueline, had been well-and-truly busted in a sting operation and sent to prison. Seth had gone to live with his aunt. She'd done what she could to tame him, but it had been a struggle. Sometimes Seth wasn't sure she had accomplished anything beyond teaching him enough so he could pass in civilized society.

"Beautiful boy" had been Marnie's first words to him, her soft hand caressing his cheek, touching him in a way no one ever had before, especially not his own mother. Marnie had driven all the way from her home outside Scottsdale to the foster home in Aberdeen, Washington, where Seth waited for the aunt he'd never met or even heard of. Over twenty-five years later, Seth could recall with terrifying clarity how deep his well of need had been, those words echoing repeatedly as they fell into him.

As soon as their coffee was finished, Seth led the way to his battered Jeep. After a few turns of the key and taps on the gas pedal, the engine caught. Yay, small victories.

"Good girl." Seth patted the dashboard encouragingly. At over twenty years old and 250,000 miles, she needed all the help she could get. And Seth could not afford a new car right now.

Sacha directed Seth a few blocks away, toward the edge of what locals affectionately called N.O.T. for North of Old Town. The street they turned onto was one of a handful still paved with cobblestones, and it was one of Seth's favorite blocks in the historic section of Skagit. His scalp started to tingle the farther down the street they traveled. No way.

"That one there, on the left." Sacha pointed at a building in the middle of the block.

"No way." Seth said the words out loud; he couldn't believe it. Pulling the Jeep to the curb, he gaped. His mouth hung open, he snapped it shut so hard his teeth clicked. A SOLD banner was plastered over the FOR SALE sign Seth had seen over the months he had been in Skagit. Seth did not believe it. This guy, this *complete stranger* was the person who'd purchased one of the old buildings he was most fascinated by?

Even if he hadn't already offered him a shower, this was practically a sign from the gods that Sacha was safe. Seth loved, *adored*, the old buildings in Skagit; he'd spent his down time researching many of them. Some of them had protected status, but this one did not. Yet. Probably because of the hideous 1960s-style remodel that hid its best features.

"No way," he repeated stupidly. "You bought the Warrick?" When he first moved to town he'd spent several days wandering around N.O.T., setting his internal compass to the layout of Skagit. He could have found the Warrick in his sleep. "I can't believe this."

Seth opened his door, sliding out of the car. Sacha followed without comment. They stood shoulder to shoulder on the sidewalk, gazing at the old building. Sometime in its history, city planners or possessed architectural designers had covered the building with a façade that made it look like the movie set for a juvie detention center. Tiny windows with a flat, personality-free exterior. More recently someone, probably Sacha, had pulled a little of it away, revealing stained white granite cowering underneath.

"It could be really pretty under all that sh—stuff," Seth breathed out, staring reverently at the building. "I've seen some pictures in the county archives, and the local newspaper did a spread on Skagit's history a few years ago that I found online; the Warrick was one of the buildings they featured. How'd you know what was under there?" Seth glanced at Sacha. Was it too much to hope he had met a fellow history nerd?

Sacha looked slightly embarrassed. "I like old buildings, especially in little towns like this one. I was looking at some old photographs of Skagit and wondered about this place. If it was still around. One night I kind of broke in and checked it out. Made an offer on it the next day. Got a screaming deal too. I guess the family has been sitting on this pile for a long time." Seth nearly swooned.

Inside didn't look much better than outside. It was dark, grimy, and smelled of disuse. There had probably been a big open space originally, but at some point occupants had divided it up into several sections, none of which made sense to the original layout. A metal staircase against the back wall led to the second floor.

Copper piping and old wiring lay in tangled heaps on the floor alongside sheets of plaster, shattered two-by-fours, and what appeared to be cabinets ripped from the walls. Along parts of the exposed floor, Seth could see shadowy outlines where walls, or maybe counters, once stood.

The ladder was in the front room beneath a hefty hole in the ceiling plaster. "You fell off that? You're lucky to be walking."

"Yeah, yeah," Sacha muttered while he bent down and dug around in a pile, which turned out to be a duffel with a tangle of clothing spilling out of it. "All right, let's go."

Seth thought he spied a sleeping bag on top of a very flat air mattress tucked in a corner. He twisted around, trying to get a glimpse of the rest of the space, but Sacha definitely needed a shower. Acting the tourist could wait.

"Thanks." Sacha's voice jolted him from his thoughts.

"What?"

"Thanks. For the shower. I appreciate it."

"Anytime."

Seth's little rental was on the east side of town. It wasn't considered a nice neighborhood by anyone but the folks who lived there. The neighborhood had become (from what Seth had learned) more transient as longtime residents moved away and a younger generation moved in. Because of its location perched above the freeway, it was doubtful the neighborhood would ever become anything more than transient student and seasonal housing. The tiny box homes built after World War II were not suitable for today's families, too used to their personal space. Too small, usually two bedrooms, with tiny kitchens. Seth didn't miss Sacha's flinch when they crossed I-5 and kept going.

"So, are you new to Skagit?" Seth asked, wondering how Sacha had discovered the Warrick.

"Not really, but I moved here very recently." Seth glanced over at his passenger, expecting a little more, but Sacha was silent, staring out the windshield at the neighborhood flashing by.

"I recently moved here too," Seth offered. His passenger didn't respond. Seth glanced over again to see Sacha still looking the other direction. Seth hoped he hadn't judged too quickly, thinking it was safe to bring this particular stray home.

"Sacha—is that short for something? Or is it a nickname?" Seth had always been slightly envious of kids with good nicknames, as his was too short to become any shorter, and his fellow students had thought names like "Beth" or "Sloth" were funny.

Sacha looked over at him like he'd lost his marbles. He muttered something Seth couldn't quite hear.

"What?"

"It's short for Alexander," he muttered louder, *still* looking out the window and not at Seth. Seth was pretty sure that was *not* what he'd said. The man needed another coffee, or maybe he hadn't eaten breakfast. He *had* been out looking for coffee, and it was early; likely he hadn't eaten yet. Seth was going to ignore the rude behavior as low blood sugar.

"Sacha, huh? It suits you better than Alexander."

Sacha took a deep breath, visibly making an effort to relax.

"I promise I am safe. Not that you aren't big enough to take care of yourself." Seth flashed a quick grin toward his passenger. "I guess it's weird going to a stranger's house, but I'm pretty good at reading people. Otherwise I wouldn't have offered you a shower. Sacha suits you better than Alexander, or even Alex. Nice to meet you, Sacha." *Shut your mouth, Seth. Quit rambling, Seth.*

Sacha shook his head at him, but Seth saw the corner of his mouth lift in a half smile. "Nice to meet you, Seth. I do appreciate the shower. Please excuse my mood. I could say I'm normally better mannered, but my family would tell you that is a lie."

Chuckling, Seth took the turn toward his house and managed to drive the rest of the way without asking a single question, setting some sort of personal record.

The tiny shotgun-style house was rented from a senior couple who were currently RVing across the southern US. They didn't live in this house, but in another one a few miles away that Seth kept an eye on while they were gone for a discount on his rent. Meaning he watered the lawn and made sure the mail didn't pile up in the box.

It was nothing special, dirty white on the outside with beige walls inside. His half-brother Adam, the reason he had moved to Skagit, had taken one very quick look at it and hated it. But Adam wasn't the one living in it, so he could fuck right off. Adam had given Seth a laundry list of reasons why the neighborhood wasn't ideal, even going so far as to send him an email with the crime statistics for the area. Seth had rolled his eyes and deleted the message.

Sacha followed him from the car up the two concrete steps to the front door. There was no porch, only a 4x4 cement pad. When it was raining, Seth had a practiced method of getting from his car to the door in as little time as possible. Today however, the sky was clear and blue as it could be, promising another incredible afternoon. So far, Seth did not miss the Arizona summer at all.

"Nice place," Sacha commented once they were inside. He sounded surprised. What did he expect? Because Seth chose to live in this neighborhood he would live in squalor? He wasn't the one camping out in a construction zone. Seth had done the best he could to create a living space he was comfortable in.

The living room and kitchen faced west and had larger windows, serving as Seth's house-plant hospice. He was forever going through Fred Meyer or Home Depot and bringing home half-price plants, the ones they had forgotten to water, or those some tiny human who should have been stroller bound had gotten hold of and abused. It was a little jungly. During the time he'd been in Skagit, he'd managed to collect quite a few patients.

Two bedrooms and the single tiny bathroom opposite faced north-east. There was nothing Seth could do about how dark they were. He'd painted his bedroom a soft blue and hung white curtains to encourage light, but that side of the house was cave-like. Most of the mismatched furniture had come with the house, adding to the sense of living inside a thrift store.

"I like it. Shower's that way." He pointed toward the tiny hallway.

Sacha moved in the direction Seth indicated, clearly wanting to get cleaned up as soon as possible. He didn't so much walk as stalk, Seth observed. For a big man—and he was big, possibly taller than Seth's own 6'2", and definitely bulkier—he moved like a cat. Long legs, and sinuous upper body flowing rather than jogging along. He probably could walk a block with a book balanced on his head. The gracefulness in that large a man was breathtaking.

Seth realized he was staring when Sacha turned and caught his gaze. Oops. Turning back in the direction of the bathroom without comment, Sacha went in, shutting the door firmly behind him.

Seth shook his head at himself. What was he thinking? He hung out with Adam and his boyfriend, Micah, and many of their friends who were gay, bi, or very accepting, but that didn't mean the rest of Skagit was the same. And Sacha was a complete stranger. Seth futilely wondered if Sacha was into men; could the universe be that kind? Had it been Seth's imagination that Sacha considered Seth a beat too long and with... approval?

Wandering into his kitchen, Seth continued unsuccessfully to try *not* to imagine the handsome and dangerous-looking man naked in his bathroom. The more he tried, the more his brain kept showering him with images. Showering. Gah. It had been way too long since he'd had sex.

One of his few framed photos caught his eye. He'd been a goofy twelve-year-old, and his aunt had surprised him with a summer road trip. They'd ended up at Glacier National Park in Montana. The photo was taken along Going to the Sun Road with the Rocky Mountains looming behind them. He stood next to his diminutive aunt, a huge grin on his face. Marnie had been everything. His aunt, a true flower child, never cared about who Seth dated, fucked, loved, or hung out with. She wouldn't care that he was ogling a stranger, one clearly older than him. She wouldn't have blinked at him bringing a stranger home. She absolutely would have agreed that Sacha also being interested in old architecture was a *sign*.

The shower turned off. Seth shook off his ridiculous thoughts to dig around in his fridge for something to eat. He'd make it, and Sacha would eat it. The man had to be hungry and probably had manners enough not to refuse food.

Pulling eggs, an assortment of veggies, and ham out of his fridge,

Seth began putting a scramble together. He always enjoyed cooking; the various steps involved—chopping, organizing, cooking, and then plating—were a calming routine for him. Baking was good too, which reminded him of the bread he had baked yesterday, perfect for toast.

He *barely* managed not to stare when Sacha came into the kitchen toweled off, wearing worn blue jeans, a sinfully tight black T-shirt that accentuated his meaty biceps and well-defined chest, no socks, bare feet... the stuff of fantasies. Seth gestured toward the table where the veggie scramble and a stack of toast were waiting.

Sacha's hair was dark, nearly black, with a little salt sprinkled through it, more at the sides. Seth loved salt-and-pepper hair; older men turned his crank. The long scratch above one dark eyebrow made Sacha appear slightly rakish. Seth wasn't sure how much older Sacha was, but enough that Seth knew he'd have a body full of history Seth could map with his tongue.

"Breakfast?" Seth offered, cutting off his inappropriate thoughts. Again. A gurgling sound from Sacha's stomach answered his question.

"Breakfast sounds fucking amazing."

They sat at Seth's little table eating in a not-entirely-uncomfortable silence. Even if Seth had hoped to chat, Sacha was ravenous. Seth stared out the small window while his guest ate.

Sacha devoured his plate of eggs and all the toast before glancing sheepishly at Seth and breaking the silence. "Thanks. I was hungry."

"No prob. My pleasure." Seth leaned back in his chair and crossed his arms over his chest. "Tell me about the building; what are your plans? Information in exchange for food."

Sacha grinned at him. The smile transformed his grim façade. Gone were the slightly brooding air and vague sense of mystery. Smiling, Sacha was breathtakingly handsome, the delicate crinkle of smile lines along the corners of his dark-green eyes giving him a slightly mischievous look. "At this point I think I must have been knocked harder in the head then I thought. The place is a wreck. My interest in local history ran by my common sense and stole the fucking baton."

"Oh, yeah? You really are a history buff?" Seth *loved* history, the quirkier the better. He and his aunt had spent several summer vacations hunting down, for lack of a better term, "weird" history.

"Kind of, I guess. I've always liked small-town history. I mean, these places were often at the forefront, right? Of the gold rush, or land grabs, or the industry of the moment, and now they're sleepy little places that people have mostly forgotten about."

"So you've traveled a lot?"

"I guess, around the US. I've been pretty lucky to have traveled to almost all the states. In my downtime I would visit the local museums, stuff like that."

Seth wondered what he had done that gave him the chance to travel so much, but something told him if he asked, Sacha would shut down the conversation.

"I'm guessing you came to Skagit, and that's how you found the Warrick?"

Grimacing, Sacha pushed his chair away from the table and stretched his long legs out in front of him before answering. "Pretty much. I had a window of opportunity; it was either take the chance or quit bitching about my day job... among other things." A haunted expression flashed across his face. "I decided to take the chance. Once the decision was made, it was easy. Although now I realize I didn't plan for things like regular showers or missing having a kitchen."

"That was a sleeping bag then; you're staying there while you remodel?"

"Yeah. I mean, it's just me, and why waste money on a place to stay?"

"Except when you need a shower and a hot meal?"

"Except for that." There was that grin again.

"Do you have any pictures of the building? In its," Seth snickered, "natural state? Before someone with the design sense of..." Honestly, he couldn't think of anything bad enough to describe what had been done to the historic structure.

"A monkey on meth? Bauhaus gone bad? Neo-structuralism? Yeah, I've got a few back at the building," Sacha answered after gulping down the last of his coffee.

"More toast?"

"No, that's okay. Thank you for breakfast; it was delicious." A faint blush spread across his cheeks.

"Lemme give you a ride back, then I can come in and see the photos you have."

FIVE

SACHA

They cleaned up the dishes together. It was the least Sacha could do after Seth fed him and let him take a shower—close to the best shower of his life. The house was a piece of shit, but he could see that Seth took care with it. Why did a nice guy like Seth live in this neighborhood? Many of the homes had peeling paint, the lawns full of weeds and trash. One a couple doors down had an ancient, rusty barbeque sprawled at the end of the driveway. Were the occupants hoping it would disappear one day? Melt into the pavement so they wouldn't have to look at it anymore?

He and Andriy Sokolovic, the Russian mobster he'd nailed earlier in the year—may that bastard rot in prison for the rest of his life—had used a couple of places a few blocks from here when Sacha was undercover. His skin crawled, thinking about what he had had to do to break the human trafficking ring and bring as many of the perpetrators to justice as possible.

It had only been for a few days, but the memory of the shivering kids locked in a storage container continued to haunt him. Sacha still dreamt of them now and then. For a while it had been nightly that his sleep was haunted by moaning children, none of them crying for their parents or family because they had already been slaves for most of their short lives. They had been resigned to their fate. It had been hell.

"Why this neighborhood?" Sacha asked as he carefully rinsed dishes under the running tap, trying to shake the memory of the trafficking victims. He placed the two plates into the dish rack before searching in the warm dishwater for the remaining silverware.

"Why not?" Seth replied. "It's cheap. As long as I mind my own business, no one bugs me."

"You got business to mind?" He probably sounded like a dick. Actually, there was no question that he sounded like a dick. It was harder than he'd thought to shed the US Marshal persona and become Sacha Bolic, ordinary citizen. He naturally assumed the worst of most people. Changing his deeply ingrained suspicion of people in general to something like "Give everyone a chance" felt like turning his brain inside out.

Seth grinned, surprising Sacha with his good humor over the rude question. "Nah, cheap. I'm trying to grow my landscaping-slash-yard-work business. This fits my budget."

Back in the car, Seth cheerfully pointed his ancient Jeep back toward N.O.T. and the building, or what Sacha was beginning to secretly call the folly. Never in his life would Sacha have defined himself as impulsive. And yet wasn't he trying to change his life? Maybe a little impulsive behavior would do him good.

When he'd first seen the Warrick, he'd *suspected* it was hiding something. The owners had been so grateful for his offer he'd almost felt guilty lowballing them. Historic building or not, it had been on the market on and off for over two years. Of course, now that he'd been in there for over a week and had a better grasp on what he'd taken on... well.

He grimaced.

"You doing okay?" They had stopped at a red light, and Seth was watching him.

"Yeah, thinking about the remodel." Among other things. Like life choices, change, and the fact that he had no idea what he was doing.

Not the remodel part, that's what YouTube was for, but what he was doing trying to live a civilian life.

"Have you had the time to dig in and do some real research? Like into who Warrick was, that kind of thing?" Seth grinned again. "I love research. I bet we could find some pretty good information if we tried."

"Meh. Not anything significant." Sacha furrowed his brow. What was this "we" business, anyway? He was wondering if he would regret accepting the offer of a shower.

His inner critic chided him. After a lifetime in law enforcement, his instincts were very good, and Seth did not strike him as a criminal or unstable. Maybe terminally inquisitive, but not a nut job. It was his own intentions Sacha was having a hard time with.

Ten minutes later he unlocked the frosted-glass front door, letting them both back inside. Seth had parked his Jeep down the street and silently followed him to the front entrance. The mess Sacha had abandoned hadn't cleaned itself up while they were gone. Sacha dropped his gear on top of the personal belongings stacked in the far corner, then dragged out the slim file folder with the information he'd collected about the Warrick Building.

"Here." He shoved the folder at Seth. "You look at this. When you're done, I'll give a tour, if you want." Sacha was inexplicably embarrassed that his duffel bag was lying splayed open, vomiting his belongings out onto the filthy wooden floor, the rumpled sleeping bag and flat air mattress adding to the general air of untidiness. And now he'd offered up a tour. Whatever happened, it was going to be purely his own fault.

While Seth flipped through the folder, Sacha attempted to stuff his jeans, boxers, and other clothing back into the bag. He'd lived out of a bag for years. He didn't know why it was suddenly bothering him. Maybe it was the shower, or falling off the ladder. Whatever, he couldn't stand his shit being all over the place.

"Man, I wish there were more of these," Seth said. There were a few photos of the building before the 1970s included in the file Sacha had. One was from 1901; the building must recently have been finished. Two men with somber expressions stood to the side, and empty fields spread out behind and beside it. Skagit had been a very young city at that time.

"There are more in the county archives. These came along with the sale papers," Sacha answered. Shoving his duffel into a corner, he also folded up the mattress and sleeping bag. There wasn't a lot he could do about the half-empty case of bottled water, bag of protein bars, or random remodeling supplies stacked along the walls.

Seth looked up from the file, paying attention to the building's interior for the first time. "What's with the hole in the ceiling? And where is all your stuff? In storage?"

"So many questions." Sacha grinned to take the sting out of his next words. For whatever reason, he didn't want Seth to leave thinking Sacha was a total jerk. "Didn't your parents tell you cautionary tales about children who asked too many questions? 'Curiosity killed the cat,' something along those lines?"

"I was brought up by my aunt, who encouraged questions, and I'm a curious guy. Besides, the entire proverb is, 'Curiosity killed the cat, but satisfaction saved him.'" Seth smiled back. Was Seth flirting? Sacha needed to smack himself in the forehead. He needed a warning label, like when nice people adopt old abandoned pets with issues. *Bites when approached: use caution.*

Stuff. Sacha didn't have stuff. He'd been undercover for the better part of two years. Before that, well... How much stuff do you need when you're constantly out on a call, flying or driving to arrest and transport a circus of fools ranging from parole violators and fugitives to witnesses of all types, to murderers and those who merely attempt murder? His place in Kansas City had resembled one of those sleeping pods at Japanese airports.

Now, three months after retiring from the US Marshals, he was the proud owner of the Warrick Building. Instead of sandy beaches and sweet cocktails, Sacha was tearing out ceilings, starting the hard work of bringing the building back to its former glory.

"The hole is where I was checking to see if there was a tin ceiling, like I suspected. And my stuff is all over there." He waved toward the bags, wondering why he was answering Seth's questions. Maybe he should start asking a few of his own.

Seth ignored his tone and most of the answer. "A tin ceiling? Can I see?"

Before Sacha could reply, Seth was scrambling up the ladder. He stood at the very top, above the warning in huge red font stating, "This Is Not A Step." Balancing precariously, he pulled a cell phone from the back pocket of his shorts. He lit the phone's flashlight feature and shined it around the gap in the ceiling.

"Whoa, it looks intact! Somebody painted over it, though. Hand me a rag." The ladder bounced a little with Seth's evident delight, and Sacha's heart shot up into his throat, nearly choking him.

His own dirty laundry half-stuffed into the duffel was the closest possibility. Without taking his eyes off the ladder, he backed up and felt around for something to give Seth. Handing over a dirty T-shirt, Sacha wondered how many years had been shaved off his life watching this guy stand fearlessly above him. Seth, on the other hand, was vibrating with excitement.

Stretching as high as possible, Seth rubbed the fabric against the ceiling. Sacha's gaze was caught by a strip of pale skin as Seth's T-shirt slid up, revealing a peek of a flat stomach and dark hair trailing downward. A sting of chagrin, from brazenly ogling another man, coursed through him, and he jerked his eyes away—even if the man in question had no idea Sacha was looking.

A flash went off, and Seth looked down, pure joy in his expression. "I think I got a pretty good shot. We can look it up on the internet. I've never seen one like this before. It has a face in the middle. Check it out."

Bending and twisting to climb back down the ladder, Seth misjudged, or the ladder tilted, or the planet wobbled. He slipped, probably exactly like Sacha had earlier, but instead of crashing to the ground, he landed with a laughing bump against Sacha's chest, still talking excitedly about the photograph and tin ceilings. While Sacha was dizzy from the planet wobble, his arms automatically went around Seth to keep them both from falling. Seth seemed not to notice Sacha's confusion, pulling away with an "I knew you'd catch me" before swiftly returning his focus to his phone where he was punching in... something. Words, probably. "Huh. Cool. Maaaybe..."

Sacha still felt the press of Seth's body against his own, but he managed to gather himself together enough to focus. "Maybe what?"

The phone waggled in front of his face, but all Sacha could see was blurry light. He grabbed Seth's wrist to hold it still. The phone showed a grainy picture of a tin-stamp ceiling tile with what looked like a man's face. The warmth of Seth's skin under his palm was distracting, and Sacha shook himself, snatching his hand back as if he were holding a burning ember.

"What am I looking at?" he growled. Because he had no fucking business looking at Seth in any way other than as a nice guy who had helped him out. He'd known the guy for four minutes.

And what?

He was expired goods, that's what. Even if Seth was gay or bi, as Sacha suspected, why would an attractive younger man want to have anything to do with the mess that was him? Fumbling around in the dark was all he had ever done; now he was trying to learn how to date men in the daylight and probably making a mess of it.

Seth was oblivious to Sacha's stupid. Thank fuck. "Could be a rare tin-stamp ceiling, meaning it could be worth bank. Not that you wanna to sell it or anything. You'd have to have a real expert look at it, though."

"How do you know about this stuff?"

Seth looked at him, focusing for the first time in minutes, his brown eyes dialing in on Sacha's disconcertingly.

"Jack of all trades, really. I've done a little of everything. My aunt was into restoration for a while when I was a teenager, so I've done some stripping—not *that* kind of stripping. I should add 'master of none' as a caveat, so you know." He chuckled, looking down at his phone again, lost to the online trail of breadcrumbs.

Sacha prodded him. "No, really, how do you know about tin-stamped ceilings and old buildings?"

"Oh." Seth interrupted his online sleuthing to focus on Sacha. "I was a failed history major in college. Mostly I was a failed college student. I still love history, as you can see. I stopped taking classes but never lost my interest in history."

"What happened?"

"What do you mean?"

"Why did you drop out?"

"Oh." Seth broke eye contact. "My aunt died unexpectedly, and I had to take care of her estate."

There was more to the story, Sacha was certain. But he understood taking care of those close.

"What about you?" Seth prodded.

"What about me?" He knew perfectly well Seth meant how had he become interested in small-town America and its history. Sacha wished there was an explanation that didn't involve telling Seth he'd been a US Marshal. The last thing he needed was a law-enforcement groupie. And yeah, he had no way of knowing if Seth was one, but Sacha had experienced it enough to shy away from sharing his past.

Seth raised an eyebrow, waiting, not letting Sacha off the hook. Sacha rolled his eyes before finally answering, "Partly the job I had often required local knowledge, then it turned into a hobby. I like old buildings, I like trivia... the rest, as they say, *is history.*"

"That's a terrible joke. Ugh." Seth leaned against the outside wall, giving Sacha his full attention. "But now, regardless of your awful taste in puns, you've saved an old building. I'm impressed. Kind of like Superman, saving buildings in single bounds, or something like that."

"Something like that." His throat was oddly dry. Sacha needed something to drink, but all he had on hand was water. "Water?"

"Yeah, cool." Seth's attention was drawn away again, back to the smartphone screen he was typing something into. Sacha grabbed a couple bottles of water from the open case in the corner. Tossing one to Seth, he twisted his open and gulped it down in seconds. Lukewarm water spilled out along his cheek and down his neck; he didn't care, he only needed to quench his thirst.

While Seth continued reading up on antique tin tiles and what-the-fuck-ever else was holding his attention, Sacha walked over to stare out one of the tiny front windows and try to ignore the earth wobbling underneath his feet again. Seth was pushing all sorts of buttons Sacha didn't know if he was prepared to deal with.

The much-larger original windows and frames still existed underneath the lath and plaster, Sacha was almost certain. He didn't think the original structure had been compromised. Remodelers had most likely built frames in the smaller size they wanted, leaving intact the nearly-floor-to-ceiling original windows seen in older photographs. Much easier than refitting an entire building. Which was good, because if Seth stuck around much longer, Sacha was going to need bigger windows and a lot more fresh air.

The tour was quick and relatively painless. Seth listened intently, asking a few questions while Sacha walked him through the building. The ground floor was a largely open space (or it would be when he was done with it) with a hallway at the back leading to a tiny room occupied by a single toilet and hand sink.

It hadn't been difficult for Sacha to imagine what it'd looked like during its first few decades of existence, when it was a bank. There was an old photograph probably taken from the staircase, customers in dark suits and bowler hats posed leaning against a long-gone marble countertop, staring seriously into the camera lens. Sacha had found it tucked, or fallen, behind shelves he tore out the first day. In the hallway, perhaps under the stairs, would have lurked an enormous steel safe, the kind only seen in old movies nowadays.

The staircase was across from the front entrance. Sacha thought the original bannister must have been lovely, but it too had disappeared. Upstairs was where upper management had housed themselves. Later it had been divided into several tiny rooms, only one of which had a window. More prison cell than office.

Reckless interior remodels over the years had left the Warrick entirely stripped of its original fixtures, except maybe the toilet. His plan was to flip the building. N.O.T. was a neighborhood on the verge of change, and a restored old bank building would be a hot commodity as the market began to heat up. Once the wiring and plumbing were up to code, which unfortunately was not something he felt comfortable doing himself, he would start putting feelers out for future buyers.

Four hours, give or take, after Sacha had fallen off the ladder, he tried to hustle Seth out of the Warrick into the late-morning sunshine. Sacha had a ceiling to uncover, but Seth clearly wasn't quite ready to leave.

Sacha almost asked if Seth wanted to stay and help out, but instead offered a lame, "Thanks for the shower and breakfast."

The thing was, Sacha was pretty sure *he* wanted Seth to stay, wanted to get to know him, but navigating a casual relationship, was uncharted territory. Also terrifying. He hadn't even made an effort to reconnect with people he knew in Skagit since moving from Kansas City for Christ sake. The idea nauseated him.

"Thanks for the tour." Seth stood outside the door, shuffling from foot to foot. "Um, look, I know this is random, and we just met, so you don't know me or anything, but if you'd like to get coffee again or something? Maybe not after falling off a ladder next time?"

He could do coffee. "Coffee sounds good."

"Yeah?" Seth beamed. "Cool, I know the perfect place."

"You, uh, know where to find me." Sacha almost shut his eyes against his own awkward response. Please, please, could the earth open now? This was exactly why he shouldn't be allowed in public.

"We should probably exchange phone numbers. What's yours? I'll call you, that way you'll have mine." Seth looked expectantly at him, and yeah, no way was he going to refuse.

Sacha recited his number, and moments later his back pocket buzzed.

"See ya around." Seth sketched out a half salute before tucking his phone away and walking toward his Jeep.

Sacha's pocket buzzed again. It couldn't be Seth, and there was only one other person who had his new number. When he'd quit the Marshals he cut all ties. New life, new number.

"What?" he demanded while watching Seth head to his Jeep, cataloguing the sway of his hips and the way his T-shirt stretched across his shoulders. Seth turned and waved as he opened the car door, then with a beep of the horn he was gone, and the morning was somehow dimmer in his absence.

"How rude. You know better than to answer the phone like that." His foster sister's irritated tone rang clear over the thousands of miles stretched between them.

"I knew it was you. Does that make it better?"

"Because I am the only one with your number." Mae-Lin sighed. "You need to quit hiding."

"I'm not hiding. I am taking a much-needed break."

"From—you know what, never mind. I didn't call to argue."

"Why *did* you call, then?" All they ever did was argue—in a very loving and supportive way, of course.

"Parker hasn't been in touch and hasn't returned any of my phone calls."

The throb in his forehead, which had mostly gone away, returned with full force.

"His number has been disconnected or changed, and when I called that pathetic boyfriend, roommate, whatever he is, he claimed Parker had left and taken most of his things with him."

"He's thirty-two, an adult who can make his own decisions." Admittedly, Parker's track record was poor. Sacha had not met the roommate/boyfriend, and Mae-Lin didn't like anyone anyway, unfortunately Sacha's foster brother had a record of terrible choices in careers and boyfriends. Although he'd been with the 'new guy' for almost a year and was trying to start fresh by going back for a degree in finance. Yawn.

Parker was a natural caregiver who jumped in headfirst... and was generally the last to realize he was being used. As a wallet, or even as a dupe, in the case of his first job out of college. Parker led with his heart, and too many shitheads had found him impossible to resist.

The kid would literally give the shirt off his back. Sacha wasn't quite sure how Parker found these people. He'd finally concluded that Parker was a magnet for them but had hoped Mae-Lin was wrong about this one.

"He didn't call on my birthday." She sounded smug, like that sealed the argument... and it did. The three of them had a tradition of talking on their birthdays. And, yeah, sometimes one of them forgot, but they always called within a few days... and sent the required extravagant apology present. Realization struck him, and he groaned.

Sacha shut his eyes in a grimace, even though she couldn't see him. "I fucking forgot your birthday."

Mae-Lin snickered evilly. "I'll send you a few links." Goddamn, missing her birthday would cost him.

"I'll see what I can find out, but let's give him a little time. He may only need to regroup."

After clicking off he tried Parker's number. Sacha was greeted with the standard out-of-service message, as Mae-Lin had said. Parker was a lot of things—irritating, impulsive, occasionally irresponsible—but he was not the one who forgot Mae-Lin's birthday. That was Sacha.

Still, Parker *was* an adult. He'd get in touch soon, probably, and Sacha would help him put the pieces back together like he always did. To soothe his conscience Sacha made a quick call, confirming that Parker's number went straight to voicemail. Mae could be a *tad* dramatic. He left a message instructing Parker to call one of them back or *else*. Sacha hadn't decided what 'else' would be yet but as a coercion tactic it usually worked pretty well on Parker. Ten minutes later his phone chimed announcing an incoming text.

I'M FINE BIG BROTHER. THINKING.

Sacha quickly forwarded the text to Mae-Lin and shoved the damn phone back into his pocket.

Back up the ladder with work gloves on, Sacha was inspecting the false ceiling and removing a few of the obviously loose pieces of plasterboard when there was a tap on the front door. Debating whether he would answer became moot when whoever it was boldly opened the door and came inside.

"Hello?" The stranger looked right and left before spying Sacha on the ladder.

He was in his late twenties, with short light-blond hair and a smattering of freckles across his nose and cheeks. The gray suit and dress shoes were out of place. Suits were not normal attire in Skagit, where the dress code ran more toward clean cargo shorts and a T-shirt in the summer and clean jeans and a T-shirt paired with a flannel or sweatshirt in cooler weather. Sacha stayed on the ladder, forcing the stranger to look up at him.

"Hello!" The man repeated enthusiastically before extending a hand upward with a business card in it. "Christopher Meyer, representing the Skagit Chamber of Commerce. Wanted to give you a personal welcome." Dammit, Sacha had been playing tag with this guy for a few weeks, ever since the sale papers had been signed. Sacha didn't take the card. His hands were full of old plasterboard he let fall to the ground with a crash, and dust billowed up where it hit the pile of debris.

"So, uh," Meyer continued awkwardly, stepping back from the mess, "we wanted to extend a welcome."

"You said that. We?" Sacha looked around for evidence of *we*.

"We, the, uh, Chamber of Commerce." Meyer paused. "So, what are your plans for the building? We have resources if you need anything. We are touching base today with, uh, the neighborhood. Getting the word out and all that."

"Great." Sacha replied in a way that hopefully made it crystal clear to Meyer that Sacha couldn't give a shit about the Chamber of Commerce and whatever their agenda was.

"Any chance of a tour?"

Sacha squinted at him. Was this guy for real? Hell. Fucking. No "Nope." *Don't let the door hit your ass on the way out.*

With no other recourse except extreme rudeness—and the guy was not in the same league as Sacha there—Meyer turned around and left the way he'd come. Good riddance.

Peace and quiet descended. Sacha loved being in the Warrick by himself, listening to the sounds of traffic and the neighborhood along the street outside. It was soothing. If not for recurring thoughts of a slender—almost skinny—guy with tousled brown hair and matching eyes, who made Sacha contemplate things he'd pushed to the side for a very long time, Sacha might have been able to get some work done. Instead ladders, coffee, and Seth Culver hijacked his thoughts.

SIX

SETH

The mattress springs whined, protesting underneath Seth's restless body as he tossed and turned, trying and failing to find a comfortable position for sleep. He couldn't reach that delicious edge where merely relaxing a little would allow him to fall into a peaceful dream.

Instead, his thoughts relentlessly drifted toward the man he had met that morning. Each time his eyes slid shut, images of a tall, dark-haired man with wide shoulders, a broad chest, and heavy Eastern European features, salt sprinkled through the hair on his head and on his chest, his thick eyebrows still black as night, jerked him away from sleep.

It had been a very long time since Seth had been attracted to someone outside of a club or party, where the intent was to get laid after a few drinks. Not that he hadn't had sex, but being interested enough that the few hours they had spent together left him hoping for more? That hadn't happened since before his aunt died. He and Sacha hadn't even touched, except when Seth had slipped down the ladder and smacked into his broad chest. Seth was pretty sure, as he ran the replay through his head, that the way Sacha's gaze focused on him wasn't because he was disgusted. It seemed quite the opposite.

As cliché as it sounded, even in the privacy of his own head, it was something about Sacha's eyes. The whole package was pretty fucking incredible, but it was his eyes. When Sacha had realized what he looked like and why strangers were looking at them funny, his laughter had changed his entire face.

It had been automatic for Seth to offer help. He had trained as an EMT, although he'd only worked for a few months in Arizona before quitting. It had been too hard after Marnie died. Everything had been too hard.

Then the guy had laughed. Genuinely laughed, and he'd gone from slightly worrisome-looking to devastatingly handsome. The laughter had awakened something in Seth that had been quiet far too long.

The whole exchange had been a kind of out-of-body experience. Not that Seth was shy in any way, but inviting a stranger to come to his home and take a shower? His common sense had fled.

Rolling onto his other side, he twitched the covers off and punched the pillow before lying back with a groan. He tried shutting his eyes again, only to be flooded with more images. The inner slide show began with the moment Sacha's expression turned from suspicion and confusion to laughter, and his eyes had changed from a murky green to a clear agate. Seth's heart had lurched in his chest.

When Sacha had straightened to his full height, looking Seth directly in the eyes, proving he was a few inches taller than Seth—rare enough—he'd looked right into Seth's soul. Seth felt exposed, like he had left a hidden door to himself open without realizing it, allowing the handsome stranger a peek inside. He'd had to go and get the man a coffee to mask the effect Sacha'd had on him. It unnerved him. Seth stayed in control of his interactions, both social and sexual.

He shifted again. Crud, at this rate he might as well get out of bed and do something productive. Picking up his phone, he checked the time. 02:33 glared from the screen. Seth rolled over onto his stomach, pressing his face into the cool side of the pillow.

After experiencing a bizarre negative space inside himself since his aunt died, he didn't exactly trust his reaction to Sacha...

Could a person travel from below zero to deep attraction in a few short hours? Seth knew nothing about Sacha, only that he appeared to be a history junkie like himself and had taken on the task of bringing an old building back to life.

Annnd, he was back to thinking about those eyes, laugh lines like starbursts, a smile that took Sacha's face from being imposing to... something else, something Seth wanted to hold in his hands.

Seth became aware of an answering tingle in his groin. If he wasn't going to sleep, he might as well rub one out. Flicking back the covers, he reached down and pulled off his sleep shorts—commando, who wanted sweaty balls? The cool night air caressed his skin as he reached down to stroke himself. His half-hard cock felt good against his palm; jerking off was always one of those weird dual experiences because both his cock and his hands liked what they felt.

A few languid tugs, a twist at the top and a thumb along the tip, and Seth was as hard as a rock. Bending and then spreading his knees a little, he reached down with his other hand and began to roll his balls around. Fuck, it felt good. Not as good as if someone else was doing it, but enough. He wasn't going to feel the remotest bit guilty if a virtual stranger's face helped him focus.

He wanted to draw the sensation out longer, but once he got started—the iron-hard slide of his erection under his palm, precome oozing from his slit—he couldn't stop himself from coming and didn't want to. Thrusting into his hand in earnest, pumping himself harder and faster, he came with a breathless grunt, spilling over his hand and onto his stomach.

He lay there panting for a few minutes before getting up and wiping himself off with toilet paper. Back in his bed, he left the sleep pants off and covered himself with the top sheet. The next thing he knew, it was morning and bright sunshine was trying its hardest to stream into his bedroom.

The sunshine was about the only thing bright. Seth logged on to check his bank account, and it reminded him that, sooner rather than later, he needed to make the rounds again giving out flyers for his budding landscaping business. Perhaps even resort to checking his email.

Of the trades he had tried his hand at, landscaping was his favorite.

He and Marnie had gardened together, as much as they could in hot, dry Arizona. Shaking himself out of his reverie, Seth headed out to mow his front lawn. Neighborhood be damned, he would have a yard —garden—to be proud of.

Earlier in the year he'd discovered hellebore. Subtly beautiful and mysterious, its foliage and flower were often close to the same color, and the flower was a perfectly shaped bell, a perfect crown for faery monarchy. It came in a variety of shades from green to cream, purple to pink, one so dark it was almost black.

The plants didn't like much sun; the home Seth had found for them along the side yard was perfect, and they were thriving there in the near-constant shade. He enjoyed them, picking out the vagaries of color that made them so interesting and complicated.

Several hours later, Seth surveyed his morning's work. If he was lucky, between the night-blooming nicotiana, bee balm, Russian sage, and buddleia, he would have hummingbirds and honeybees visiting on a regular basis. If he was patient, maybe he would discover their hoard.

SEVEN

SACHA

Sacha stood back, surveying his handiwork. About a third of the false ceiling lay on the wood floor, and Seth was right, the tin tiles were gorgeous. Each one was about the size of his hand, and the center stamp was a stylized green-man emblem surrounded by a frame of leaves. Absolutely worth the effort to clean up and restore.

His stomach rumbled loudly, expressing its displeasure at being ignored since before lunchtime. Circling around the first floor, he dragged the day's debris into a pile against one wall. Then he made an attempt to clean up using the hand sink, digging around in his duffel for a semi-clean shirt. No point in playing zombie again.

There was a bar a few blocks away; he'd driven past it several times, taking note of the sandwich board on the sidewalk advertising the daily specials. It was as good a place as any to escape his thoughts... or brood, more likely.

Work on the Warrick, while physically demanding, was mindless, giving him far too much time to think. Sacha had spent more than a few hours over the past week wondering if he had misread Seth's interest. Wondering about him in general. Obviously Seth was a nice guy; maybe he always invited strange men home for showers? Made them breakfast? Pretended to be fascinated by endless construction projects? Maybe Sacha had confused interest in the Warrick with interest in him. The thought depressed him.

Seth was probably gay. He was at least bi. There'd been a few too many appraising glances when Seth thought Sacha wouldn't notice. Sacha hadn't been a US Marshal for twelve years only to be the least observant person on the planet once he retired. And he was done trying to fool himself about his attraction to men. Because the gay bars he went to and men's beds he ended up in were by accident? In the military he'd been able to claim it had been convenience: a hole was a hole. That excuse didn't hold any longer.

Out on the street, the sunshine felt overly bright and new, shining into corners previously populated by shadows. His truck sat waiting. For a moment Sacha considered walking but, fuck it, he hadn't changed *that* drastically.

He stopped short at the entrance to the Loft. There was a little rainbow sticker in the corner of the front window. He felt stupid for not noticing it before and hesitated a beat before pushing the door open. Then he felt like a shit. Wasn't he trying to change, to accept himself? Hadn't he moved to Skagit with the intention of not hiding anymore? Of at least hoping to quit living in the closet and fucking men in the dark? The door swung slightly ajar, and cool air from inside washed over his skin. He took a deep breath and entered.

He wasn't struck by lightning. Only the bartender noticed him— and since that was the guy's job, Sacha didn't think he suddenly had a sign around his neck proclaiming his gayness.

The place wasn't full. It was still early and a weekday. Which one was to blame, Sacha didn't know. He plopped down at the end of the bar near the servers' station. He couldn't stand sitting at a table by himself.

"Hey." The bartender greeted him, sliding a coaster across the bar. "Can I pour you a drink?" If Sacha wasn't mistaken, he was being eyed appreciatively.

"A pale ale?" A little discussion and Sacha was given three local ales to choose from. Taking a long, satisfying sip of something with cascade hops and a citrus flavor, Sacha shut his eyes for a moment, enjoying the bitter flavors on his tongue.

"Long day?" The bartender was still watching him. Sacha couldn't tell if it was out of boredom or something else. "You want the food menu?" He was a younger guy, younger than Sacha was comfortable with, but he was good-looking, with curious, greenish eyes and a mop of auburn hair. What he *wasn't* was a rumpled, tall, tangle-haired guy named Seth with a smile that made his entire face light up.

"Yep, to both." He *was* being scoped. There was no stopping his grin from forming. He might still be working a few things out, but it always felt nice to be appreciated.

"Are you new to the area? I haven't seen you here before."

Sacha took another sip before answering, "I recently relocated, but I, uh, did some business here over the last couple years." By business he meant undercover as a Russian human trafficker. Another reason why he was reluctant to tell the people he did know in town that he was here. He felt weirdly exposed. Before, he'd been undercover with a script to follow; now he was plain old Sacha, struggling with life choices.

"I'm Cameron."

"Sacha." They shook hands across the bar, and Cameron grinned at him. There was no denying he was attractive. He had the same kind of open smile Seth did. Unreserved and unabashed.

The hum of the bar increased, and Cameron turned away to help a few other customers who had wandered in. When he came back, Sacha was ready for another beer and ordered a burger and fries. It felt good to be sitting and listening to the swirl of conversations around him as other customers came in for a drink or a meal.

"You don't seem like our usual type." Cameron was back in front of him.

"Whaddya mean?" Sacha cocked his head at the young man. "Explain."

Cameron polished an invisible speck off the bar top, obviously embarrassed that he'd broached the subject of Sacha's appearance in the Loft. "Um, geez, I told Sterling I wasn't ready for prime time."

Sacha waited for him to continue. "I, uh, am usually pretty good at telling, you know, and…well I haven't seen you here before." A blush crept over his face, and his words halted. Sacha turned to see what had caught his attention. Cameron's gaze was glued to a very handsome man around Sacha's age. His hair was almost completely silver, with a little dark sprinkled throughout.

The man looked over at the bar area, spotted Cameron with his tongue practically hanging out of his mouth, and quirked a black eyebrow before changing course to go sit in the dining area. Cameron muttered something under his breath. It sounded to Sacha like "arrogant motherfucker," but he couldn't be sure.

"Friend of yours?"

Cameron's blush deepened further once he realized Sacha had witnessed the exchange. "He thinks I'm too young."

"Oh. Um, how old are you?"

"Twenty-two. Ira's," Cameron waved a frustrated hand in the other man's direction, "I dunno, your age? Maybe a little older. I heard the lady at the Booking Room talking about his birthday being a big one, so he's probably going to be forty soon." Cameron sighed, his eyes still on the mysterious Ira.

"Well, I guess you'll have to convince him you aren't too young." And how did he end up at a gay bar giving advice to the bartender? Weren't there rules about this sort of thing? Maybe there was a good reason Ira thought Cameron was too young.

"He won't even look at me, much less talk to me. How am I gonna convince him?"

Sacha considered Cameron's words. "There's that old saying: actions speak louder than words. Maybe he needs to see you doing something else, not only being here. Are you in school or anything? What else do you do?"

A customer tapped on the bar, and Cameron went to take their order. On his way back, he picked up Sacha's burger from the kitchen. The tantalizing scent of grilled beef and melted cheese had Sacha's mouth watering before Cameron set the food down in front of him. Sacha took a huge bite, chewing while waiting for Cameron's answer.

The burger practically melted in his mouth, and the fries were cooked in some sort of fancy truffle oil. Delicious.

"I'm kind of still getting on my feet. Sterling let me work as a busboy before I turned twenty-one. Now he's giving me a few bartending shifts, so I'm making more money." Cameron's gaze shifted inward. There was more to this story, and Sacha had a feeling he wasn't going to like it. He already had a soft spot for the kid. Young man.

At twenty-one Sacha'd been in the military kicking ass overseas, pretending to be an adult. He'd had to make adult decisions daily and live with the consequences. Looking back through a lens of experience, yeah, he'd been young, but he hadn't been innocent.

"My parents threw me out of the house when I came out. I'd like to do more, but I'm still working at making sure I can pay the rent and buy groceries. Plus I have some medical bills I gotta pay," he mumbled.

"Hey." Sacha reached out, surprising himself, covering Cameron's smaller hand with his own. "Don't beat yourself up. Look how far you've come. If this Ira guy can't see that you're an adult, you either gotta show him or quit moping about it, because that shit won't change anything."

Cameron grinned back at him, seeming to have regained his earlier good humor. "Yeah, screw that."

Hell *had* frozen over. Sacha had given advice to a gay man and had dinner in a gay bar without the earth swallowing him. The world hadn't ended. As he finished his burger and fries, he allowed himself to think about Seth and whether they would meet again.

Sacha wasn't superstitious, didn't believe in God—had seen way too much bad shit happen to good people for that—but it was impossible to contemplate recent incidents in his life without wondering if maybe he should be paying a little more attention. Falling off the fire escape in Kansas City had brought him to Skagit. Falling off the ladder the other morning had led him to Seth (who, remarkably, had not run screaming in the other direction).

It seemed the universe was trying to tell him something, and if

Sacha sat on his ass watching the world go by instead of participating, he was not going to hear it. He needed to take his own advice to Cameron, modify it a little, but the core message—actions spoke louder than words—held true.

If he was going to change his life, *keep* changing his life, both metaphorically and for real, he needed to quit using the Warrick as an excuse to avoid seeing people he might know. Which meant Mae-Lin was right, he *was* hiding. Groaning quietly at the realization, he leaned on the bartop, his head in his hands, pulling the hair at the back of his head. He hated it when Mae-Lin was right.

Being in the military during DADT, and then a US Marshal, had fed his innate tendency toward hiding. Maybe some guys felt safe enough being more open, but he never had. The wall he'd built around himself was so high and deep he wasn't sure if he would ever be able to break it down, but he was damn well going to try.

Straightening from the bar, Sacha squared his shoulders. He could do this. Deep breath. He had Seth's cell number. Tomorrow he would call, and they would have coffee, and maybe Sacha wouldn't make an ass of himself.

A face appeared in his memory, one that haunted him with some regularity even all these years after he'd come to the States. Sacha had been the one to find him, bloody and lifeless; if he'd ever known the boy's name, it had been forgotten over the intervening years. In the filthy alley, Sacha wouldn't have recognized him if not for the bits of clothing clinging to his remains. Sacha'd seen him around—he hadn't been too much older than Sacha—laughing with other boys and older men before disappearing behind a shop or down an alley. The strange boy had been untouchably beautiful, until he was dead.

Sacha himself had been an outcast, left at a state orphanage in Bosnia when he was a toddler—a family with too many mouths to feed, maybe, or a single mother; he didn't know the reason. When the orphanage closed its doors a few years later, Sacha found his way to the streets of Sarajevo and eventually to a missionary group that brought him and several other children to the United States. A long, strange trip indeed.

He'd never forgotten the lesson, though, about who it was accept-able to be with. That boy had been careless, gone with someone dangerous, and it had cost him the most precious thing he had to give. Even apart from that boy, there had been the anti-gay graffiti, the daily rants blaring from radios and TVs.

A shuffling noise caught his attention, and he raised his eyes to the mirror fixed againt the backbar. Behind him a familiar figure stood, eyebrows bunched in confusion, squinting at him. The fucking universe. He'd met Joey James back in December when he'd been finishing up his undercover assignment.

"Oh my God. It *is* you."

He twisted around on the bar stool to face the young man standing behind him.

"I thought it was you, and then I thought it couldn't be. But I looked again and I knew it had to be you. I can't believe you're here. What are you doing here?"

Joey was irritating and tenacious, but Sacha respected his bravery and smarts. He hadn't told him, but it was true. Joey was the reason Sacha didn't have worse nightmares about the young trafficking victims he had been trying to save.

Before he could say anything, Joey launched himself at Sacha, embracing him in a full-body hug, somehow ending up mostly in Sacha's lap. Boundaries were not Joey's strong suit.

"You're ruining my reputation, kid," Sacha growled as he hugged Joey back. Nearly a foot shorter than Sacha, Joey was a lot of energy packed into a small body. Sacha wondered how his boyfriend managed, although being big enough and Nordic enough to pass for Thor probably helped. The two of them were clearly very well suited for each other.

"Ppphhft, your reputation. Come sit with us. I want to hear all about it all. Why you are here... wait, are you—" Joey's voice dropped to a loud whisper, "—undercover?"

"Well, if I was, *you* just blew it." Joey's eyes widened and a horri-fied expression crossed his face. Sacha took pity on him. "I'm not, though. Actually, I retired from the Marshals."

"Okay, now you are required to come sit with us." Joey disentangled himself enough to point at a table across the bar where three other men were watching with amusement. One of them was Joey's boyfriend, Buck Swanfeldt. Another was Adam Klay, a local fed who had assisted with the Matveev case. Adam cocked his head, indicating the open chair next to him.

Fuck, he was going to do this.

The third man at the table was introduced as Nate Richardson, an agent who worked for Adam. Nate was around Adam's age, maybe younger, bright red hair and an astounding amount of freckles. He'd recently joined Adam's team from the east coast. He seemed on edge, and soon after Joey dragged Sacha over he made excuses to leave. Sacha wanted to beg him to stay; as soon as Nate left, Joey would begin his relentless questioning.

"New guy." Adam smirked, watching Nate leave. "I make him nervous, but he bravely joined us for an impromptu happy hour. Although I don't know why the fuck I am hanging out with these two."

Sacha respected Adam. He had good instincts and wasn't as much of a tool as most of the feebs Sacha had had the misfortune to work with. Adam was shorter than Sacha, but he was built, heavily muscled, still looked like the football player he had been in high school. He was also the son of a prominent local artist who had passed away last fall.

"Because your boyfriend is on a business trip and you are sad and lonely. And we are the only people who will put up with your cranky ass."

"There's that," Adam muttered.

Joey leaned across the table toward Sacha. "Okay, why are you here? *Here*, here. You do know the Loft is a gay bar, right?"

"Joey, you don't ask people that," his much-smarter boyfriend interjected, eyebrows raised almost to his hairline.

Joey didn't take his eyes off Sacha, narrowing them as if he was threatening. "I disagree. Sacha won't tell us unless we ask."

"Unless *you* ask. Normal people don't ask that kind of stuff." Buck rolled his eyes at his boyfriend.

"Fine, I'm not normal. Well?" He tapped his index finger impatiently on the table. Sacha shook his head in disbelief.

Adam watched the exchange with amusement, leaning back in his chair with his arms crossed over his chest. Doing nothing to rescue Sacha from the interrogation. Asshole.

"You know, I could have been hungry." Joey glared, and Sacha continued, "But I still came in when I saw the rainbow sticker." He interrupted himself. "I need another beer." If he was going to do this, he was only going to do it once, and there was no way he was getting through it without alcohol. "This story is longer than gay or straight, or whatever."

"You stay here." Joey practically bolted to the bar in search of a beer for Sacha. When he returned moments later, Sacha took a long drink before continuing. Pondering life changes, about being open about who he was. That, even though he hadn't known this group of men very long they were people he trusted. He felt like he owed it to himself to be completely open, to tell the entire story. Anything else would smack of avoidance.

"It's not like I recently discovered I'm gay. But I was born in what was then Yugoslavia, which was not known for its progressive politics." The boy's battered face came to the forefront of his memory again. "When I came here I was placed with a conservative Christian family. They weren't horrible, but their attitude didn't help, plus I was already different enough. I never considered coming out. Then I was in the army during DADT and, as you know, a US Marshal."

Adam was nodding as Sacha spoke. "I'm a little younger, but law enforcement hasn't changed overnight. My team is lucky to have a great leader. For the life of me, I do not understand why who we fuck affects our day jobs."

"Don't interrupt, I want to know the rest. You left without saying goodbye!" Joey legitimately looked upset that Sacha had left Skagit without contacting him.

"Aw, did you miss me?" This earned Sacha another glare from Joey and a quiet chuckle from Buck.

Taking another sip of his beer, he continued, "Yeah, anyway, getting shot and losing my spleen wasn't so much fun. Then some other things happened after I returned to the Marshals service that made me take a long, hard look at my life. Long story short, I retired and decided to move here."

"And do what? Where are you living? What are you doing?"

"I'm surveying the best locations in the county for shallow graves so when I get tired of all the questions I know where to hide the body," Sacha grumbled. The other three men burst into laughter, and Sacha noticed a glimmer on Joey's left hand. "Wait, what's with the ring?"

By the time he extricated himself from the welcoming committee, Sacha had been invited to the social event of the following year. Buck and Joey were getting married, and the entire population of Skagit was descending on Maureen James's house in the spring to watch the event. Sacha had, in fact, not been invited but *commanded* to attend.

Adam had laughed before admitting that he and his boyfriend were attending as well. His phone buzzed and the screen flashed at the same time, and the laughing ended as Adam's expression turned serious. "I've got to take this, duty calls."

Sacha left along with Adam, gladly escaping to the peace and quiet of the Warrick.

EIGHT

SACHA

Warmth cocooned Sacha. Cool hands soothed his overheated skin. They were big hands, ones that could hold him down and do what they wanted. But they didn't; they felt safe, soft, gentle, skimming across his pecs to lightly tweak a nipple. No one had ever touched him there, and the action sent a jolt of lust directly to his rapidly hardening dick as if there was a direct conduit between them no teacher had bothered to tell him about in sex ed.

He moaned under the attention. His body yearned. Yearned so much. Weight pressed against his back, he didn't panic; it felt right and good for the weight to be there. One strong hand continued to roam across his chest, the other still playing with that nipple. He needed it to touch his other nipple. He tried saying the words, but he was overcome with pleasure, speechless. He jutted his hips forward, silently begging for attention.

If he could form words he would demand *more* and *harder*, but he couldn't. Instead he offered his cock, needing touch, caress, the pressure of a hand to find him, dripping and desperate, to stroke him and rub his erection until he came. The hand finally moved down, gripping him briefly before moving farther, taking himself in hand.

He was surrounded by heat and fresh sheets. Visceral desire

crashed against his carefully maintained barriers, a wave on a rising tide. He moaned again when hot breath warmed the back of his neck. Was that the wet tip of a tongue? One hand on his nipple, leaving the other throbbing with want; the second hand gently rolling his balls, occasionally changing it up to massage his perineum, which had him begging for more, further—but he couldn't think about that, couldn't go there, because teeth bit down on his earlobe and Sacha came, bucking into his own hand, covers and bedding tangling around his legs, trapping him. All the things he'd fantasized about, broke through —broke *him*, leaving him a sweaty, sticky, hot, fucked-up mess after the most fucking incredible dream he'd ever had.

Sacha bolted upright, wisps of the dream disintegrating as he became aware of his surroundings. The sleeping bag was tangled around his hips, and he'd come all over his stomach. His breathing was ragged, chest heaving like he'd run a marathon. The digital clock was blinking 4:45 a.m. He dug around in his duffel for hand wipes and did the best he could to clean himself up. The box was half-empty by the time he finished.

The twenty-four-hour gym opened at five a.m.—which he didn't understand, but he was thankful they were open at all. The locker room was blissfully empty. Sacha took one of the stalls at the very end of the shower room. If he quietly jerked himself off to the image of Seth completely naked with a raging erection all for Sacha, dribbling precome and begging for Sacha to *do something*, no one was going to judge him but himself. This time of the morning was too early for judgment.

The dream stayed with him long after his come washed down the drain.

He made the drive to the gym three mornings in a row. It was embarrassing that at his age he couldn't stop thinking, or dreaming, about another man who he hadn't actually touched yet. He kept putting off calling or texting Seth, not because he didn't want to but because he didn't want to fumble the call. And, going for the win, he had a bad case of nerves making him feel about fourteen years old.

Sacha was also... unsuccessfully trying not to worry about his foster brother. Since Mae-Lin's phone call he had tried to get ahold of Parker again. There had been no further response to his emails or phone calls, only the single text after his first call. As far as Sacha could tell, Parker hadn't updated any of his social media accounts either. Sacha was giving him another day to hide and lick his wounds before calling some old law enforcement acquaintances... assuming he hadn't burnt those bridges and the forest around them when he left Kansas City.

An email had pinged his inbox yesterday, no subject and a link and an already 'filled' virtual shopping cart. Wonderful. He dropped an unholy amount of money on Mae-Lin's birthday gift. A pair of fancy shoes, for fuck's sake, but he'd felt his savings balance plummet when he clicked on the 'place order now' button.

Carefully backing down the ladder, Sacha used his T-shirt to wipe the sweat from his face. He was going to have to invest in a fan, or AC. He cringed at the prospect of going out in public again; running into Joey and the gang had been awkward enough. This personal-growth shit wasn't for cowards. Maybe he could order an AC unit online, a big one with enough BTUs to cool the entire building.

A noise jolted him from a waking fantasy involving huge amounts of cool air blowing across his sweaty body. An indistinct figure was outlined on the other side of his front door. Groaning, he pulled his dirty shirt back over his head. It was probably another neighbor inter-rupting his work for a building tour who then would stand around expecting Sacha to fucking chat.

Worse, when he opened the door, it was the guy from the Chamber of Commerce again. Sacha had kind of hoped after the guy left his card the other day he was done pestering him. He hadn't exactly kept his card. It went in the recycling as soon as Mr. Chamber of Commerce's ass had left the building.

"Is there something you needed?" Sacha asked. He hoped his voice transmitted his lack of enthusiasm at the interruption.

The man seemed unfazed by Sacha's manner. "Christopher Meyer from the Skagit Chamber of Commerce. Checking in on you again."

Could the guy not tell how little had changed since the last time he'd been by?

"Well, I'm still in the process of tearing out the old before I decide what to do with the new." How was that for a non-answer? And, weirdly, it resonated personally: Sacha himself was a bit like the Warrick. Fuck, this self-reflective shit was ambushing his brain.

Meyer eyed him warily but continued, "We can provide you with contact names in city hall to help you with the permit process if you need. We have a network of small business owners who specialize in all aspects of the remodeling process. If you come to our meetings, you will meet other people like yourself." Sacha tuned his words out; obviously the guy wasn't going to take a hint and leave. Instead he looked at him carefully, comparing this man to Seth. Testing himself.

Meyer was good-looking, he supposed, and he did have a nice ass. Average height, blond hair cut in businessman style. Unlike Seth's unruly hair, which, regardless of his attempt to control it, had been slipping out of a hairband falling nearly to his shoulders when they had met. Sacha had liked Seth's hair a lot. The suit did nothing for Sacha, either. He'd seen enough of those to last him a lifetime.

There was no spark, nothing about Meyer that made Sacha curious to know more about him. Nothing that would have Sacha waking up in the middle of the night after some of the most erotic dreams of his life. Nothing worth changing his life for. Which was ridiculous, because for all of his replaying their meeting over and over, including Seth's obvious excitement when he learned that Sacha owned the Warrick, there was no magic that would tell Sacha Seth was interested in *him*.

Except he didn't think he'd imagined the reaction when he caught Seth falling off that ladder. Replaying the laughing brown eyes looking up into his own and supple lips in a wide smile was fast becoming a pastime. It was on a fucking repeating loop in his head.

"Mr. Bolic?" Meyer interrupted his train of thought.

"What?"

A file folder appeared in Meyer's hand. Where had he pulled that from? "Here's a brochure about our organization and a list of city numbers that could be helpful. The Chamber meets the first Tuesday of the month. Welcome aboard!" Sacha took the folder, and Meyer stuck out his hand for Sacha to shake. Reluctantly, Sacha took it. Meyer's grasp was firm and slightly sweaty. Once Meyer was on his way out the door, Sacha wiped his hand on his shorts.

Had he agreed to attend a meeting? Sacha wasn't sure. He'd kind of lost track of the conversation somewhere in the middle... thinking about Seth Culver's *hair*.

NINE

SETH

Luckily for his bank account, the flyers Seth had posted were beginning to pay off. It had been a couple of weeks since he had first posted them around town, and people were starting to email. After one no-show asshole (Seth had even called *again* to confirm the evening before), his first actual appointment was easy. Mrs. Anderson, one of his friend Micah's neighbors, needed her front yard refreshed. She was too frail to do the work herself any longer but missed the annuals she'd cheered herself up with over the years.

They met at her home and set a date for Seth to pick her up so they could go the nursery together and pick out the exact plants she needed. Mrs. Anderson seemed a little lonely, and Seth looked forward to spending time with her. He knew she wouldn't be able to stay inside while he worked on her flower beds.

"Will, Mr. Anderson, passed away three years ago," she said when she saw him glance toward the photograph on the mantel. It was a black-and-white wedding picture from the late fifties, if the dress was any indication.

"I'm sorry for your loss."

"It's part of life, but I would be lying if I told you I didn't miss him every day."

"My aunt, who raised me, died a few years ago. I still miss her." Sometimes it was almost unbearable. He figured it was because she had been the one certainty in his life, and when she died he had no one to act as his center. The grief had dulled but hadn't disappeared, he supposed it never would. Marnie wouldn't want him to grieve so hard, but he couldn't help it. Missing her felt like a splinter he couldn't quite remove; a little of it was left behind to fester.

Mrs. Anderson was very astute; she cocked her head at him. "Is your aunt the one who taught you to garden?"

"She was." He smiled. Marnie had brought home several packets of seeds. Together they had planted them in tiny pots, watered them, and waited for the first seedlings to poke through the soil. She had taught him how to water, to gently separate the plants. Seth hadn't wanted to go to school, worried that something would happen to the seedlings while he was gone.

"What a wonderful way to honor her memory."

As he was leaving, she tried to give him a check, but he refused to take any money until the work was done. As he drove away he set an internal note to ask Micah who else, if anyone, spent time with her.

His second—or third, depending on how he was counting—appointment of the day was outside of town. A little farther than he would like, but he couldn't complain when he needed the work. So here he was out in the east county following his GPS to gods knew where. Finally, the female voice directed him to take a right, and Seth parked in the driveway of a slightly disheveled mid-century two-story home with an unkempt yard. Seth's mental hands were rubbing together with excitement; this kind of yard was a blank slate and a moneymaker. He grabbed his notebook and headed for the door.

A youngish guy met him on the porch. "Hi, you must be Seth. I'm Greg. Would you like something to drink?" Greg was cute: big brown eyes, stick-straight brown hair longer on one side and currently tucked behind his ear. Seth would have had a pretty good idea which team he played for even if he hadn't been wearing a pink T-shirt with PRIDE imprinted in huge letters on the chest.

"No, thanks, I'm excited to take a look at your yard. Take me on a walk."

"Cool." Greg shut the door behind himself and motioned for Seth to follow him.

They walked around the property, a great deal of which was covered with invasive blackberry; they found two rhododendron bushes Greg hadn't known about and generally got an idea of what it would take to clear it out.

"So, you think you can pound it into shape?" Seth shook his head and smiled. Did the guy have these lines written up beforehand?

He quickly sketched out a map of Greg's yard and added some notes so he wouldn't forget. "I think so. How about I send you an estimate with three levels of work, and then we talk again." He looked up from his notepad, smiling at Greg's appraising glance.

"Still nothing to drink? I've got iced tea or beer." Definitely a suggestive eyebrow wiggle.

Seth thought about it for a second, but Sacha Bolic, with his salt-and-pepper hair, broad shoulders, and wary eyes popped into his head. No, he thought better of a quick afternoon delight with a stranger and possible client. Ethics and all that. "I better not; I have one more appointment waiting. No rest for the wicked."

By the next day he had two possible jobs – but he was pretty sure about Greg – and one potential customer trying to get work done for free. Seth valued himself more than that. No amount of hinting that she would "spread the word" had him offering several days of free labor. Next on his list was a visit to the Warrick building: if the coffee date wasn't going to come to him, he would take himself and coffee to Sacha.

PUSHING open the door of the Booking Room, he half-waved to a few regulars he recognized. Thankfully Ed Schultz wasn't there, or he would have been stuck gossiping for hours.

"Hey, Sara." Sara, Ed's daughter, owned the place. As usual she was behind the counter making the world turn, churning out coffees and plating pastries.

There was a new kid behind the cash register. Sara tended to hire lost souls, and Seth wondered where she had found this adorable limpet. He couldn't be more than eighteen, with jet-black hair that hung across one eye and porcelain skin goths would kill for. His eyes were a striking ice blue with a darker ring around the iris, set in an elfin face. The name tag hanging from his apron said "Rich."

"Hi, Seth. How's it going? What can we get you? Why don't you take this one, Rich?" She indicated Rich, who seemingly turned to stone at the request, his mouth opening and closing before he was able to reply.

"Um, hi. How can I help you?" Rich managed to ask.

"Don't worry, Seth doesn't bite." She looked at Seth. "Rich had an encounter with Mrs. Behn, and before that Jack Summers was in here with one of his sycophants."

Seth nodded in sympathy. Mrs. Behn was very particular about her pastries and the temperature of her coffee. She always repeated her orders to the staff several times, louder with each repetition, as if they were deaf. No matter that she always ordered the same thing and everyone had it memorized. Seth had seen her in action several times. Ed told him she had been a school teacher for forty years, and that explained everything. As for Jack Summers, he was SkPD and unfortunately believed the world revolved around him.

Ten minutes later, Seth left with a bag of mouthwatering pastries and his thermos full of coffee. Let 'Operation Drop In Unannounced' commence. He'd given Sacha a week to call for a coffee date, but who knew, maybe he hated texting or using the phone. O was shy, but he didn't think that was it. It was time for a direct approach. Seth didn't want to come across as a stalker, but his curiosity had been piqued.

As he parked, the door of the Warrick opened and a blond man in a gray suit exited the building. Seth narrowed his eyes. Who was this guy? Seth had first dibs. Stopping short outside the entrance, the stranger turned back and frowned. Seth was pretty sure it wasn't the building he was frustrated with. After a moment, the man shook his head and walked up the block.

From where he was parked, Seth could see Sacha's shadow moving around inside. Sometime in the past week Sacha'd pulled much of the façade away from the first floor. Three enormous windows were now exposed, extending almost from floor to ceiling on the first floor.

The windowpanes were opaque from years of built-up soot and dust, but Seth could see where Sacha had managed to crack one of them open a little. The revealed granite of the original fascia was grimy from being stuck behind cheap veneer for so many years, but damn, the Warrick would be extraordinary when it was finished.

"Hey, you found the windows. I can't believe someone covered them up like that."

Sacha didn't seem surprised to see him, offering a small smile before stepping back so Seth could come in. Seth wondered how often Sacha smiled, if it was something he wasn't used to. "Spent all night doing it. It's probably a good thing I don't have any neighbors," he grumbled.

Sacha looked exhausted, worn thin. There were bags under his eyes, and it was obvious he hadn't shaved; his stubble had more salt and pepper than his hair and was sexy as hell. Seth wanted to run his fingers across it—was it soft, or rough? Not that it mattered; either way, Sacha was a living, breathing fantasy come true. His height, breadth of shoulders, muscles that weren't from a gym. A little older than Seth, for sure, and that was icing on the cake. Or maybe Danish.

"It's good to see you. What brings you by?"

Seth held up the bag, shaking it a little. "I brought treats." He didn't imagine the charge of attraction; it was practically a living thing, a downed electrical wire sparking between them, waiting for one of them to make a move.

TEN
SACHA

Sacha tried to rub the grit out of his eyes. A heat wave had made it impossible to sleep for several days and showed no signs of letting up. Instead of sleeping, he'd spent the last night wrenching ancient drywall and two-by-four framing away from the boarded-up front windows so a breeze could hopefully sneak inside. Frustration-fueled and poorly planned, the "five-minute" project had turned into hours when it became clear that he would need to pull all the drywall and plywood away from both inside and outside to allow even the smallest breeze access. When five a.m. rolled around, sleeping had been pointless.

*He'd finally gotten rid of Chris Meyer, again—the man was relentless—when, from his side of the frosted glass, Sacha spied a lanky figure bouncing back and forth on the balls of his feet. His heart pounded in his throat, making him slightly lightheaded. Sacha had hoped Seth would stop by; he was too old to start texting and couldn't bring himself to call. He knew it was ridiculous; Seth had *given* Sacha his number. It didn't help that in the days since the coffee-zombie incident Seth had managed to insinuate himself into Sacha's daily thoughts and fuel his nightly fantasies. It was inexplicable. They had known each other for three or four hours, tops.

Besides, Seth was far too nice for him, and younger. There was no reason to imagine a hot younger man would find anything about Sacha compelling. It was pathetic. A laughable fantasy to imagine the minute Sacha decided to live "out" he would meet someone; life didn't work that way. He turned the doorknob anyway, heart pounding.

"I brought treats," Seth said after admiring the results of Sacha's overnight labor's. He held up a small white paper bag, the kind pastries come in. "Fresh out of the oven." In his other hand he held a dented silver thermos. "And coffee. Lots of it."

"Danish?" Sacha reached to snatch the bag out of Seth's hand, but the asshole jerked it out of range.

"Ah, ah, ah. You must want these pretty bad. What are you willing to do for one?" Seth teased, a wicked gleam in his eyes.

Seth looked good enough to eat, and Sacha was a starving man in more ways than one. Without thinking, Sacha moved toward Seth. Their chests were touching while Seth still held the bag of pastries out of reach. Seth's breath was hot against Sacha's cheek; his pupils dilated, reducing his irises to a strip of chocolate brown.

"Oh yeah?" Seth cocked his head to the side, exposing more of his neck. Seth smirked and the pink tip of his tongue swept out, moistening his lips. "I dare you."

Fucking hell, he'd never backed down from a dare in his life. Sacha growled under his breath before inhaling deeply, worshipping the lingering scent of sweat and maleness that was Seth-specific. The striation of browns that made his eyes appear caramel when the light hit them right was easy to see and impossible to look away from. A week of this man in his dreams and he had no self-control.

Seth was playing a dangerous game. Sacha's hands dropped of their own volition to rest on Seth's hips. Seth's lips parted. Sacha didn't miss the invitation. Ignoring the cacophony of voices in his head telling him this was a bad idea, he pressed his mouth against Seth's.

Fucking hell, it was perfection. Like a confection, sugary, hot, and sweet. It was impossible to resist sweeping his tongue across Seth's lips.

Sacha loved kissing. When he'd slept with women it was his

favorite part, almost always better than the long drag toward orgasm. This kiss was explosive a ticking bomb ready to go off. If they kept going, eating at each other's mouths, licking, nipping, sucking, Sacha probably could come from that alone.

Seth murmured something when Sacha abandoned his lips to trail hot kisses across Seth's cheek and down his neck where he stopped nipping, now gently sucking where Seth's neck and shoulder met. The low groans and murmurs coming from the man in his arms spurred him on. Abandoning Seth's neck, Sacha returned to ravaging his mouth, sucking on his lower lip and his hot, eager tongue.

"Jesus Christ, Sacha, just... ungph." If Seth could speak, Sacha was doing something wrong.

A hard thump against his hip had Sacha pulling back and looking down. Seth was trying to grab onto him but still had the thermos in one hand and the pastries in the other.

Sacha chuckled. "Don't you even think about dropping that bag."

"Dude, please. You're killing me." Seth's body shuddered against Sacha's, his eyes half-mast and his lips swollen from their kissing.

"I don't think so. You were asking for punishment."

"Shit." Seth shivered against him.

Sweeping his hands underneath Seth's T-shirt, Sacha slowly traced his fingertips up Seth's flat stomach to his nipples, which were hard under his touch. Sacha rubbed them both with his thumbs before flicking one of them, making Seth moan decadently and shudder against him again.

"So fucking responsive," Sacha ground out. The thermos thudded against the hardwood flooring, and Seth used his free hand to grab at Sacha's hip, pulling them closer.

They needed to stop before they ended up writhing and naked on the floor of the Warrick. In theory it sounded hot, but Sacha suspected one of them would end up with slivers in his ass.

Before pulling away, he whispered into Seth's ear, "I think I've earned a Danish now." Seth was flushed, and his hair had gotten tugged out of the band holding it away from his face. Sacha couldn't recall when he had run his hands through Seth's hair, but he had dreamt about it more than once over the past week.

"I'm going to start bringing pastries every day," Seth said, breathless. "Holy fuck." He swiped a hand across his mouth before handing the bag to Sacha. "You can have first choice. I think I blew a fuse."

The apricot Danish was very good. It almost melted in Sacha's mouth, but it didn't hold a candle to the taste of Seth on his lips.

"I'm finishing getting the ceiling down." Sacha pointed at the wooden slats the plasterboard had been mounted to. "I ordered some cleaning supplies to strip the tiles, which is going to take a fuck-ton of time."

What he didn't say was that he needed a distraction before he dragged Seth over to the tangled mass of sleeping bag and mostly flat air mattress. He had a feeling there wouldn't be much protest, but Sacha needed a breather, self-control. As short a time as they had known each other, and now knowing what Seth tasted like, Sacha needed this *whatever it was* to matter. He hadn't imagined the chemistry between them.

He had to adjust himself before he got back up on the ladder. Seth smirked and licked his fingers suggestively. Sacha groaned. He was in capital-T Trouble.

"Hey." Several hours later, Seth's voice dragged him from reliving the kiss. Again. Sacha'd finished pulling down the remaining ceiling plaster on the main floor and was propped against the ladder, planning the best way to get the rest of the wooden framing down with as little damage as possible. He could see where workers had fastened the frame into some of the tiles with woodscrews.

Seth had stayed to help, and Sacha enjoyed having the company. Seth proved to be quietly efficient, not asking a lot of questions or engaging in meaningless chatter. Without asking, he had sorted the trash and recyclable materials into separate piles. Then he had found a spare set of gloves and worked on removing the remaining framing around the huge windows.

"What?" Sacha didn't look at Seth, instead planning for the next stage of deconstruction.

"Why don't you come back to my place for a shower again? Bring your stuff; you can toss it in the wash. You won't be able to finish any of this tonight."

The right thing to do was to say no. He had already accepted a great deal from Seth. But Christ, a shower and clean clothes? That was an offer he couldn't turn down. Not only could he not bring himself to refuse, he wanted to run out to his truck and roar over to Seth's, running every single stoplight along the way to stand under the cool rain of a shower until he couldn't feel a single speck of dust on his skin.

Something must have shown on his face, because Seth grinned. Setting the broom he was holding aside, he tugged off his gloves. "All right then. My place it is. You wanna to ride with me?"

Sacha followed Seth in his truck, parking on the gravel strip in front of his house. Seth waited for him before unlocking his front door and stepping aside so Sacha could bring his duffel in.

"You hop in the shower. I'll throw these things in the washer for you."

Sacha hardly heard a word. He was so fixated on rinsing the sweat and grime off his body, it was like he couldn't breathe. Unlike the gym, here he could take his time and not feel weird about it.

Like the house, the shower was a tiny piece of shit. Sacha barely fit inside the flimsy beige enclosure, and he had to scrunch down to get his head under the spray. Regardless, the experience was bliss. He was so tired of having to go to the gym to get cleaned up. Scrubbing the plaster dust and dirt from his skin and hair, he gloried in the cool water splashing across his shoulders. An indecent groan of pleasure escaped his lips. This shower was better than any sex he'd ever had. Yet.

He still remembered his first hot shower on American soil. It had been both glorious and frightening. Glorious because, he had been filthy from months, if not years, of systematic shelling and ongoing skirmishes even before the outbreak of war in Bosnia. There had been no facilities for orphan street children. Frightening because it finally hit him that he was never going back. That his life was now in the

United States and he had a responsibility to make the best of it. Hot water gushing over his shoulders and tears running from his eyes Sacha washed his homeland from his body.

When Sacha'd arrived in the United States in 1990, aged 12, filthy, terrified, the American family that had taken him in already had five other kids. A couple of their own, the rest homeless like himself. There was never enough of anything to go around: food, clothing, beds, space, or comfort. Still, Sacha hadn't cared that he shared a bedroom with a seven-year-old, nor about hand-me-downs or a lack of books and toys.

That reminded him that he still hadn't heard from Parker.

Parker Crane and he ended up being roommates for the six years Sacha had been in foster care. Sacha refused to contemplate what kind of trouble Parker might have landed in this time around. After almost twenty years in law enforcement, he still shook his head over Parker's escapades... and, somehow, Parker had nearly always managed to include Sacha in them.

There was the time Parker had been certain the creepy neighbors had abandoned their dog in the backyard. That had ended badly. The dog had been left out in the yard because they were cooking meth in the basement. Those neighbors disappeared and new ones moved in. Parker convinced himself that they were spies. They weren't spies. The husband was, however, having an affair while his wife was working swing shift.

He turned the shower off. Stepping out of the tub, he hesitated before grabbing a towel off the rack. He should have brought his own.

There was a soft tap on the door. Seth's voice followed it. "When you're dressed, come out to the backyard. I got the barbeque going. It's really nice outside." Sacha heard Seth's footsteps fading to silence as he walked away.

Finishing drying off, then dressing in shorts and a T-shirt, the only clothing still clean, Sacha glanced at himself in the tiny mirror over the matching tiny sink. The salt was overtaking the pepper in his hair. Tired eyes, a few new lines on his face; better not to look.

Wandering through Seth's tidy house on his way to the backyard, he noted that while there were a lot of plants there wasn't much that was personal. A single framed photograph, no knickknacks, nothing that screamed "Seth" to him. He snorted. Like he knew who Seth was.

"Hey, how was the shower? You look better." Seth was sitting in one of several ratty plastic lounge chairs, long legs stretched out in front of him, an open beer on a small side table between the chairs.

The slight breeze fluttering into the backyard, across his body, and through his damp hair cooled Sacha's still-overheated skin. Flopping down onto the chair next to Seth with a groan, he leaned back and shut his eyes.

Lack of sleep and exhaustion from the unending construction threatened to overwhelm him. Sacha was suddenly so tired forming words was impossible. So he didn't; he lay back in the creaky chair and let the breeze, the sounds of the neighborhood, and the fragrant scents from Seth's garden wash over him.

A light touch grazed his shoulder. Snapping out of a hazy dream, he grabbed the wrist of whoever touched him. Seth, of course, his brain told him. Awareness sizzled under his skin. He knew Seth felt it too; he dropped Seth's arm before he pulled Seth onto his lap or down to the ground so he could further explore his body like he wanted.

"Didn't mean to startle you." The sun was directly behind Seth, so Sacha couldn't see him clearly, his face thrown into deep shadow. "I'm gonna grill chicken and veggies, sound good?"

Sacha's stomach rumbled. Seth chuckled.

"I'll take that as a yes, big guy." He turned and headed into the house. Sacha was momentarily blinded by the glare of the sun as he moved away. "While you were napping, I called a friend. His boyfriend got called out of town, so he's at loose ends. He's going to be here in a few."

"I wasn't napping," Sacha mumbled, but Seth was inside already and didn't hear his ridiculous protest.

Sacha's ass was still firmly planted in the lounge chair when Seth's friend arrived. He was a little shorter than Seth, slender, with crazy curly brown hair. He nearly tripped on the way down the back steps, nearly losing hold of the six-pack of beer he had in one hand.

"They don't call me Grace for a reason." Smiling, he stuck a hand out. "Micah Ryan, thanks for letting me crash your dinner."

The two men were funny; clearly there was significant affection between the two of them. Seth brought up the Warrick, and the three of them spent the rest of the evening discussing the building, renovations, and general Skagit history. Micah was a local and knew a lot of random facts about Skagit.

"So, yeah, the Warrick brothers were local lumber barons who cashed out their investments in land to start a bank. This is all before any kind of banking regulation, and the brothers were somehow ousted and replaced by the Cutler family. I think one of the Warrick brothers lost the bank in a bet?"

"No way!"

"It was a pretty big scandal for the time. Skagit had like 2,000 permanent residents at the time, so everybody knew everybody's business. Kinda like now." Micah snickered.

"Skagit is still pretty small."

"Man, if I wasn't so busy with work right now I'd totally come over to help you out. Maybe I'll stop by, if it's okay, and get a tour?"

Sacha found himself agreeing.

The evening light faded, and Micah gathered himself to leave, muttering about his evil cat. Sacha made to leave as well, but Seth stopped him with a hand to his shoulder as Micah headed out to his car. He exited through the side gate, managing not to trip this time.

"This may sound crazy, but you're welcome to crash on the couch here. It has to be more comfortable than the pancake you've been sleeping on."

It was probably the beers that had him nodding without hesitation, or maybe his near inability to move. Lack of sleep, beer, and the thought of something not hardwood underneath his body as he slept sounded like nirvana. He wasn't certain who was more surprised that he accepted, him or Seth.

"I'd offer you the spare room, but it's still full of boxes from when I moved in. I haven't bothered to unpack everything yet. I'd offer you my bed but," a naughty grin spread across Seth's face, eyes filled with blatant appreciation, "when I get you in my bed it's not going to be for sleeping. And sadly I think that's what you need most right now."

Sacha found himself prone on a lumpy, slightly musty couch hardly long enough for his body, a sheet and light blanket thrown over him. He barely heard Seth as he moved around, locking up the house, before falling into a deep, mostly dreamless sleep.

ELEVEN

SETH

When he offered up his couch, Seth was certain Sacha would refuse and drive himself home. And Seth would have had to argue with him about it because the man was clearly too worn out to drive on top of two beers. But no, he'd accepted, and now there was a hulking form snoring softly on the couch in Seth's tiny living room.

They hadn't talked about the scorching kiss Sacha had laid on him. Seth had thought about it, though. Seth had thought about almost nothing else. He probably wouldn't be able to eat Danishes ever again without popping a semi.

Before heading to bed himself, he tossed Sacha's laundry into the dryer and started a second load. Stripping his own clothes off, he took a quick shower before crawling under the sheet in his own bed.

The next morning he wasn't surprised to find the sheet and blanket tidily folded on the couch, the laundry gone, and no sign of Sacha. Shuffling into the kitchen, he found a pot of coffee already made and a note from the man himself.

Thanks for dinner and the couch. —Sacha.

He grinned and tucked the note into his junk drawer before heading out to spend the day remodeling people's yards. Life didn't get much better.

* * *

THE FRONT DOOR of the Warrick was unlocked again. Letting himself in with impunity, Seth glanced around, cataloguing what had been done over the course of the morning. Sacha was nowhere to be seen. Muffled pounding and cursing floated down from the second floor. Heading up the staircase, Seth was unsurprised to find Sacha wielding a huge sledgehammer, battering down an offending wall. Shirtless was a benefit.

Not desiring a repeat of the evening before, when he startled Sacha and nearly ended up in a choke hold, Seth waited until the pounding came to a stop before making himself known. Taking the time to really appreciate a half-naked Sacha. As he'd suspected, there were several scars marring his torso. Two Seth recognized as old bullet wounds, plus another much fresher of the same. A single small tattoo along his rib cage; what it meant Seth didn't know, the words were inked in what was maybe Cyrillic.

"Thanks for the coffee this morning." And the view right now. As if reading his mind, Sacha grabbed the shirt hanging on the metal railing and pulled it over his head. Damn. Sacha probably thought he was a stalker, but Seth hadn't been able to stop himself from dropping in. He was fascinated by both the building and the man trying to save it.

"No problem, thanks for the couch and dinner." Sacha peered behind him. "No Danishes?" He waggled his thick eyebrows.

Heat flooded Seth's body with the memory of yesterday's kiss. "If I thought bringing Danishes would get me another kiss, I would have brought a baker's dozen."

Sacha's body language morphed from casual to dangerous. He prowled closer to Seth, stealing his oxygen, making breathing difficult. "It's probably a good thing, because I want in your bed, and I'm too old to fuck you on this floor."

The air rushed out of Seth's lungs and he tried unsuccessfully to breathe. "Yeah?" he rasped out.

"Yeah." Sacha stalked closer. "Except now I'm thinking it would be worth it."

What was that about being a predator right up until you became the prey? Seth wasn't in the same league as the man in front of him.

Careless of the now-open windows, Sacha tilted Seth's chin and brought his mouth down on Seth's. Seth was too lost in the kiss to realize he was being slowly pushed backward until he felt the rough edges of exposed brick against his back and shoulders. He sagged against it, letting Sacha and the wall hold him up.

Sacha pressed his chest against Seth's, and Seth could feel the larger man's heart drumming against his own. Sacha's wicked tongue dipped into Seth's mouth, a flicker touch sending a flash of desire directly to Seth's groin. He couldn't help the moan that escaped; after yesterday his body responded immediately, wanting what it hadn't gotten then.

Seth didn't care who walked by or into the Warrick at this point. The mayor could have been there and it wouldn't have stopped him. He ground back against Sacha, reveling in his heavy erection through the fabric of the shorts they were both wearing. He lost himself in the sensation of kissing and rubbing against each other. Sacha managed to get one large, rough hand down the back of Seth's shorts to massage his ass and slide a finger in and out of his crack.

"Jesus fucking Christ, please, please, don't stop."

"What do you need? My hand or my mouth?"

"I, uh, uh... fuuuuck."

Sacha dropped to his knees, popped open the snap on Seth's shorts, and pulled everything—shorts, boxer briefs—down past his knees. They both looked down at Seth's cock jutting out of his dark pubes, and it pulsed as they watched, pushing precome out of the pink tip.

"Please," Seth begged, out of his mind.

Grabbing the root in one hand, Sacha pulled Seth's erection toward his mouth, licking off the precome before opening wide and sucking him down. The sensation was so intense Seth banged his head back against the brick wall trying to keep himself from coming. That was before Sacha snuck his other hand around, sliding his index finger back into Seth's crack, dragging it around his hole and pushing a dry finger slightly inside. Seth couldn't take it anymore; there was no way he could hold on or warn Sacha. Grabbing Sacha's head, he came into his hot, wet mouth and down his throat, thrusting against him with no finesse. He would have been embarrassed, but he came so hard he literally had spots in his eyes from forgetting to breathe.

Sacha slowly stood up and wiped his mouth with the back of his hand before leaning in to ravage Seth's mouth again. Seth managed to fumble into Sacha's shorts and take his thick, throbbing cock into one hand to pump it. Sacha stopped kissing him, short, hard breaths panting into his ear. Softly, slowly, harder at the top, a little twist, a thumb in the slit wringing gasps of pleasure from the big man. Sacha's body stiffened against Seth's. Grabbing Seth's chin again, Sacha plundered his mouth, their tongues dancing and twisting as Sacha's orgasm overwhelmed him.

They stood pressed together for eons trying to catch their breath, hanging on, neither ready or willing to pull away or speak, breathing against each other, eyes closed and foreheads pushed together.

"That was fucking amazing," Sacha whispered into his ear, so softly he almost didn't hear it over the pounding of his heart. "I'm pretty sure when we actually fuck, it's going to be an out-of-body experience."

"I'm not sure I will survive, but I'm game to try."

Sacha grimaced. "My knees would prefer carpet next time." He moved away from Seth. "I'm not sure what you see in me. I'm old and broken."

"Well, I'm broken too. You just can't see it. Quit fishing for compliments; you're fucking hot. What does your tattoo mean?"

Sacha looked down along his rib cage, which was amusing because he had a shirt on. "An adolescent mistake."

"Oh come on, at least it's not a tramp stamp. I know one guy who has a ladybug on his hip. I have no idea what he thought he was doing, but it's been there long enough that it looks like a melanoma now."

"It's Russian, 'It's better to be slapped by the truth than kissed with a lie.' I was eighteen and very dramatic. It was before I joined the military, and I thought I was a badass when I was really only a punk."

"So, you're Russian?"

"Bosnian, but I also speak Russian and Croatian. I have a knack I guess, it came in handy when I was in the military. I came to the US when I was twelve. Look, this is going to sound shitty, but I don't like to talk about it. I left, I was glad to leave, I probably would be dead if I hadn't left. I was one of many orphans living on the streets, but I am the only one I know of lucky enough to have escaped." He paused, and Seth thought maybe he was done talking, but then he continued. "I'm not explaining this well, but... my childhood, it was a war zone, and I feel guilty about escaping. I can't change what happened, but I also don't like to talk about it."

"Okay. Believe me, I understand." And he did. Seth never told anyone about his early childhood, not if he could help it. Over twenty years since his mother's arrest and he still had nightmares. Dark hallways, closets, strange voices, hunger, being too hot or too cold featured in all of them.

Downstairs they did their best to clean each other up with hand wipes. Seth's shirt was totaled, so Sacha loaned him one of his. It was too large, but Seth got a kick out of wearing a T-shirt emblazoned with "US Marshals Service."

"Come back upstairs, I wanna show you something."

Sacha had been working in one of the small offices on the second floor, as evidenced by the gaping hole along the back wall and the exposed red brick behind it.

"That's pretty cool. You going to leave it open like that?" Seth was slightly behind Sacha going into the room.

"Somebody dumped a bunch of shit behind there, boxes and old tools, trash. So, yeah, going to have to leave it like that, at least for now, while I drag the crap out of here," Sacha grumped.

"Lemme help." Seth moved to his side. They stood side by side, taking in the mess. The interior wall had about twenty-four inches of space between it and the red brick behind it. Tucked into what should have been empty space between the walls were several wooden crates, the type fresh fruit had been packed in back in the day. One of the crates was crushed and splintered where, presumably, the sledge- ⟩ hammer had come crashing in on it.

"Wow, when I was wondering what kind of secrets these walls were hiding, I didn't mean literally."

"What are you talking about?" Sacha asked, looking at Seth like he was addled.

"On my way over here, I was thinking about how long the building had been around and what kind of history it had seen that we, I mean you, would never know."

"Well, all I'm thinking right now is that this stuff is a pain in my ass."

Seth rolled his eyes. "It's not the end of the world. Let's pull it out of there. I'll drag it downstairs so you can get back to bludgeoning the wall into submission."

They got the crates out, and then Sacha picked up the sledge-hammer again, hefting it over his shoulder with ease. His back muscles flexed under the shirt, leaving Seth a little breathless. He lugged the boxes downstairs, dust, grime, and spider corpses be damned. Two of the boxes were filled with random tools and metal pieces. The third, the one the sledgehammer had hit, was packed with old paperback books, postcards and pictures wrapped in twine, loose papers, and a folded-up piece of fabric. At the bottom there were a couple of tin cups, an old pair of spectacles, and some half-disinte-grated balls of string.

Since there was nowhere else to put them, Seth stacked the crates against the wall away from the enormous pile of demolition debris. Gently, he tugged one of the books from the box. The slim volume was battered and torn. Whether from today's beating or from wear and tear before it had been hidden away, it was difficult for Seth to tell.

Holding it carefully in one hand, he did something he'd learned from his aunt. Before paging through books they found at thrift stores and yard sales, Marnie would try to learn as much as she could without opening the cover. Was it heavy or light? Well cared for or rumpled? Was a section dog-eared or bookmarked? If not, she would hold the book spine down and see if it opened to a particular page or section.

Once inside the cover, she checked to see if the book had been inscribed to or from anyone. Was there anything tucked in the pages: receipts, love notes, a phone number or address, photographs? Lastly, she smelled the book. Seth drew the line at that, but Marnie had sworn she could smell lingering cologne or perfume. She'd believed the scent of perfume meant the book was a gift of love.

This was a book of poetry, small enough to fit comfortably in one hand. The volume was battered, tattered, dog-eared in several places, and had been in a box hidden behind a wall for too long to open automatically to a favorite passage. Seth didn't find any scraps of paper tucked inside, or photographs. It was a collection of poetry by W. H. Auden, not valuable given its condition, but clearly well loved.

Thoughts of what he and Sacha had done earlier and even the jarring banging and crashing noises from above couldn't keep Seth from poking through the rest of the crate. A few more books of poetry, dime-store detective novels with lurid covers, a package of letters and postcards that he set aside to look at later, a silver call bell, several ancient pens and pencils (one covered with bite marks), as well as a tiny pair of glasses wrapped in a scrap of velvet. Hummingbird hoard, his aunt would have said. Seth wished with all his heart that she were alive to see it.

Seth was so engrossed he didn't realize the pounding had ceased until Sacha snuck up behind him.

TWELVE
SACHA

At first, Sacha ignored the buzzing coming from his pocket. After years of reacting to every phone call, that had been the easiest thing to let go of when he left the Marshals. Unfortunately, the buzz persisted. Sighing, he put the sledgehammer down and tugged his phone out to see who wanted him now. Now that Seth, Joey, and Adam all had his number, he didn't expect the buzzing to be a series of texts regarding Parker.

Why he was surprised was anyone's guess; he needed more than ten fingers to count how much trouble he'd bailed Parker out of over the years. One of the reasons he'd distanced himself once he became a Marshal had been that Parker got in enough trouble on his own. He didn't need to be around the kind of trouble Sacha found himself in on a regular basis.

The most recent text read, "He's coming," with an airline abbreviation and ETA. Sacha scrolled back to read the first texts. They were from Mae-Lin, of course, expletive-laden commentaries on both Sacha's and Parker's life choices. She was very tired of the nonsense. *Ha.* Sacha wondered who else had pissed her off recently. People always thought he was kidding when he told them *he* was the nice one.

The flight was late in the evening; there would be time to plan before his arrival. Parker wouldn't wander around Skagit looking for him. Or, for fuck's sake, show up unannounced at the Warrick, although how he could know about that, Sacha couldn't fathom. Parker had an uncanny way of finding out things normal people and criminals preferred to be left hidden.

Realization hit him. Groaning, Sacha thumped his head against the door frame in frustration. In his post-orgasmic state he hadn't put all the pieces together. Where the hell was he going to stash Parker? Not here amongst the construction debris and dust.

The Warrick felt quiet. Where had Seth had disappeared to? Maybe he would have an idea. It wasn't like Sacha could go rent a house in an afternoon, and a hotel was out of the question since he had no idea how long Parker would be staying... or why he was coming.

Abandoning the sledgehammer, he headed to the ground floor. Seth sat cross-legged in a corner, sifting through the boxes Sacha'd found stashed in the walls. Sacha clomped down the stairs, but Seth was so engrossed he didn't hear him approach. Sunlight struggled in through the filthy windows, soaking Seth's sun-kissed skin, highlighting the curves and dips of his form.

It gave Sacha pause, watching Seth unawares. It was private. The too-large T-shirt hung from his lightly muscled body; the cargo shorts and practical hiking boots did not detract from his natural presence. Nothing about him was fancy or impractical, or soft—he was very much male, and he carried himself with an *acceptance* Sacha envied.

"What's in the boxes?"

Seth startled, turning to glare at him. "Fuck, do you not make noise? You are practically a mountain!"

Smiling, he shrugged. He hadn't intentionally snuck up on Seth. Not really, but he'd gotten caught up watching him. Not only was being light on your feet a good characteristic for US Marshals, it got truant, quasi-criminal kids away from the scene of the crime before the cops arrived. Most of the time.

"I walk, like a normal person."

"I beg to differ." Seth waved a hand. "Doesn't matter. Check it out, this box is full of cool old books and stuff."

Not wanting to loom, Sacha crouched down next to Seth and peered into the boxes. Two were stuffed with tools, unidentifiable pieces of metal, a couple tin cups, and other construction paraphernalia from the past. The third was currently empty, the books and other items Seth had pulled out of it in a pile on the floor.

"Why would anyone stash this behind a wall?" Seth wondered.

"Probably trying to clean up fast, didn't feel like moving it." He picked up one of the battered books, flipping the cover open. The title page was inscribed:

To my dear Owen, may these words find you. TG

Sacha stared at the spidery words for a long while, wondering what TG meant, who TG was. A sister, brother, lover? Along with Seth, he was curious how such a well-loved little book ended up behind the walls of an old bank building.

Flipping to the copyright page, he noted the volume: *Another Time*, poetry by W. H. Auden, published in 1940. He placed it gently back in the box. Seth was scanning through a small stack of postcards and letters.

Sacha's attention was captured by the late-afternoon light accentuating Seth's profile. His features were sharp and intelligent, yet he was a gentle soul, curious, naturally happy. Things Sacha was not, but found himself drawn to.

The sun shifted, sliding closer to the horizon. Even with the open windows, there was no breeze, and the building was stifling after another day of unrelenting heat. Sacha suddenly needed to get out for a while.

He reached out to touch Seth's shoulder, enjoying the feel of him through his T-shirt. "Any chance you'd let me treat for dinner tonight?" What was he doing? Inviting trouble was what he was doing. Changing a lifetime of hiding who he presented to the world was fucking exhausting.

"If by dinner you mean barbeque and a couple beers in my backyard, yes. I'm not going out anywhere. Can I bring this box?"

Sacha had a feeling his answer to Seth would always be "yes." That however this whole thing played out, Sacha would be saying "yes," and he looked forward to it.

THIRTEEN

SETH

Out on the sidewalk, Sacha grabbed Seth's shoulder, stopping him from heading immediately to his car. Seth swung around, wondering what this was about. Hadn't they decided to go to his house? If Seth had any luck at all, they would end up in his bed later.

"Um, so." Sacha sounded unsure of himself, which was kind of endearing. "My foster sister texted me and apparently our foster brother, Parker, is arriving in Skagit late tonight. I'm picking him up at the airport. There's some kind of *emergency*." He said emergency like it was a bad word. Or perhaps overused.

"Where is he staying?"

"I was wondering if you had a suggestion. Obviously I can't bring him back here."

Seth had a terrible habit of finding strangers interesting and pursuing them. It was a tendency that had made his aunt bestow her most gentle smile on him, probably because for a short time after he went to live with her he could have gone either way. Trust in strangers had not been a strong point.

"You're like a hummingbird, Seth," she'd said. "People are your flowers. You flit from person to person collecting interesting tidbits and taking them back to your nest where you hoard them or share, whichever you choose."

He'd been a quivering, spindly nine-year-old, thirsty for anything to help him make sense of the world. "Marnie," he'd said, because she'd told him to call her by her name, not a societal construct, which confused him, "hummingbirds don't hoard. Dragons hoard."

"How do you know hummingbirds don't hoard?" she'd replied, her beautiful face glowing with laughter.

Her question stuck with him over the ensuing years, rolling around in his head, evolving into a personal touchstone—comforting and solid as river rock in the palm of your hand, still warm from sunshine. As a nine-year-old it had blown his mind, like the first time he'd looked into a kaleidoscope.

He didn't even have to think about it.

"You know I am going to offer to have both of you stay at my house."

Sacha looked skeptical. "Parker is a handful. Also," now Sacha looked slightly guilty, "I, uh, haven't seen him in years."

The dominoes that would unlock the mystery of Sacha were beginning to topple. Seth could almost hear the snick of tiles clicking against each other as they cascaded.

"Stay at my place until you figure out what you and your brother are going to do. If it's one day or a few weeks it's fine. If you feel like a burden, you can help with rent and groceries."

He could see the cogs turning as Sacha considered his offer.

"You know this is a bad idea."

"Why?" Seth leaned back against Sacha's truck, ready to argue his point.

Sacha prowled close, hooking a finger through Seth's belt loops. "Because I want to get to know you better, and if I am in your house all the time I am going to want to fuck you. And fucking you could get in the way of actually getting to know you."

Seth swallowed. "I think we could do both. Maybe." A fission of anxiety snaked through his belly, he ignored it for the time being. The lure of having Sacha nearby, to comfortably delve into his secrets, for the moment outweighed the lingering anxiety of letting someone, the first since Marnie died, get close.

FOURTEEN

SACHA

Seth insisted they stop at the grocery store on the way home. Sacha followed behind him in his truck again. Sacha paid since they were getting food for three. They ended up with enough for a small army.

Today Sacha better appreciated Seth's backyard. It was an oasis. Quiet, peaceful, and set away from the street, an abundance of flowering shrubs encouraged honeybees, butterflies, and birds. When he sat down, a flash of wings turned out to be a tiny brown hummingbird hovering over a blue cone-shaped blossom.

Seth puttered, insisting on cooking since Sacha had paid, getting the grill ready for the chicken they'd purchased and watering the shrubs and flowers that were desperately thirsty after the sweltering day. Sacha had offered to cook; he could, after all. But Seth insisted.

"You mind if I turn on some tunes?" Seth asked startling him from his lazy observations.

"Sure?" Sacha didn't really do music. Seth took his quasi-answer for a yes, racing inside for some kind of portable speaker. Soon enough there was music to go with their dinner.

"I'm pretty eclectic; there's a little of everything on my playlist," Seth commented.

It was unnervingly pleasant to sit in Seth's backyard sipping a couple of beers and eating dinner off real plates, not paper or out of a bag. Both things Sacha had done with some regularity over the past two years, as well as before that. He cooked for family once in a while, for the occasional friend, but not much more than that.

"So, what do you think about that box of stuff? Pretty cool, huh?"

"Yeah." He'd forgotten about the wooden crate of mementoes he'd nearly crushed into kindling. "What else was in there?"

Grabbing a napkin, Seth wiped his hands before getting out of his chair. Sacha saw the stack of photos or postcards sitting on the little metal side table.

Seth grinned at him. "You fell into my hastily laid trap." Sacha found himself grinning back. That shit was infectious.

The collection consisted of nearly twenty postcards all addressed to Owen Penn, four badly faded handwritten letters, and a single photograph of two young men laughing, their arms around each other's waists. The postcards were from parks and cities across the US. The farthest away was from Acadia Park in Maine; the closest had been postmarked at Marble Mount, which was about a hundred miles away in the North Cascades National Forest. The same spidery handwriting flowed across the four letters, much too faded to read in the dying light of Seth's backyard, possibly too faded to read at all. Sacha turned the photograph over. On the back was written: Owen Penn, Theodore Garrison Lake Chelan. It was dated 1939.

He stared at the photo, hoping to divine its secret history. The boys, young men really, looked happy, laughing over a secret or merely smiling for the camera. The picture was black-and-white, of course, but one of them had darker hair and was a little taller than the other. They were skinny in a way people weren't anymore, wearing similar dark work pants and white button-up work shirts with the sleeves rolled up. Sacha wondered who had been on the other side of the camera. A friend? A passing stranger? What were the two of them doing at Lake Chelan in the late 1930s as the world was going mad?

Seeming to share, or understand, Sacha's thoughts, Seth broke the silence that had fallen between them. "I wonder why these were hidden? Clearly, this Owen person saved everything." Leaning over, he tugged the photo from Sacha's limp grasp. "I wonder which one he is?" He stared at it for a few moments before tucking it back in with the postcards, gingerly, as if it were the most precious treasure.

Seth looked up, his gaze catching Sacha's, and an intense spark crackled inside Sacha's chest. He felt short of breath. Dropping his eyes, he found himself mesmerized by Seth's lips. Seth bit his lower lip shyly before breaking into a broad smile and taking Sacha's breath away again. The moment lasted forever, shattering time barriers, and was over far too quickly, leaving Sacha reeling. The feeling in his chest expanded, and he looked away, afraid of what unfamiliar emotion was showing on his face. He was used to sex, fucking, but had never allowed an emotional connection to form before. It almost hurt.

A gentle hand tugged his chin. The chairs were close together; there wasn't much distance between the two of them.

"You wanna kiss?" Seth asked quietly, brown eyes looking directly into Sacha's. Sacha nodded, mute. *Yes*, he wanted to kiss under the broad blue sky and the sun that never changed no matter where it shone. The same sun that shone over Kansas City, over Miami, Paris or Sarajevo. He wanted to be absolved, to be clean, unsullied by life, the sun shining down on him free of judgment.

"Is that a 'yes'?"

Heat flared across his cheeks. His expression must have encouraged Seth, though; he leaned forward, gently touching his lips to Sacha's.

Sacha's lips opened of their own volition, desiring more, but Seth merely pressed their mouths together, a barely there touch. A touch so strong it was close to sending Sacha into orbit. He breathed in, smelled the beer they'd had, felt Seth's warm breath mingling with his own. Felt.

If Sacha knew one thing, it was that he was in trouble. A whole hell of a lot of trouble.

TOGETHER THEY STRAIGHTENED up the little house. Seth dug out some blankets and sheets for Parker; he would be sleeping on the couch. Not that Parker was going to need blankets, or even sheets, since it was still fucking hot enough to fry an egg on the sidewalk.

Together they moved the last of Seth's moving boxes from the spare room to the living room, then they tackled the air mattress. A half hour later, Seth declared victory.

"Duct tape really is a miracle."

"It won't hold." Sacha groused.

"Quitter." Smiling, Seth led the way back out into the living room. "Besides, you know where my bed is if you find yourself sleeping on the floor."

Leaving both the front and back doors open to encourage a breeze, Sacha stared outside into the offending early evening sunshine. The neighbor's pathetic wind sock didn't even twitch, only hung limply from her porch.

What in the fucking hell was he going to do with Parker? Why was he coming to Skagit? Mae-Lin didn't tell him anything. Claimed she didn't know. Besides, she never involved herself in Parker's drama any more than she had to. Sacha felt this was a copout, seeing as both he and Parker jumped to her assistance whenever she called.

Somebody in the neighborhood was hosting a BBQ or something. Street parking at Seth's was a little dicey, seeing as there were no sidewalks and residents parked wherever, and however, they felt like. As he stared out the front door, trying to make some sense of Parker's arrival and what was possibly blooming between himself and Seth, he watched a shiny black late-model four-wheel-drive circle the block.

The driver deftly maneuvered the vehicle in between two other equally large and unwieldy ones about halfway down the street. He didn't know if it was Parker's imminent arrival that had him on alert or something else he wasn't able to put his finger on, but he continued watching until a family spilled out to unload their vehicle, a multitude of screaming children, strollers, and bags of what looked to be drinks and to-go containers spewing from inside.

He wandered back into the kitchen and, apparently inevitably, Seth. "Is there anything I need to know?" Seth asked over his shoulder. "You know, a deathly seafood allergy, won't step on cracks, do I need to put away the silver?"

Sacha snorted. "I guess we'll find out."

Seth stood from where he'd been putting the contents of the cooler back into the fridge. Seth's hair was a mess. His T-shirt was, as usual, untucked, and his ratty shorts hung low on his hips, exposing a sliver of skin that Sacha longed to run his fingers across.

He couldn't keep his hands off of him. Didn't want to.

Stepping into Seth's personal space, Sacha focused on Seth, letting his body do the talking. Placing his hands on Seth's hips, he tugged him close, sliding his hands up under Seth's rumpled shirt, feeling the soft bumps and curves of his torso, smooth beneath the tips of his fingers, and Seth shuddered.

Without stopping, without hesitation, Sacha lowered his mouth to Seth's. This kiss was a rocket. Hard and explosive. Seth opened for Sacha, flicking his tongue along his lips and inside his mouth. Sacha couldn't help releasing a low groan, feeling Seth's response. Seth's arms came around him; there was no space between them as they touched and explored each other's mouths, lips, faces, bodies. In the middle of Seth's kitchen.

Sacha couldn't stop caressing Seth, molding himself to the slighter man's shape. Couldn't stop running his hands across as much of Seth's skin as he could reach. Frustrated by their clothing, he pulled Seth's shirt off, following it with his own, discarding them onto the kitchen floor.

They came back together skin to skin, chest to chest, hips pressing together. Sacha groaned again, louder and longer. He almost (*almost*) didn't need any more than Seth's mind-blowing touches. His body sought more, though; demanded it. Sacha felt himself harden further and twitch against Seth's hip. Seth skimmed his fingers along Seth's back. He shivered, not knowing what to do next, where to put his own hands, needing to be everywhere.

Long, gentle fingers skimmed further and paused on the button of Sacha's shorts. Seth cocked his head again, questioning. "Yes," Sacha rasped, "please."

The shorts were quickly dispensed with, leaving Sacha in his boxer briefs. Seth started to take off his own, but Sacha stopped him. Leaning his forehead against Seth's shoulder, he unbuttoned them carefully, pushing them down over Seth's hips so they landed in a heap on the floor. Watching as Seth was exposed to him, thick erection bobbing against his groin.

Sacha was conscious of his scarred and battered body. In the daylight there was no way for him to hide the myriad battle scars from the life he'd led. His imperfections were obvious, both the physical and the emotional.

As if he'd read his mind, Seth began to trace a gentle finger along his scars, from bullets, knives, flying glass, a very old one from before he'd come to America when he'd been hit by a car. So many.

"I love your body, how it tells your history. Maybe someday you will tell me where these all came from."

"Jesus Christ, the things you say…"

Seth leaned in and began to kiss him again: hot, open mouth; thrusting tongue; sucking lips. Sacha wasn't going to be able to hold off, didn't try. His uncertain hands ended up on Seth's ass. Lost in the kiss, feeling the flex of muscle under his palms, the drag of Seth's erection against his own, he was living a fantasy barely conceived.

"My room?" Seth whispered into his ear.

"Yes."

Taking him by the hand, Seth led him into his tiny bedroom. He crawled onto the bed, a double mattress and box spring directly on the floor, and turned to lie on his side. Sacha followed. They lay chest to chest, anticipation surrounding them like a heavy blanket.

"I don't want to hurt you," he whispered, hoping Seth understood he meant more than sex.

Seth took his face between his hands. "I'm a big boy, in case you haven't noticed." They both looked down at Seth's cock nestled next to Sacha's like it belonged there. Yeah, Seth was nicely built.

"That's not what I meant." Sacha chuckled.

"I know." He smiled, eyes locking onto Sacha's. "Trust me? Trust me to know what I can handle?"

Sacha laughed into Seth's neck. "Yeah, I think I can manage that." Sticking his tongue out, he licked Seth's neck, reveling in his salty flavor.

They became... a tangle of arms, legs, and touching. Sacha stripped his briefs off, pressing his naked body against Seth's, nearly coming from that too. Pushing him onto his back, Seth straddled Sacha's hips before he could figure out what was happening, leaning forward and tracing the tattoo with his tongue. Sacha melted into sensation. He moved over to Sacha's shoulder, to his left side. Sacha realized Seth was tracing his scars again. The ones on the outside of his body. Maybe someday he would tell him about the ones on the inside.

Helplessly turned on, he thrust his hips upward against Seth's weight. Seth answered with his own before wrapping a hand around both of their cocks and bringing them together using the precome dripping from them as lubricant. Sacha lost himself in sensation again, wondering that he'd finally managed to get to this place where he was with another man and the world wasn't crashing around him.

Orgasm surprised him, although they had been chasing it for several minutes. His balls tightened, a spark of lightning sizzled along his spine, and Sacha was coming so hard it ached; he had to wrap himself around Seth to make himself stop shaking. Seth's face pressed into the crook of Sacha's neck, and then Sacha felt the answering warmth of Seth's come on his stomach. Fucking amazing.

Lying with Seth covering him like a blanket, Sacha felt the most at peace he'd been maybe ever in his life. The mattress was lumpy, the covers had been kicked aside, both of them were drenched with sweat, and there was no mistaking the sharp smell of come. Sacha shut his eyes and let himself drift for a few minutes.

Seth slid off him. "That was amazing," Sacha huffed out.

"Yeah?"

"Yeah."

He opened his eyes, and deep brown ones looked back, a little question lurking in them. Sacha squeezed him. "Really."

"Tell me something about yourself. I know it's backward—sex first, questions later..."

Seth tucked up against his side while Sacha stared at the ceiling. The sense of peace had still not disappeared, emboldening him to speak. "As I told you, I am originally from Bosnia—well, Yugoslavia. Bosnia became a separate nation after I was brought over here."

"Yeah?" He turned his head so he was face to face with Seth and his compassionate gaze.

"I lived there until I was twelve." Drawing a deep breath, he continued with his story, one he hadn't told more than a handful of times over the years. "I was brought over as part of a humanitarian effort. Somehow I ended up homed with a very conservative Christian family."

"What happened to your own family?"

"I don't know. I was left at an orphanage when I was young, but then it closed. You have to understand how chaotic things were back then. We, Bosnians, had been fighting for years, but to the rest of the world, the war had just begun. I'd been on my own for a long time before I was evacuated. Probably at least a year." His memories were vague. "A lot of us were forced to live on the street—war orphans, dispossessed, some runaways."

"You lived on the streets of... Sarajevo?"

"Yeah. Then I came here and wasn't on the street anymore. But other than that, not a whole lot changed."

"Plus you had to learn another language, right?" Sacha nodded. "And meet all new people and live in a scary new country."

"Street rules are universal though, and I was a fast learner. And I'm good with languages." He wasn't lying when he said the rules were the same. "At least in the US I wasn't constantly cold and wondering where my next meal was coming from. The Finlaysons may have used the system to line their own pockets, but they were forced, by random inspection, to provide somewhat regular meals as well as a roof over our heads. Being small, with a foreign accent, and hand-me-down clothes that didn't fit or match was a worse offense." Hence Sacha's drive to shed the accent.

Seth didn't say anything for the longest time. Sacha started to worry; about *what*, exactly, he wasn't sure.

Seth rolled against his side and pressed his face into Sacha's neck, still not saying anything. Sacha swore he could feel Seth's body shaking. "Are you okay?"

It was difficult to understand with Seth muttering into his neck, but he thought he heard something about hummingbirds.

Seth came up for air. "What time do you have to be at the airport?"

Parker. He'd managed to forget about that. "Fucking fuck. I have to take a fucking shower."

FIFTEEN

SACHA

The trip out to the airport was uneventful. The other drivers seemed to sense Sacha's heavy mood, slowing down and pulling to the right as he approached. Or it could have been the roar of his engine as he gunned it down the two-lane road behind the airport property.

The terminal was like every other small-town airport Sacha had ever visited. The exception was the 5'8" pissed-off man waiting for him at the curb outside baggage claim. Sacha didn't have to get out of his truck to know Parker was out of sorts; he wore his moods like clothing. Sacha had no idea what he could have done to irritate him after so many years.

Leaning across the cab, he pushed the passenger door open. "Get in."

Parker picked up his bag and tossed it into the truck bed before climbing inside. "Nice, the first words you bother to say to me in years aren't 'Hey, Parker, I missed you,' it's a grumbly 'Get in.'"

Parker had more lines on his face; his hair was a little less blond, his body lankier than Sacha remembered. He still had the grace of an athlete, though, which was evident as he gracefully climbed into the truck.

"Damn, Sacha, why do you have to drive these monsters? They make me feel like a toy human," Parker groused.

"How was your flight?"

"Horrible." He pouted. "I had to sit next to someone who took their socks off, and their feet smelled like tuna fish."

"Buckle your seat belt." Sacha pulled away from the curb, sliding into the traffic leaving the airport.

The snick of the buckle engaging reached Sacha's ears. "Yes, Mom."

"Why are you here?"

"Do we have to talk about this now? I'm tired and hungry." Not irritated, then; hangry.

"I'm staying with a friend; tell me now or tell the both of us." Why he would threaten Parker with Seth made zero sense. It was like threatening Parker with a kitten.

"I can stay in a hotel." Parker looked out the window instead of at Sacha, his shoulders now slumped and tense.

"Bullshit, Seth already made space available."

Still looking out the passenger window, Parker asked, "Who's Seth?"

The million-dollar question. He wasn't sure how to answer it. Was he anything, yet? Did he need a label for what they were exploring? He settled on, "A guy I'm staying with while some work is being done on my building." He immediately felt like shit for downplaying what was happening between the two of them. Even though he was practically a caveman, he knew it was more than nothing.

"Your building." Parker paused and glanced over at Sacha. "A guy. I think we have a lot to talk about."

Fuck if he was going to talk about fucking anything. Parker could take his talk and shove it—

"I can tell when you're thinking asshole thoughts inside your head."

The rest of the drive from the airport to Seth's house was made in complete silence. Sacha couldn't see how this was going to go. Things with Parker historically went sideways.

Seth's front door was still open when they arrived. What the fucking hell was with that? Was Seth really clueless that this neighborhood was not great? Creeps lived right up the street and would be perfectly happy to waltz in and fuck up his shit. He slammed the truck door, the sound ricocheting across the street, before stomping up to the house, ready to give Seth a piece of his mind. Parker trailed along behind, probably thinking Sacha had lost his marbles. Which he had.

He stopped short at the sight of Seth through the open door, causing Parker to smack into Sacha's back.

"Jeez, give a guy some warning," Parker groused.

Seth was in his tiny kitchen with the music player on, cutting vegetables or something while moving to the beat, dark hair pulled back out of his face in a sort of artful tangle. He'd showered and changed into a pair of thin cotton sweatpants, which clung to his butt as he danced.

Parker cleared his throat, looking around Sacha. "Like that, is it? I wondered. It's always the quiet ones."

"What?" Then, deciding denial would get him nowhere, he added, "Fuck off, Parker," using his most threatening growly voice. Because, no, he had never actually come out to his foster brother. Between one thing and another, Sacha's sexuality had never been up for discussion.

Seth heard them over the beat of his music, and he grinned as they walked in. The force of his smile was a velvet slap in the face. "Hi, I'm Seth. You must be Parker. I've heard absolutely nothing about you." He walked forward to shake Parker's hand. "Sacha, put his things in your room." He turned back to Parker. "You need a shower? It's not the best, but it does the job."

Sacha pointedly ignored the raised eyebrows from Parker. Regardless of the years since they had seen each other, Parker knew that Sacha did not take direction very well. Or at all. Fuck that; he was trying. New fucking leaf or something. Picking up Parker's bag from where he'd dropped it, Sacha stomped into the tiny bedroom.

Seth'd put on a ratty T-shirt while Sacha was following directions. Thank fuck. Bad enough Parker was here, with his knowing glances and mocking smile; he didn't need Seth parading around half naked.

Thankfully, Parker opted for a shower, giving Sacha a few more minutes to collect himself and prepare for the inquisition.

The already-small house was going to feel like a sardine can with the three of them here, and it was too fucking hot. Sacha didn't know what was going to happen. Between the distraction known as Seth and whatever was going on with Parker, something was going to give. Collapse, more like.

"So, Parker?" Seth interrupted his wandering thoughts.

He quelled his irritation at Seth's question. The man was, after all, generous enough to offer a place not only to Sacha but to his semi-estranged/deranged foster brother as well. "I haven't had a chance to question him yet." Like he was a suspect or something.

"Did you piss him off already? That was quick."

Sacha grinned, because Seth did have his number. "Maybe. But he's pretty good at pissing me off too. Always has been."

"I imagine that's not very hard."

"Fuck off." There was no heat behind his words, though. He leaned against the kitchen counter watching Seth work.

"See?" Seth returned to cutting veggies and sliding them onto skewers before laying them on a cooking sheet and brushing olive oil, or something, over each one. There were burger patties laid out as well. "Does Parker eat meat?"

"Hell, yeah," said the man in question.

"Fuck's sake, Parker, can you not?"

"What? And miss a chance to see you get all riled up? I haven't taken that quick of a shower since you and Mae-Lin played the trick on me with the garter snake."

"Jesus Christ, don't bring that up again, we fucking apologized. We had no idea they actually bit. It's not like it was poisonous."

"You put a snake in the shower. While I was in it. You still owe me. And they are in fact poisonous." Parker emphasized his point by jabbing his index finger against Sacha's chest.

Seth had stopped prepping and was doubled over laughing. When he got himself under control, he chuckled, "This is going to be awesome."

This was so *not* going to be awesome. And if Parker thought Sacha had forgotten he'd travelled across the country to include Sacha in his Big Drama, he had another think coming.

BY MUTUAL AGREEMENT they headed out to the backyard, where Seth had the grill going. Sacha ended up sitting between the other two men. Seth dragged over a wooden bench to use as a setting spot for their plates and beers. It was much more pleasant than inside the tiny house. With all the windows open to relieve the heat, Sacha was having to put aside some of his misgivings about the neighborhood. The family parking their car, for instance, was probably merely that: a family parking their car.

Parker had bulked up a little over the years. As a kid he'd been chubby, and then in high school, when the bullying began, he got way too skinny. He was wan under his tan, though, the lines on his face exaggerated as the sun began to set, and dark circles lurked under his eyes.

Tired or not, he looked like he took care of himself, which, Sacha supposed, he'd been doing for at least ten years. Sacha watched as Parker mowed through a huge burger and helping of vegetables while they enjoyed the slightly cooler evening temperature.

As if reading his mind, Parker remarked, "Is it always this hot here? I thought it was supposed to be cold and rainy."

Sacha's mouth was full. Seth answered, "This is my first summer here. I'm from Scottsdale. This winter was brutal. I've never been somewhere where it rained every day for literally months. I'm not complaining about the heat."

Swallowing, Sacha added, "Last couple summers have been pretty hot." Seth's sharp gaze jerked over to him, his eyes narrowing. Sacha replayed what he'd said. Ah. Fuck. "I was here on assignment," he mumbled. He watched Seth tuck the information away and wondered when he would be on the receiving end of an interrogation.

"Assignment?" Seth prodded.

Parker put his plate down and leaned forward to peer around

Sacha. "Yeah, the US Marshals. You know, like that old movie, *The Fugitive*."

"You're going to be a fugitive if you don't shut your trap." Sacha enjoyed Tommy Lee Jones, but that fucking movie drove him crazy. In fact, all cop shows drove him up a wall. When he watched TV he preferred stuff like *House Hunters*, but there was no way he was telling these two.

He'd been so careful, keeping his worlds separate. It occurred to him that that wasn't going to be possible any longer. Maybe he didn't care enough or have the energy to keep things in their tidy little cubbyholes. The reasons why he'd distanced himself from Parker were gone. The reasons why he hadn't allowed himself the kind of relationship he yearned for, also gone. A gaping hole where he used to hide... was waiting to be filled.

"No Parker, keep going," Seth quipped.

They both laughed out loud, a wholesome sound that reverberated across the yard. Something he hadn't heard much. Sacha was mildly irritated, but also flattered that Seth was curious enough to pump Parker for information.

"Seeing as the information I get is second hand because he cut me off for years, I can't guarantee any of it is still correct."

Human trafficking cases and witness relocation were low on the list of subjects Sacha cared to chat about.

"So, Parker, the time has come for you to 'fess up. What has you fleeing the East Coast, giving Mae-Lin enough of a sob story that she told you where I was? What's going on with you and that *roommate* of yours?"

Parker shifted in his seat. Running his hand through his disheveled blond hair, making it stand on end, he took a deep breath. Sacha braced himself.

"Quit stalling. And don't even think about leaving anything out," he snapped. "If we're going to figure whatever this is out, I need *all* the facts. What hornet's nest have you disturbed this time?"

"Okay, so, I left Zeke, kind of." Parker's voice was quiet.

"Kind of?" He sent up a quick prayer for patience. "You either did or didn't. Pregnant, not pregnant."

Parker squinted at him. "You know we can't do that, right?"

"Quit trying to avoid the subject. Which is you right now, and why you're here."

"I got tired of Zeke's bullshit, ghosting me when it wasn't convenient to have a boyfriend. Then when he was lonely, or what the fuck ever, he acknowledged I existed."

There was more to that part of the story, but it could wait.

"It was stupid, I know, but I was fed up. All my friends spent so much time warning me and then saying 'I told you so,' acting like they knew everything and never messed up." He sniffed, and Sacha wrapped an arm around his shoulders, pulling him in tight. "Sometimes, you know, you don't need that kind of response, you need someone to say, 'Hey, that's fucked up, let's get drunk and plot his death.' Not really, you know; imaginary." He twisted to look at Sacha.

"Yeah, I know. Keep going." Parker snuggled into him.

"So I packed my shit, but the only place I could think of to stay was his boat. I borrowed the keys. I was only going to stay there a night. Two at the most. I needed to think about stuff."

"What is a cop doing with a boat?" Cop salaries were not *that* good.

"I don't know. He's had it as long as I've known him. He said something about family." He said bitterly, regardless of Parker's front, he was still smarting from what had happened between himself and Zeke. "Anyway, I was asleep on the boat. I didn't bother having lights on—I wasn't supposed to be there, right? I dropped my stuff and went to bed."

Sacha hadn't been paying much attention to the news, but even he'd caught the coverage of a huge marina fire in Florida. He'd been at the gym, maybe, and the newscaster kept talking about the millions of dollars in luxury yachts that had been lost. Some dot-com guy had his second boat stored there, and it had gone up like a Roman candle.

"Please tell me you were not sleeping on a boat berthed at that marina in Melbourne that burned to the fucking waterline a while back." Sacha had a headache, and his brother hadn't even been in Skagit an hour.

Parker hunched further inward and whispered, "Uh. Yeah. Can't do that."

Jesus. Fucking. Christ. The footage from the fire had been horrifying. The fire had been huge, with flames reaching thirty feet and higher into the inky darkness of a Florida night. Fuck, he could have lost Parker forever and this cringe-worthy moment might never have happened. He thanked whatever deity he needed to for his little brother still being alive.

Seth broke the silence. "Anybody else for another beer? I know I need one."

"Bring out the whole pack. I'm going to need more than one. Please," Parker asked.

Seth disappeared inside, taking their dinner plates with him. Sacha heard the fridge open and him rummaging around. Silence settled over the backyard like a blanket. He heard the fridge door shut and Seth's footsteps fading further into the house.

"So, Seth, huh?" Parker nudged Sacha with his knee.

"Do not try to redirect."

"I'm not; I'm glad for you. I've always thought you were lonely. He seems like a nice guy. Different from the macho Marshal types."

The things Parker got him to talk about. Probably why he'd avoided him for so long.

"Have you always been into guys? Or both? Any women?" Parker tilted his head. Trust Parker to go for the jugular.

"A couple. No one worth changing my life for."

They could hear Seth doing something in the kitchen again, pouring chips into a bowl, maybe.

"No one cares anymore. Not really," Parker said into the darkness.

"I know." It was Sacha's turn to rub his hands on his face, wanting this conversation to be over but needing it so badly. "It's hard."

Parker snickered. "In all seriousness, it's not that hard. You make everything harder than it should be. He likes you; kiss him already and see where it goes. I don't think he'll punch you for it."

"You've always been out, Parker."

"Yeah, not by choice," he muttered.

"True, but I was never out; it was much easier for me to hide. And I'm learning it's a hard habit to break."

No way was Sacha going to tell him what they had already done, that Sacha's world had already changed for the better. He hoped. It was hard to change a lifetime of ingrained hiding and subversion. Probably it was partially his personality, but almost everything he'd experienced in life added to his innate need for self-protection. Until Seth, there'd been no reason to try.

"What'd I miss?" Seth had a six-pack in one hand, a plate with some cut-up cheese and apples in the other. "Just a sec, lemme grab the crackers." Sacha watched as he climbed the three steps into the kitchen.

"Jesus, if you don't do something you're going to explode. Maybe I should kiss him for you?" Sacha whipped around to glare at Parker; fucker had a knowing smirk on his face. "I bet I could make it good for him, even though he's not my type."

Seth returned, plopping crackers on the small side table and handing beers around before sitting back in his lounge chair. He stretched out his long legs and looked expectantly at Sacha and Parker, eyebrows raised. Grinning, Parker chuckled, and Sacha groaned inwardly, sending up another prayer for patience. "Shut it, kid," he grumbled.

Parker picked up where he'd left off. Although there wasn't much more to the story, unfortunately it was the important part.

He'd been asleep when he smelled the smoke, and awoke confused and disoriented but alert enough to know he needed to get out of there. When he heard terrifying pops and crackles getting closer and smoke began to pour into the cabin area, he cut his losses and ran as fast as he could. He'd barely managed to escape with his backpack and the clothes he was wearing.

The marina went up fast, because nothing burns like boats with tanks full of fuel as an accelerant. The fire burned so hot engines couldn't get close, and even the fireboat was restricted. Parker ran and didn't look back. The next day, when the fire was all over the news, he learned there had been a body floating amongst the burned-out fiber-glass shells of the yachts... a body that was apparently connected with the de Vega crime family. It was a good thing Parker had never been struck by lightning; he would absolutely be one of those people it hit twice.

"I didn't have anything to do with it!" he protested, seeming to know the path along which Sacha's mind had wandered.

"Zeke seemed pissed and worried, apparently. Mae-Lin talked to him when you didn't call her." Sacha waited a beat to see if Parker would realize what he'd forgotten.

"Fucking fuck, I missed her birthday."

"I already got her the shoes; you're going to have to fork out for the bag."

Sacha noted Parker's lack of reaction to the fact that his ex-boyfriend still seemed to have some kind of emotional investment. He wondered if Parker really understood what it was like to be an out gay cop. Every day worrying and wondering if, when push came to shove, the people you needed most would have your back. If instead they would help put you six feet under. There were places he'd heard weren't so bad, but Sacha himself couldn't have done that. He could relate to Zeke, and that's why he'd never pursued anyone before. It wouldn't have been fair.

"Busted. Anyway, he had no idea where you had gone. Why come here?"

"It's far away from the East Coast," Parker mumbled. "I need time to think, I guess, get away from everything."

"I get that, I do, but does everything have to be so fucking dramatic with you? Couldn't you have had an adult discussion with Zeke? Instead, as usual, you react and get yourself involved in a fucking arson and probable murder—and then you flee the scene so you look like you have something to hide. And, by the way, although I am shocked that Mae didn't say anything, I retired, so if you need help getting out of a jam it's going to be a little harder."

"You retired?" Parker squeaked. "I mean, that's great."

Seth piped up, "We could call Adam, see if he can find something out."

He'd been so quiet Sacha had mostly put him out of his mind.

Sacha narrowed his eyes, a slippery half-thought trying to make itself known. "Adam?" There was only one Adam in town Sacha knew, but it was a relatively common name.

"Adam Klay, Micah's boyfriend. My half-brother. He's not a Marshal, he's a Fed."

"Fuuuuuck." Adam fucking Klay. Right. Because of course Seth was Adam's half-brother. He should have seen the resemblance. The two men did look similar now that he knew. He should have known; fate liked her little jokes.

"Parker…" Sacha looked over at one of the few people he considered family. "What the fuck am I going to do with you?"

Parker cast a tragic glance at him. "I dunno. I'm sorry I'm useless. Everything I do ends up in a big clusterfuck." He sniffed. "I'm tired of feeling like nothing matters, like I'm inconsequential with nothing anybody wants."

This was the Parker who really scared Sacha. He could handle the dog rescuer, signing on to be a summer nanny only to discover the parents were swingers and tried to include him in their fun and games, or the accidental accountant for the mob… but a defeated, scared, *hopeless* Parker, that's the one who always got him in trouble. People looked at Parker—slight, cute boyish looks, blond hair usually cut in a kind of party-boy style, and thought he was simple, easy.

"The first thing we have to do is reach out to some people and see what the authorities aren't telling the media. We need someone to talk to your boyfriend—"

"Ex-boyfriend."

Sacha waved a hand. "Whatever, ex-boyfriend. I'll make some phone calls… and yeah, I should probably reach out to Klay." He ran his hand through his short hair, tugging on it painfully. "Fuck. First, Parker, I need some answers."

SIXTEEN

SETH

"Where have you been since the fire?" Sacha's focus on Parker was intense, laser sharp. Seth wouldn't last under that hard stare—or maybe he would; it was pretty hot.

Parker winced, his blond eyebrows coming together in a V. "I didn't know there was a security camera at the marina. I was trying to save my life, not play 'Unnamed Male Character first to die" in Bond movie.' With all the fire trucks and other responders arriving on the scene it was chaos, and I managed to slip out. I freaked out because... you know..."

Sacha nodded.

"Yeah, so," He paused to take a gulp of his beer. "When I saw on the news that a body had been discovered, I didn't know what to do. I'm an accountant, not a cop. After I finished freaking out I went and took out as much cash as I could. Then I holed up at a motel for a while."

Sacha snorted. "Only you would become an accountant, inadvertently find your first job with a firm fixing the books for a company claiming to be a nonprofit, and end up being a whistle-blower at the ripe age of twenty-five."

"Really?" Seth looked back and forth between the two of them.

Parker answered, "Yeah, really, mad skills. Kind of why I'm not an accountant anymore and have a thing for cops, I guess. What else did Zeke have to say?" Whatever Parker claimed had motivated him to leave his boyfriend, he wasn't as done with this Zeke guy as he claimed.

"You'll have to talk to Mae," Sacha taunted.

Parker grimaced.

"Anyway, I mostly laid low, waiting to see if the cops would catch the real criminals who did this and not some lowlife trespasser who'd been illegally staying on his ex-boyfriend's boat." He took another long gulp of his beer.

Night had fallen; the backyard was in complete darkness except for the light leaking onto the yard from the open kitchen door, but Seth didn't need to see Parker's expression to know he was lost and a little scared. "So, what are we going to do?" he asked. Privately Seth thought that Parker should be more scared but maybe it was the 'Sacha effect'.

Sacha narrowed his eyes. Seth felt a delightful shiver run down his spine. "Don't you fucking dare. *I* take care of my own."

"Dude, the lone cowboy thing is not going to fly. Seriously, call Adam."

"Oh, wow. This is going to be awesome," Parker breathed. "I want popcorn with my front-row seat." Seth chuckled. Parker was funny, and it was awesome to see Sacha flustered and protective. "I can tell we're going to get along."

Sacha groaned, covering his face with his hands. Seth made eye contact with Parker, and they both snickered.

"Fine. I'll call Adam, but for my own sanity I am waiting until tomorrow. I can't handle any more of this crazy right now. For the rest of tonight we are pretending everything is normal." He raised an eyebrow in Parker's direction. "As normal as it can be, at any rate."

Parker sputtered and muttered something about showing Sacha who was normal.

Taking pity on both of them, Seth handed Sacha another beer. At this rate someone was going to need to run to the store for more.

Sacha snatched it from him, popped the cap, and guzzled half of it while Parker and Seth watched in silence. As he set the bottle down, a breeze finally mustered the strength to make itself felt, and the three of them sighed in relief. It wouldn't be the heat that killed them tonight.

Relaxed Sacha was hilarious. He and Parker regaled Seth with stories from their childhood. Sacha steered clear of stories about being in the Marshals, but he did tell a couple pretty funny ones from when he'd been an MP.

"I was so green, not prepared for the on-base domestic calls. Most calls we got were for drunkenness or domestics. My favorite was when we stopped a woman for weaving all over the road. My partner leans in the window, 'I need some ID, ma'am.' She asks, 'Which one?' then opens her wallet and she has two different sets of military ID." He snorted. "She was so drunk she forgot she was committing bigamy, married to a seaman and an airman. We laughed about that for months. Drunk driving and bigamy."

"No way."

"Yes, way."

And so it went.

THE WEATHER BROKE LATER that night, or morning. Sometime around three a.m., before true light but long past midnight, clouds rolled in, blanketing the region and lowering the temperature significantly. With all the windows open, his house was freezing. Seth'd woken up shivering, the blankets on his bed long crumpled into a heap on his floor in favor of a single sheet. They'd all gone to sleep in separate beds, otherwise he would've wrapped himself around the warmth of Sacha's body.

"Crud," he muttered. He dragged himself up and searched groggily in the half-light for the sweatpants and T-shirt he'd taken off the night before. Stumbling out into the living room, he found Parker asleep huddled under a throw blanket.

Quietly, Seth made his way around the house shutting windows, trying to stay as asleep as possible. He turned from the last window, the one over the kitchen sink, and slammed into a hard chest. Before he could cry out, lips came down on his, swallowing the sound. Sacha's tongue licked his lips, requesting entrance. Of course he could come in. He could come anywhere he wanted.

He welcomed Sacha's invasion, their tongues dancing together and against each other. It was heady; Seth was having a hard time remembering to breathe.

"I missed you in my bed, next to me."

Seth's stomach clenched. The things Sacha said messed with his resolve to keep things casual.

"Yes. But *my* bed, not that thing you are sleeping on," Seth whispered back.

"Whatever you want," Sacha growled before pushing him up against the counter and trapping him there with his long arms.

"My bed," Seth repeated.

Sacha manhandled him across the kitchen and down the tiny hallway into his bedroom. Seth could have sworn he heard a snigger from the living room but chose to pretend he didn't. It was incredible how Sacha changed when they were in the privacy of the bedroom, self-assured and comfortable with what they were about to do.

They fucked and weren't quiet about it.

PARKER GLARED at them when they emerged several hours later.

"What?" Sacha asked, as if he hadn't gotten Seth so wound up and turned on that by the time he came it was doubtful the entire neighborhood didn't know he was getting laid. The man had a very inventive imagination, put to good use on Seth's body. He tried hiding his smile, but Parker spotted it.

"I don't even know you anymore, but seriously? I am not old enough for all of what I heard going on in there. And you could have told me you were, you know, sexing it up already."

"Ear plugs, Parker. Ear plugs," Sacha teased.

Parker grumbled something under his breath and pulled the

blanket closer around him. His hair was sticking up all over the place; he looked like a cartoon character.

"You could at least feed me. And I couldn't find any coffee." His eyes widened dramatically. "Please tell me you drink coffee," he begged Seth. "You're not some kind of healthy-living guy."

Seth rummaged through his spices-and-other-stuff cabinet. "After all the beer we had last night? I don't think so. I think I am out of coffee, though. Damn."

"I'll go. You two," Sacha pointed a finger at both of them, "stay here." He went into his room for a few minutes before coming back out dressed for public in shorts, a worn gray T-shirt emblazoned with "Property of US Marshals," and an unzipped plain black hoodie. He jammed his bare feet into the shoes lying by the front door. "I mean it: stay here," he said before shutting the door behind himself. The roar of the truck's engine echoed across the neighborhood when he gunned it down the street. Damn, he was sexy.

"Jesus, I hate that truck." Parker turned to look at Seth, who was standing between the kitchen and the living room. "So, you and Sacha. We need to talk."

"Talk? About what?"

"About you and Sacha," Parker repeated. "We may not be blood related, but he is my family."

"I'm pretty sure Sacha and I are both adults. We can figure this out by ourselves."

"Hmm." Parker nodded. "You are both adults. But I don't know you. I know Sacha." He patted the cushion next to him.

God help him if Seth didn't walk over and sit down as bidden.

"I've always suspected Sacha was gay, or bi, I guess."

"Uh, okay." Seth wasn't sure where Parker was going with this or why it required sitting down on the couch.

"I was seven when he came to live with us."

The ends of Seth's fingers tingled. The nervous, anxious feeling fluttered in his gut.

"Okaaaay?"

Parker took a deep breath before continuing. "Look, we grew up in foster care. It wasn't a nightmare; it wasn't great. The family had their own agenda, and I guess, since we are still alive and none of us has had too much therapy, it wasn't too bad. But Sacha, he's a different kind of person. Like, he is wired to protect. But also, mmmmm—" another breath, "there's no natural trust, right? You have to earn it. He's always taken care of himself and a few very lucky other people."

"You and your sister, Mae-Lin."

"Yeah." Parker narrowed his eyes. "And, I think, you."

And damn if that didn't make the nervous fluttering in his stomach intensify. Seth tried to choke it back, to swallow the swirling unease.

He hid it with a chuckle that probably sounded more like a whinny. "Nah, we're pretty casual."

"Casual." Parker spat the word back at Seth. "I don't think you understand what I'm trying to tell you. When Sacha decides he's in, he goes *all* in. There's no middle ground where he is concerned. We may not have talked much in the past few years, but *I know* he hasn't changed. Lemme give you an example."

He smoothed the blanket on his lap. "He was like a wild animal when they brought him to the house. He had nothing, not even a bag like the social workers normally hand out for kids belongings, only the clothes on his back. He spoke very little English and basically refused to acknowledge any of us." Parker snorted when Seth rolled his eyes. "Yeah, that went on for a few weeks. We shared a room. At first I was scared of him, because he never spoke. That changed when Sacha was assigned to the same school as me. One day he was out during recess and saw me being bullied by some other kids. It was probably pretty harmless, but all I remember is him standing between me and them, yelling at them, protecting me."

Parker looked at Seth, his blue eyes serious. "After that, I never worried about feeling safe. Poor guy, I bonded to him like a baby duck or something. But the thing is, I hadn't felt safe since the fire that took my family... and suddenly somebody had my back. Sacha has never wavered from that. Even though he thinks he has been protecting me the past few years by staying away, see... he was still protecting me."

He narrowed his eyes at Seth. "I see what's happening. If you aren't dead serious about Sacha, then you better back the fuck away, right now."

"I, uh—" Seth stammered.

"Yeah, that's what I thought. Asshole."

"Hey!"

"Me and Mae have been worried about him being alone. But this is worse. If you fuck up… if you break him…"

"Are—are you threatening me?" Seth couldn't believe this conversation, and before coffee too.

"I'm telling you to be careful. To think about what you are doing and what you intend."

AVOIDING Parker and his knowing gaze for the rest of the morning—an absolute necessity—proved to be easy. After coffee, Sacha took Parker to go find some new clothes to replace the ones that went up in flames with the marina. Seth spent the morning researching Theodore Garrison and Owen Penn. Owen proved to be elusive, although there was a Penn family that had lived in eastern Washington that might fit. For Theodore, the likeliest candidate seemed to be Theodore Garrison, Emeritus Professor of English at the large state university in Seattle.

The problem was—in Seth's mind, anyway—Theodore was too young, his birth year recorded on the university website as 1922. Seth stared at the picture of the two men. It was impossible to tell their ages. The men in the picture could be anywhere from fifteen to thirty. They wore cocky grins like they had a secret. Or Seth could be projecting.

The grainy quality of the black-and-white photograph didn't help. He stared at it for several minutes, until it swam out of focus, before sliding it back on top of the stack of documents. The postcards were no help, and the letters' handwriting was too faded and spidery to read. Dammit. He *knew* the biggest clue was the battered book of poetry with the dedication on the title page. The words seemed bittersweet. Where had Theodore gone that he could only hope?

Sighing, Seth stretched, his shoulders and back popped from sitting too long at the table. Where were Sacha and Parker? It couldn't possibly take this long to decide on clothing. In any case, he had clients to keep happy and an anemic bank account to bolster.

Sacha and Parker returned as he was headed out the door. They were in the middle of an argument. Seth couldn't tell what it was about; he thought it was mostly that Parker liked to argue with whatever Sacha said, and Sacha had the whole bossy, in-control thing going on. Seth was glad for the excuse to leave them to it, because he suspected whatever was happening between Sacha and himself pushed up against a personal boundary. One he wasn't sure he was ever going to be prepared to move across.

SEVENTEEN

SACHA

The laughter booming over the connection was not funny.

"Bolic, you are fucking kidding me, right?" He heard Adam dragging air into his lungs so he could speak. "Lemme recap so I get this straight—so to speak." Sacha rolled his eyes, even though Klay couldn't see. "You leave Skagit after being undercover for years, go back to Kansas City, decide to retire. Move *back* here, and the first person you meet is my half-brother, who you are 'kind of seeing'— which I am not going to think too deeply about—and now your foster brother shows up and he appears to be a witness, maybe the *sole* witness, to a marina fire in Florida. You do know, when the flames cooled enough for investigators to go in, they found a body, right? And Diego Smith did not die of smoke inhalation or drowning; he was leaky as a sieve with three bullet holes in his back."

"Yeah. That's pretty much what happened." Adam's summary didn't make the situation sound any better. As soon as Seth had left that morning, Sacha'd hopped on the internet to see what he could find out about the marina fire. It hadn't been good. Regardless of who or which side of what organization killed Diego Smith, the de Vega family would be out for blood, and Parker appeared to be the single witness. Investigators were going to need to talk to him... but Sacha was more worried about the de Vegas.

"Well, let me call some people and see how they are going to proceed."

Sacha ran his hand through his hair again, fighting the urge to pull it out. "I know you gotta look at everything, but no way was Parker involved in this; he was there by chance. He is freaky scared of fire—his family was killed in a house fire. It's a miracle he got out. He..." Sacha looked to the ceiling as if it was going to offer advice, "he has this knack for finding trouble. I kid you not. Law enforcement should hire him, use him as a divining rod for criminal activity."

"Yeah, okay." Adam was silent for a minute. "Look, I'll do what I can. Keep yourself available."

Because he had to stay busy or go insane, Sacha left Parker at Seth's hiding in the second bedroom, and headed to the Warrick to inflict damage on walls, both real and metaphorical.

"ARE YOU DONE HERE?" Seth's voice broke into Sacha's thoughts. Seth must have known he would be hard at work. The interruption was welcome; Sacha didn't hesitate to put down what he was working on, pulling the paper mask from his face so he could talk. Stripping tiles was not his idea of fun.

They stopped at the grocery store again. The checkout clerk had served them several times now and greeted them with a cheery hello and a knowing smile.

"Grilling again?" Fucking great, the kid remembered what they had bought before.

"Yep, my buddy is hungry from a day of manual labor."

The kid eyed Seth with a different sort of interest, one that put Sacha on edge. His gaze traveled up and back down what he could see of Seth from his side of the counter. Then his eyes widened and jerked back over to Sacha. Sacha realized he'd stepped closer to Seth; he may possibly have growled.

Seth snickered, patting him on the shoulder. "Down, boy." Seth tried to pay, but Sacha knocked his hand away from the card reader, which for some reason made him chuckle again. Sacha grabbed the bags and stalked out to the parking lot.

"What crawled up your butt?" Seth asked from behind him. "I've grown used to the tall, dark, and grouchy part, but you've taken it to a new level."

Aside from wondering what kind of trouble Parker could possibly have gotten into over the course of the afternoon, Sacha was still trying to process his conversation with Adam. He was out of sorts and generally irritable. Seth didn't deserve that.

Sacha took a deep breath, letting it back out slowly, "Sorry, I'm fighting with the city over electrical permits and the fact that I need them this year, this century would be nice."

"Are you in some kind of hurry?" Seth stopped at his car, popping the hatch for Sacha to load the groceries. "I mean, it's not like I know anything, but I had the impression this, erm, project was running on your own timeline?"

"The city is a pain in my ass. I don't understand why everything has to take so long. I may actually have to go to a Chamber of Commerce meeting." It wouldn't kill him, but he didn't have to like it. As irritating as it was to admit, though, Seth was right: there was no time limit. He had all the time in the world. Maybe not all the money, but plenty of time. Stretching out endlessly ahead of him.

That evening the three of them avoided touchy subjects like murder and arson instead indulging in homemade pizza and since neither Seth or he owned a TV, several hours of gin rummy. Seth was a terrible card player, but he more than made up for it, distracting Sacha by running a hand along his thigh teasing, pressing, touching. Halfway through the game Sacha was hard enough he couldn't concentrate and worried he had a wet spot on his shorts.

Parker pretended he didn't know what was going on. He also won. With a look far too knowing for his little brother Parker threw his last card down on the discard pile.

"For the win," he looked at them both shaking his head, "I'm sleeping in your bed tonight Sacha, you won't be using it. I promise not to emerge before morning." With that he disappeared into the spare room, swiping a pair of headphones off the table before he exited.

Seth grinned, this time he cupped Sacha's erection through the rough fabric of his shorts squeezing a little. Sacha groaned, unable to control the thrust of his hips.

"I think you need a little distraction from permits and pesky relatives."

"Oh yeah?"

"Yeah."

Sacha scooted his chair back from the tiny table, patted his thighs, "Come here." Seth cocked his head like he was thinking about it before complying, coming to perch lightly on Sacha's lap legs spread wide so Sacha could see the bulge in his shorts.

"What do you want?" Seth asked breathlessly, scooting close so their cocks rubbed against each other in a most tantalizing way.

"Fuck." Sacha gasped out, swimming in sensation from the hours long tease fest.

"That, yeah, for sure, can I suck you first? I wanna taste you on my tongue."

Seth didn't wait for an answer which was good because Sacha's brain was off-line. He scooted back so he could unbutton Sacha's shorts. He'd opened Sacha's zipper sometime toward the end of the game sliding a finger tentatively in, stroking Sacha randomly. Sometimes using a fingernail running as far up and down the side of him as possible in the tight space, it was a wonder Sacha lasted. His heavy cock, still constrained by boxer briefs, throbbed in time with his heartbeat. Seth slid to his knees, opened his own shorts pulled his erection out, pumping himself a couple times while Sacha watched, breathing hard.

Seth tugged at Sacha's shorts, he lifted himself so Seth could pull them all the way down and off, taking the underwear with them. Sacha was splayed wide for Seth to see, taste, and touch as he wished. As he wished. Sacha had to shut his eyes for a moment.

Finally Seth put his lips against the crown of Sacha's penis pulling it into the hot wet of his mouth, Sacha moaned, breathless, "fuck, Seth."

Seth proceeded to lick, suck, and lavish up and down from base to tip and back again. His lips stretched around Sacha obscene with spit and the precome dripping from Sacha's erection. Massaging Sacha's balls but keeping a firm grip on the base, Seth leaned closer pushing his nose against Sacha's pubes breathing deeply, the scuff on Seth's cheek soft against his aching cock.

"Bedroom." Sacha rasped.

"Mmmm." Seth popped off, leaving Sacha bobbing in the cool air.

"Now."

"Oh, hot and bothered are you?" Seth leaned back onto his heels, "but – bedroom is good. Very good."

Later Sacha would not be able to recall exactly how they got from the table to Seth's bed, only that they landed on it a tangle of arms legs and naked skin sliding, a mess of sensation.

"Is this okay?" Sacha remembered to ask. He had Seth on his back, legs spread wantonly, massaging Seth's hole, pushing a finger inside.

Seth smiled up at him, eyes half closed, "Hell yeah... inside me." He pushed down a little forcing Sacha's finger further inside, groaning as he did so. "Hurry up, I'm not made of glass, I've been to the rodeo before."

Sacha tortured him a few more minutes until both their cocks were leaking again, enough precome that they almost didn't need lube. The condoms were in a plastic bag by the side of the bed. Sacha fished one out and as quickly as he could suited up. The thought that he would like to do this bare flashed through his head.

Turning his attention back to the incredible man laying sprawled on the bed Sacha asked, "How?"

"Like this, on my back."

Sacha crawled between Seth's legs positioning himself before pushing carefully into Seth's heat. He was tight and hot, Sacha was going to go insane.

"I said, I'm not glass." Again, Seth tried to take control by driving himself further onto Sacha.

"If you do that, I am going to come and I wanna try to make this last." Sacha grumbled.

"Fuck me already." Seth's mouth, swollen from sucking Sacha's cock, was irresistible. Sacha leaned down so he could lick across his lips and swallow them in a ferocious kiss, pushing his aching cock all the way into him with steady pressure until his balls rested against Seth's ass. Caving to Seth's demands Sacha set a relentless pace, pounding and from the moans and 'fuck's' he was hearing, also hitting Seth's prostate.

It was too soon when Sacha felt himself start to tighten, Seth had been teasing him for hours – he had no control.

"Do it." Seth demanded.

One last thrust and Sacha was coming hard into the condom, the intense heat of Seth's body as he pulsed into him, lighting him up. Seth's ass tightened around Sacha's now sensitive penis he pulled out removed the condom and tossed it into the plastic bag. Returning his attention to the incredible man splayed out on the bed, cock hard but looking well fucked Sacha leaned closer and took Seth into his mouth. He'd hardly closed his lips around him, reveling in the soft skin and scent of him before Seth was coming with a groan that probably shook the walls. Quiet his boy was not.

Sacha released him to slump over Seth's limp body. "That was fucking incredible." Seth murmured. Sacha was pretty sure he responded but the next thing he registered Seth was skootching around, pulling a sheet over the both of them. Sacha feel into a dreamless sleep, his arm thrown across Seth's waist his taut ass tucked into the well of Sacha's hips.

EIGHTEEN

SETH

Seth knew Mrs. Anderson would be bursting with excitement when he arrived to take her to one of the local garden centers. He'd done a lot of research since moving to town, and this particular nursery was, in his opinion, divine. Seth forced himself to stay away if he was low on funds; he *always* found something that needed a home.

Since Sacha and Parker were hunched over a laptop trying to figure out the fuck-fest Parker had made of his life, Seth was grateful for the excuse to leave. The two of them were like vinegar and baking soda... except the obvious affection between them was clear for anyone to see.

Seth considered himself experienced, worldly. An *open* person. And he loved sex. His policy had always been to have sex with pretty much anyone where there was mutual interest. There had been a few people he'd liked more than others but never anyone who dogged his thoughts. Seth figured he wasn't cut out for a long-term relationship; somehow he had been broken or born with an emotional defect that kept people at arm's length.

And now there was Sacha. Waking up this morning wrapped around him had been both frightening and one of the most peaceful experiences he'd ever had. Sacha made him feel safe and solid and ... he was afraid to trust it.

The one-sided conversation with Parker rang in his ears. He knew Parker was right about Sacha; he was not someone to take lightly, that made Seth cringe. Light was his signature. Light meant that when he and whoever he was fucking went their separate ways (and they always did), no one got hurt. Since all relationships would end eventually, Seth saved himself the heartache by never fully investing.

He'd been called on it a few times. His past partners had said he was emotionally unavailable; he didn't let people get close enough for a real relationship. They weren't wrong. He had an internal blueprint: as soon as he felt the noose tightening around his neck, he called things off. The second moving in, spending more time together, or "relationship status" came up in conversation, Seth was done.

Marnie had been very careful bringing strangers around after Seth moved in, to the point of it being the two of them against the world. He hadn't realized until much later that she'd worried that, after the revolving door of Jaqueline's vagina, Seth would have issues. She was probably right.

He'd meant his flirtation with the mysterious, sexy, brooding Sacha to be the same light, innocent fun he was used to. Okay, maybe also something of an experiment, because Seth found Sacha compelling, unsettling, mysterious. Seth was starting to realize he'd bitten off more than he could chew, but he wasn't quite ready to end things yet. Was he playing a dangerous game? Absolutely.

Engaging Sacha was dangerous, not because Sacha was an intrinsically dangerous man—though he *was*; there was no point in denying the aura of menace that engulfed him—but because peeling back Sacha's layers also meant peeling back and exposing his own. Seth hadn't realized that until too late.

"Dammit."

Mrs. Anderson was ready to go; she waggled her fingers at him through her living-room window as he parked. A few moments later her front door opened and she stepped out wearing a practical bright-pink windbreaker, white slacks, and matching pink Keds. Adorable.

Seth met her at the top of her stairs and escorted her to his car, helping her in and making sure her seatbelt was buckled. Seth wished he had a nicer car to drive her in, but she didn't seem to care about the derelict condition of his ancient Jeep.

The nursery was located on the south end of town, at the top of Old Charter, past the city rose gardens. The main building was a tiny cottage. Probably built around the 1920s, it sat on several acres of land. The current owners had packed it full of fun little treasures for the garden, houseplants, and seasonal decorations. Each nook and cranny was stuffed with surprises.

Seth parked and went around to open the passenger door. "Let's start inside first, shall we? We can get a wagon for your plants."

"Seth, thank you already for bringing me out here," she said. "I don't like to drive anymore."

Seth had spotted the decades-old Chrysler tucked under her carport. "How do you get groceries and things like that?"

She fluttered a hand. "Oh, when I get desperate I'll drive. But my car is so huge, and I'm afraid I won't see someone over all that hood."

"I know someone who might be able to help you with a smaller car, if you'd like." Buck Swanfeldt would help her out, although as far as Seth knew he was knee-deep in wedding preparations at the moment. Seth snickered to himself. Buck might as well let Joey plan the whole thing and just show up on time.

Outside the main building, rows and rows of native plants, perennials, annuals, trees, and shrubs crowded the grounds, with gravel walkways in between. There was a section displaying grasses and bamboo, a section for berry vines, a section for water plants. Several greenhouses dotted the landscape, filled with not-so-hardy herbs, fuchsias, and tender annuals. Seth felt like he was in heaven. Mrs. Anderson felt the same, if her reaction to the spectacle was any gauge.

"Seth," Mrs. Anderson sighed after a few minutes of looking at the huge selection of plants, "I want it all."

He chuckled. "Isn't that the truth." He grabbed a wagon and led Mrs. Anderson toward the greenhouses.

NINETEEN

SETH

The postcards and other treasures they'd found in the Warrick still intrigued Seth. Over the past few days he'd been close to obsessive, trying to learn as much as he could about the two men in the photo – which wasn't much. He was desperately curious about who Owen Penn and Theodore Garrison had been, what their history was, and why someone had saved the books of poetry and dime-store novels. Why had the box been tucked behind a wall in the Warrick? Their story felt important, although he couldn't explain why.

Plus, it was a good distraction from Sacha and Parker. The two of them fought like cats and dogs about ninety percent of the time. Over the few days since Parker arrived, Seth had moderated more than one "discussion" between the two. It was kind of endearing, their arguing merely accentuated how much they cared for each other, but it was stressful to be around.

Seth went to the Booking Room for some relative peace and quiet. The café was bustling, but most of the patrons were taking their drinks and snacks outdoors to enjoy the sunshine, so there were plenty of tables available.

Ira Fragale was in residence, doing his sexy, silver-haired, man in charge thing. They'd danced around an attraction earlier in the year, but it hadn't gone anywhere. They were both emotionally elusive – but in different ways. Didn't mean he couldn't appreciate the silver fox from afar.

"Hey, Ira."

"Seth."

Ira made Sacha seem like a gossip.

Snagging a table away from the noise of the espresso machine, Seth got down to business, popping his laptop open and setting himself up for maximum focus. He'd been searching all week, but he decided to start over again from the beginning. Typing in Owen Penn got him a whole lot of nothing relevant. He tried Owen Penn 1939, the date from the back of the photograph. Nothing. These guys were too old for a big social-media presence. If they were even alive.

There were several Theodore Garrisons recorded as living in Washington State between 1910 and 1930. The emeritus English professor at the UW kept catching his eye, but Seth still thought his birth year was too late... although at nearly ninety-five he was the single living Theodore Garrison Seth could find in Washington. He certainly wasn't after the guy in Iowa who was a shift manager for Pizza Hut. The internet was a weird place. He had a burst of excitement when he discovered birth records for an Owen Penn born in 1920 in Twisp, Washington, but he couldn't find anything following that.

Nothing for the two names together. He added Lake Chelan, then Chelan on its own. Then he tried each of them with the state and the year. He wasted some time following a string of names through a major ancestry site, but he didn't know if he had the right people or not. Seriously, how hard could it be to find evidence of someone from the 1930s, when the population of Washington was less than two million souls? Taking a deep breath, he tried to think of how else he could research someone he literally knew nothing about.

Somebody tapped his shoulder, interrupting his train of thought. "Your coffee is cold; more?" Ira asked.

"What?" Seth squinted up at him, eyes bleary from staring at the computer screen.

"You've been sitting here for hours, focused on whatever it is you're doing. Do. You. Want, another coffee or not?" If Seth hadn't known Ira, he would have thought he was an asshole. Actually, he *was* pretty much an asshole.

"Damn. Is that the time?" Seth shut the lid of his laptop on the mostly futile search. He'd found a few possible clues, but if he was going to figure out who Owen and Theodore were, he would need to go somewhere like the city library in Winthrop, or even the county courthouse. In the meantime, he was late for his daily check-in at the Warrick. Parker or not, Sacha would probably be there. Fragments of the other day's conversation with Parker popped into his head, but he chose to ignore them. They were both adults, and it wasn't Seth's job to guard Sacha's heart, was it?

AFTER CIRCLING the block for a spot, Seth tucked his Jeep in behind a massive trash container jammed against the curb. Sacha had caved and rented a Dumpster to haul away material from the demolition. It sat directly in front of the Warrick, and the man himself was out front, tossing offending pieces of the building's history into the trash.

Seth swallowed. Every time he laid eyes on Sacha he was hit with twin stabs of lust and longing. Even after days of having him, and Parker, in his house, Seth wasn't tired of the sight of him. Or the sound of his gravelly voice, or the smile Seth knew was his alone. Parker had shaken his head behind Sacha's back more than once, but Seth didn't have to explain anything to Parker, and frankly Parker should focus on working out his own shit.

He wondered what Parker and Sacha's home life had been like. Growing up under Marnie's wing had been the luckiest thing ever to have happened to Seth. She'd created a safe place for him to live and explore, learn and grow. No subject had been taboo; if he had a question about anything, Marnie would answer the best she could. If she couldn't answer, she'd find someone who would.

She'd never said, "Don't love your mother; she is a bad person." Instead, she'd helped Seth recover the good memories he had of Jaqueline, helped him understand that in some intrinsic, impossible way his mother was broken beyond repair... and it wasn't Seth's fault. Mostly.

Jaqueline had brought Seth into the world and therefore to Marnie, for which Marnie insisted to her deathbed she was forever grateful. When he'd been confused about his sexuality, she'd hugged him tight and said as long as he loved well and true it didn't matter who they were. He wondered what she would have to say about Sacha.

Looking back on the exact moment Marnie appeared in his life, coming through the door of the social worker's grim office in Aberdeen like some sort of hippie storm trooper, Seth could almost believe it had been a miracle. If he believed in a God, he would believe this one person had been sent for him alone. Without her, Seth's life would have had a different outcome. Instead Marnie appeared and swept him off to Arizona with her.

It hadn't been all sunshine and roses. Seven-year-old Seth had been practically feral. Which reminded him of what Parker had told him about Sacha; they had more in common than a mutual interest in old buildings. It had taken months for Marnie to gain his trust. He stole money from her wallet, believing she would put him out on the street. He kept his meager belongings packed, sleeping fully dressed, even in his shoes, because he *knew* they would be leaving in the dead of night at some point. He hoarded food in his room, because there would be a day when there wasn't any. He'd had to learn how to make friends and started school a grade behind.

Seth shook himself, bringing his mind back to the present and the compelling vision before him. Limned by the early evening light blanketing the city, Sacha was a living work of art: shirt off, muscles flexing and straining while he heaved scrap wood, plasterboard, and whatnot off the sidewalk into the skip. The sight would challenge any red-blooded human. Taking a calming lungful of air, Seth got out of his car and headed toward the man of his dreams. In, *in* his dreams.

Micah came around the corner as Seth was nearing Sacha.

"Hey!" Micah waved. "I'm hoping to get that tour."

Seth about died laughing at the expression of disgust on Sacha's face. Evidently, Sacha had hoped Micah would disregard his offer of a tour.

"Jesus fucking Christ," Sacha not-so-quietly muttered. "I will never get any work done with the two of you here. It's bad enough I have to babysit Parker."

Seth snickered. If Adam knew what a dick Sacha could be, they would either get along scarily well or there would be an epic Godzilla vs. King Ghidorah dogfight. Hard to tell who would win. Sacha was grizzly-bear huge, but Adam was crafty and seriously built. Seth had a short-lived fantasy about the two of them battling to the finish... until he squicked himself out envisioning Adam locked in a wrestling hold by a mostly naked Sacha. His brain had to shut it down; he did *not* need to be having pervy fantasies where his half-brother was an accidental co-star.

Anyway, not even Sacha could be unpleasant to Micah for very long. Micah *niced* people until they had no other recourse than to be pleasant back.

Micah was taken by the building, quickly seeing what both Sacha and Seth did: a diamond in the rough. "You could do so many interesting things with this space, and I know the Chamber of Commerce is really trying to bring N.O.T. into the economic plan for Skagit. What are you thinking about?"

"You two are like the Wonder Twins with all the questions. And the fucking Chamber of Commerce can kiss my ass."

Seth wondered what the Chamber had done to get on Sacha's bad side—not that it would have been difficult, but his response did seem particularly vehement.

Micah ignored Sacha's outburst. "There really isn't enough small office space here in town. I know loads of artists and other small-business owners who would kill to rent desk space somewhere like this. They could have a respectable address without renting the whole building. *I'd* rent space here. Or small retail could be nice, but the light in here is so amazing it would be wasted on retail. Although," Micah twitched his sweaty T-shirt away from his body, "you should think about air conditioning."

Seth couldn't tell which horrified Sacha more, the idea of Micah renting imaginary desk space or having to deal with installing air conditioning. On second thought it was probably the idea of Micah being around on a regular basis. The air conditioning would have to lie there and take Sacha's attitude.

Micah left after exacting a promise they would come over for dinner soon. Sacha and Seth stood together on the sidewalk watching him drive away.

Seth turned to Sacha. "Hey. So, did you find any more treasure today?"

"You were late," Sacha grunted unresponsively, turning to pick up a large piece of lumber and heaving it over the edge of the container. It landed with a boom, and a cloud of dust spooled upward.

He *had* been later than usual after falling down the virtual rabbit hole researching Owen and Theodore. He'd been in the habit of showing up in the early to mid-afternoon and helping out for a couple hours. They'd fallen into a routine since the day Seth had brought the Danishes.

"Were you worried?" The idea was kind of mind-boggling. Marnie had worried, in a way, but that hadn't really been how she parented. He couldn't fault her; she had been in her forties by the time he had come into her life. He didn't know how to be a kid, and she didn't know how to parent, yet the both of them had been fine.

Sacha frowned. His default expression, it didn't really mean anything. "A little." He tossed another piece of lumber into the skip.

Seth told himself to quit ogling and get to work. Forty minutes later, the skip was three-quarters full, and most of the debris was gone from inside. Sacha went to grab his shirt—a shame, even if Seth did find his attention sliding Sacha's way too many times to count. The ground floor was now empty except for what was left of Sacha's belongings. He'd even taken out the wall between the tiny restroom and the main space, leaving a depressed-looking toilet in the far corner.

From where he was standing, Seth could see that much of the second level had also been on the receiving end of Sacha Bolic's raze-everything treatment. Several large boxes stood in the main area, fixtures to replace what Sacha had removed. Original style lamps from a lighting company that specialized in old designs, two ceiling fans, a stack of what looked like crown molding and other trim. Slowly but surely Sacha was bringing the Warrick back.

TWENTY

SETH

The next afternoon Sacha was busy bullying the city, and a construction firm he was hoping to hire for a wiring upgrade and new electric box, into quickly issuing the necessary permits and generally moving faster. Seth suspected that Sacha might have met his match in the city bureaucrats, although the construction firm could possibly fall in line. The timeline for Sacha's project had been pushed back a minimum of four weeks due to a backlog of requests. Four weeks for him to stalk and prowl and generally scare the crap out of Seth if he wasn't paying close attention.

Parker was holed up in the spare bedroom again, still. He hadn't come out since lunch; when Seth had tapped on the door, he'd said he wasn't hungry. Seth didn't know how to help the younger man, who seemed a little depressed—when he wasn't interfering in Seth and Sacha's personal lives.

His front door banged open, and Sacha stomped in looking as flustered and pissed off.

"So... didn't go well with the city?"

"Fucking bureaucrats, pencil-pushing jackasses." Sacha stopped, scowled, and ran a hand through that sexy salt-and-pepper hair Seth had been fantasizing about running his own hands through. "Fucking Chamber of Commerce..." He seemed to have run out of steam.

"Water, beer?"

"Fuck, yeah. Beer, please."

Seth turned and began rummaging in the fridge. When he turned back there was no mistaking the heat in Sacha's eyes, or the direction he'd been looking. He'd been staring at Seth's ass. Seth allowed himself a small, very naughty, grin. Sacha still hadn't taken the beer from his hand. Seth moved closer, holding the beer out. Before he could change his mind, he tucked his nose into Sacha's neck, loving that they were close enough in height for this to be easy.

Seth was feeling reckless. Running his nose up Sacha's neck, Seth nipped his earlobe, then placed a quick kiss on the corner of Sacha's mouth. It was meant to tease. Instead, strong arms slid around his waist. The cold bottle trapped between them kept Seth acutely aware of the intimacy of the situation. He almost couldn't breathe.

Aside from the cold beer, all he felt was Sacha's hard body pressed fiercely against his own, chest heaving. Nothing else happened, except maybe time stopping for a minute while Sacha held him. Too soon, Sacha stepped back, taking the beer from his hand like nothing had happened, and went out into the backyard. Seth trailed along behind.

They spent the rest of the evening amiably discussing baseball, of all things. Seth discovered Sacha was sort of a fan, which surprised him because baseball was a game for the patient. On the other hand, it added to Seth's increasing hoard of information about him. Growing up in the land of spring training had its benefits. They talked players, RBIs, on-base percentages, the value (or not) of the designated hitter, and myriad other baseball stats until they were both tired.

Parker stayed in the spare room, forcing Sacha to sleep on the couch, which wasn't long enough for him. Some unnamed emotion – fear? -- held Seth back from offering Sacha space in his bed. He wouldn't let himself offer something Sacha might interpret as permanence. He couldn't allow himself to get used to having Sacha in his bed or elsewhere. Sacha didn't say anything about being relegated to the living room. He was tucked up on the couch and asleep before

Seth finished brushing his teeth. Sacha half turned onto his back, arm thrown over his head, face in repose. Seth longed to run his fingers through his hair, whisper nonsense in his ear, tell him he was afraid of the dark so Sacha would hold him tightly. Instead he went to bed alone.

Christ, he was messed up.

TWENTY-ONE
SACHA

Parker was hungry. Which Sacha supposed he should be glad of; the past few days, almost a week, with Parker holed up in Seth's house refusing to do anything but sulk had been driving Sacha crazy. He understood; this was how Parker reacted when he was hurt, and no doubt whatever Zeke had done (or not done) had hurt him. But he needed to quit the running away. Adam was supposed to get back to Sacha any minute with what information he was able to find out about the fire and the dead body, and how badly the authorities wanted to talk to Parker. Which he figured with the time it was taking Adam, wasn't terribly badly.

"There must be somewhere decent to eat in this village," Parker whined.

"Jesus fucking Christ." They were driving up State Street. Sacha could see the SkPD headquarters and knew there was a good coffee-and-sandwich spot across the street. As luck would have it, there was a car pulling out of a parking space.

The Booking Room was busy and full of cops. It made Sacha oddly wistful—a feeling he hadn't expected, missing the camaraderie of his Marshal days, shooting the breeze about cases and suspects over terrible cups of coffee.

Scanning the seating area, he stopped short when he spotted a very recognizable brown, curly head of hair. Parker nearly ran into his back.

"Did you purposefully pick a spot where all the cops in this town go for lunch?" he whispered into Sacha's shoulder.

Before Sacha could come up with a reason why they should turn around and leave, Micah looked up and saw them. Sacha could see why Adam had fallen hard for the guy; his smile lit up his entire face.

"Have you been making friends?" Parker asked incredulously, seeing Micah's reaction. "This is not the Sacha I know and love."

Micah waved them over, tucking his laptop into a ratty messenger bag as they cut through the lunch crowd toward his table. "Have a seat, it's great to see you."

They sat, and Sacha made introductions, then listened as Micah and Parker charmed each other. Sacha watched the SkPD stream in and then back out with their gallon jugs of caffeine. He recognized a few of them from when he was undercover.

Parker poked him in the side. "Order me something, will you? I'm starved."

He was finishing ordering when someone tapped him on the shoulder. Managing not to spin around like a lunatic, he plastered a smile on his face before turning to see who it was. It was Meyer from the Chamber of Commerce. The guy was worse than a tick.

One summer while Sacha still lived with the Finlaysons, he'd semi-adopted a stray dog that had been living out in the abandoned field behind their neighborhood. Meyer reminded him of the dog, except Sacha had liked and encouraged the dog. He'd been sad when it had disappeared. Meyer grated on his nerves.

"Sacha! Great to see you; what are you doing on this side of town?"

Meyer ended up sitting with them at Micah's table. There had been no way to politely—or rudely—get rid of him. The guy ignored or simply did not understand social cues. He really was like a puppy. He oozed in between Parker and Sacha, sitting far closer than necessary even though the table was small. Sacha scooted his chair away as far as he could.

Parker seemed fascinated, but Sacha couldn't tell if it was in a good way or the way a person watches a slow but inevitable car accident. Glancing up, Parker saw Sacha eyeing him and shook his head before tossing out a knowing smile. Sacha had no idea what that was about.

"Call me Chris," Meyer repeated, after Sacha introduced him as Meyer. Old habits.

And good fucking God, he'd forgotten how Parker could talk when he got going... about anything. While the other three men talked about the city of Skagit, business, random things Parker brought up—including a few stories from their shared childhoods (names changed to protect the innocent, of course)—Sacha's mind wandered. He wasn't a master of casual conversation.

He mused over the time since his return to Skagit. Seth. Almost every memory had Seth in it or some association with him. Seth returning from a job, covered in a fine coating of dusty soil held tightly to his skin by the sweat of the day. He should have smelled terrible, but instead he smelled like sunshine and the outdoors. A little bit like laughter. Seth sitting on the floor of the Warrick, again dusty and sweaty, hunched over the box of long-lost artifacts. Seth, ignoring Sacha to gather the day's debris and put it in the trash. Seth, at ease in his backyard, chatting with Sacha about mountain biking as if it was the most natural thing in the world to be doing.

Parker smirked at him as if he knew exactly what Sacha was thinking about.

TWENTY-TWO

SACHA

""Why are you being such an asshole?" Parker punched him in the shoulder.

Sacha'd gotten a phone call from an old boss, the one person from his old life he would call in a favor from. After briefly entertaining the idea of asking Rick instead, he'd called Johnny. He'd never bothered to memorize his old partner's phone number and he hadn't wanted to go through official routes.

"I heard through the grapevine that you retired. Could have knocked me over with a feather; I thought you'd die with your boots on." Johnny's deep voice rumbled over the connection.

Yes, well, that was exactly what Sacha had been trying to avoid. He'd called Johnny asking if he could find anything out about Parker's ex and the marina fire.

Parker's ex-boyfriend, while maybe not a rising star in the Miami PD, was a clean cop. And, it seemed, very concerned about Parker. Zeke had told authorities that his "roommate" often left for days at a time but that he'd never not come home before. The boat was apparently an inheritance from his grandfather.

"Parker, you're in the middle of an arson case, and we don't know why. The good news is, your boyfriend—" Sacha waved a hand at Parker's expression, "—whatever he was-slash-is, didn't have anything to do with the fire. In fact, he was at some kind of training that week." Sacha had considered that possibly this Zeke guy had light up the marina himself for insurance or something but there was no evidence at all and the boat itself hadn't been worth much.

Seth wasn't at home, but typically—and Sacha really needed to talk to him about that—the back door was unlocked, so he and Parker had let themselves in. There was going to be a safety conversation in Seth's future that had nothing to do with condoms. Seth's "but I've got nothing worth stealing" meant nothing. Lives could be stolen too. Parker went into what now seemed to be his room; Sacha headed out to the backyard.

It was after nine when he finally heard Seth's car pull up onto the parking strip. Parker had come out for a while, but had given up on Sacha being conversational and was back inside reading a book. The neighborhood was quiet; even though the sun had peeked out from behind the clouds later in the afternoon, it was still cool. A hardy mosquito buzzed around, trying to land on his arm, and he smashed it with satisfaction.

The rumble of conversation drifted out the back door. Parker laughed, and Sacha felt the sting of jealousy. He was pathetic, sitting out in Seth's backyard feeling out of sorts because the man had left for hours without telling him why.

Seth and Parker wandered into the backyard, Parker choosing to disregard Sacha's terrible humor and Seth blissfully unaware.

"Hey, guess what?" Seth was smiling as he approached Sacha, something that had not happened much in his life. Most people didn't smile when they saw him; they frowned and often ran in the other direction. He found himself drinking Seth in, memorizing what he looked like in this moment: sparkling eyes; warm smile; a T-shirt worn enough to look like he'd owned it since the early 90s, with an old rock band logo or something on it.

Parker leaned down, whispering loudly into his ear, "Man, you have it bad. You should see the look on your face."

"I may have tracked down the right Theodore Garrison," Seth

continued. "He's still alive, but I couldn't talk to him today. He has quite a wall of protectors in the English department." Seth went on to describe his visit to the university and how certain he was that this was the right person.

Seth'd texted Sacha that morning after leaving the house while Sacha and Parker were arguing over something completely unimportant, like who had used the last of the milk. The text had merely said that Seth was going to Seattle for the day; he'd be back that evening. Sacha'd been in a bad mood ever since, purposely egging Parker on, arguing about, of all things, the finale of a show Sacha had never even watched. It sounded so stupid he certainly would never watch it now.

At some undefinable point over the long hot summer, a complete stranger had become very important to him. He snorted. Important didn't really cover it, but he wasn't going any farther—not even in his head—right now. The list of people Sacha considered friends was short; the list he considered family even shorter. Family was something he protected fiercely. Family was not to be fucked with. When he wasn't paying attention, this generous, sexy, sweet-talking man had become family.

Big-hearted and seemingly carefree, Seth befriended a complete stranger who looked like he'd been in a car accident. Taken him home and, if Sacha was going to be honest with himself, he'd never really left. Yeah, he'd slept at the Warrick for the most part, until Parker arrived, but whenever he had, he missed the warmth of Seth's home.

At the same time, there were hidden depths to Seth, something lurking out of sight but not out of mind. For all of their random conversations while working and the few times Sacha had shared something about himself with Seth, it hadn't escaped his notice that Seth didn't really tell him anything about himself.

Sacha could run a background check, of course. He'd done so several times in the past, and each time had led to him ending a nascent relationship. For whatever reason, Sacha felt it important that Seth share his history himself. Whatever it was that led to him being raised by an aunt. Whatever led him to being... elusive. A laugh on the wind, a dandelion clock drifting on a breeze tantalizingly out of reach.

Now he felt stupid for being grouchy and argumentative all day and, possibly, jealous. Sacha'd forgotten about the postcards and the book he'd found in the wall. His distrustful nature had Seth going to Seattle for a different reason; he had jumped to a conclusion with no facts to support it. *He* was the one who travelled to different cities for anonymous sex, not Seth. He was mortified to have thought that Seth was hooking up with someone, when instead he had been following up on a lead that might help them discover who the boys in the photo were.

Seth kept smiling at him, a look of excitement that had Sacha grinning back regardless of his inner turmoil.

"I left my phone number and email; the secretary is going to pass them along. Professor Garrison will get in touch with me if he's interested. He's very elderly." Seth talked with his hands, and it was clear how excited he was about this possibility.

Seth said the return commute had been hellish, making Sacha feel even more like shit for jumping to an extremely wrong conclusion about why Seth had gone to Seattle.

Before leaving the Marshals, Sacha had never much considered his future. Morbid? Probably, but he'd assumed he would die in service one way or another. It wasn't a stretch to imagine that instead of that fire escape collapsing he would have been lying on the ground with a big hole in his head.

Now he had a future, and Seth kept slipping into it. Sacha wasn't sure exactly when that idea had insinuated itself into his head, but it was there, humming in the background, refusing to be ignored. It frightened him; futures required planning, and Sacha didn't even know what he wanted for dinner most days. He wanted Seth and he wanted a future.

He patted the patio chair beside him, and Seth sat down, grabbing a beer from the six-pack Sacha had brought out earlier. Parker rolled his eyes and shot Sacha a look before mouthing, "We're going to need to talk." Sacha would have to see about that. He had a plan for

Parker, and Parker probably wasn't going to be very happy about it. Too bad.

Sacha turned toward Seth, and proximity turned the careless movement into an accidental-on-purpose brush of lips in the near dark. They were so close Sacha saw Seth's eyes widen before he pulled back a fraction and licked his lower lip. The *almost*-kiss sent a pop of awareness coursing through Sacha, head to toe.

Fuck. He'd missed Seth today. Giving in, he pressed his lips firmly against Seth's. He could smell the beer they'd drunk and the scent of the day on his skin. Oh, lord, he was starving. He shut his eyes, allowing himself to fall into the kiss, their breath and tongues tentative and empowering. One of them groaned.

"Uh, guys? I'm right here."

"Shit." Sacha jerked away like he'd been stung, snatching his hand off Seth's thigh but managing a last-minute squeeze.

THE NEXT MORNING, Adam showed up. He looked tired and rumpled. Out of town on a case he'd flown in the night before, not landing in Seattle until after ten.

"The flight was ridiculous; I don't wanna talk about it."

Seth, Sacha, and Parker had been lounging in the house between the kitchen and living room area, cradling huge mugs of coffee. Sacha stood to shake Adam's hand; they did the weird handshake-backslap thing straight men and, apparently, law enforcement agents of any persuasion engaged in. Micah, a step behind Adam, shook his head at the two of them.

"So, Bolic, you come to Skagit and trouble follows. Big surprise," Adam said.

Seth and Micah chuckled; Parker pouted. It was all Sacha could do not to run screaming.

Adam turned to Parker. "You I don't know, but I have a feeling."

"Yeah." Parker stood. "Parker Crane; not sure it's going to be a pleasure to meet you."

"Parker," Sacha growled.

Parker snorted. "Your growly bear thing has no effect on me."

"Me locking you up and throwing away the key—"

"Gentlemen." Adam cut across the bickering. "I think we need to have a little chat. First we'll talk about Parker, currently the only known witness to the murder of Diego Smith. 'Witness' is pretty loose; from what Sacha told me you didn't see anything, but I gotta ask questions. Since I know Sacha, we're gonna keep this informal for now, but Agent Gonzales will take your statement later. Luckily your background check came back clean." He gave Parker a look. "Don't even think about leaving anything out." Parker huffed and scrunched back into the couch.

Parker did a good job; he told Adam what had happened that night at the marina, what he'd heard, and how he'd laid low before coming to Skagit. He remembered a few new things, but the story he told was basically the same one he'd told Seth and Sacha.

"It's too bad you didn't see anything," Adam remarked after Parker finished.

"Why?" asked Parker.

"Well, the parties involved likely think you did. The local authorities don't, but need to speak to you as a witness, not a suspect. We can take care of your official statement here. It would be nice to have some information to pass along to our team in Florida. At any rate, we're going to have to make contact with them."

Parker's whine was unpleasant.

Adam raised his eyebrows, "Does somebody need a snack before we interrogate him?"

TWENTY-THREE

SETH

The Booking Room was one of Seth's top ten places in Skagit. The downside was that it was located almost directly across from police headquarters. There were always cops in there getting coffee and chatting up the cute wait staff. Seth had nothing against cops. Or US Marshals. They made him edgy, like they were waiting for him to make a mistake so they could haul him off to jail or something.

This downside made itself apparent when he, Sacha, Parker, and Adam and Micah crowded into the café. Adam was something of a local celebrity, and even though there was historical animosity between the agencies, all the cops still stopped by the table to say hi and shake his hand.

Parker was standing next to him while Sacha went to grab a couple tables for their group to sit at. Some big blond cop was taking all of Adam's attention when Seth felt Parker stiffen and mutter something under his breath that sounded a great deal like, "Are you fucking kidding me?"

Seth turned to see what Parker was looking at, a random stranger was standing in the doorway blocking the way for everyone. Except his eyes were trained on Parker. Like he knew him.

Parker backed closer to Seth. The unknown man saw the movement, and his face changed. Not to anger, as Seth half expected, but to sadness. Resignation. Maybe worse: hopelessness.

"Who is that?"

"That would be my ex, Zeke. What the hell is he doing in Skagit?"

"If I was going to guess, from the look on his face, he came here to see you." Zeke was standing stock-still, customers flowing around him like water around river rock.

"How did he find me?" Parker's eyes narrowed at Sacha's broad back. "That rat bastard."

Seth had no idea if Sacha was behind Zeke's appearance but thought Parker was probably right.

A skinny, twitchy-looking guy came in and bumped into Zeke from behind. At first it looked like he was trying to push through the crowd where Zeke was standing, but then Sacha exclaimed, "Jesus fucking Christ, Sigurd Jacobsen?" The next thing Seth knew, Sacha was shoving past him and the skinny guy had turned and bolted back out the door. Plates, glasses and coffee mugs clattered across the floor many shattering as tables were pushed aside and tipped over.

The neighborhood was teeming with cops, but it was Sacha and Zeke who chased the guy down the street and tackled him before he got more than half a block away. Adam followed the two men a bit more slowly, cell phone in one hand an espresso in the other.

Parker grimaced. "Oooh, that had to hurt."

Did the guy not know they were right across from the police station? Most of the civilians in the café were watching the action through the windows; everyone else had rushed outside to see if they could help and were now standing in a circle around the three men. The guy was putting up a fight, yelling something Seth couldn't make out, but in moments he was in handcuffs with Sacha's knee crammed in his back. Start to finish the incident lasted about sixty seconds.

Adam was standing over the guy—Jacobsen?—shaking his head. Sacha slowly got to his feet, and Seth saw him wince.

"Quit fucking struggling, or the closest officer gets to shoot you," Adam barked at Jacobsen, who seemed to realize Adam meant every word and went very still. His bloodshot eyes finally focusing on the crowd of law enforcement surrounding him.

Seth was relieved when Sacha separated from the group and limped over to where he and Parker were waiting.

Before Sacha could speak, Parker went on the attack. "You asshole!"

"What?" Sacha looked confused for a second before he looked back in the direction Parker was pointing, "Oh, yeah, by the way, I called Zeke. Don't even think about running away without talking to him."

Seth tried to distract both of them from yet another argument by gesturing toward where Jacobsen was being led away. "What was all that about?"

Sacha ran a hand through his hair and shook his head in disbelief, "My past life coming back to haunt me."

How fucking crazy was life, anyway? It seemed the now handcuffed Jacobsen was a low-on-the-totem-pole junkie, running drugs and whatnot for anyone who'd let him... which included some big-name crime syndicate from the Ukraine. But apparently he'd grown up in Skagit.

Adam walked over to join them, listening to Sacha's story.

"From what he was babbling, during a visit to his childhood home at some point over the past couple of years, he got mixed up with the Russian mob here in town. He 'borrowed' some inventory and then took off back to the sunshine and beaches," Sacha said. "Then, last March, when my partner and I were assigned to bring him in as a witness, he recognized me from here and ran because he thought the Russians were after him."

"He recognized you from...?"

Sacha's mouth flattened. "I was undercover for... a long time."

The warning look in Sacha's eyes stopped him from asking about it.

"Okay," Seth said slowly. "He, um. He thought you were a Russian mobster or something?"

"Something like that." Sacha agreed, scowling over where Jacobsen still lay on the sidewalk.

Seth had to admit, Sacha probably played "bad guy" remarkably well.

Sacha glared at the ground a moment before continuing. "Anyhow, he got away—a god dammed fire escape collapsed from underneath me—but like a recurring rash he's here visiting family again, saw me walk in and panicked. Such a devoted family man, visiting his sick mother and all." He shook his head. "It doesn't make a lot of sense, but I'm thinking his light bulb is pretty dim."

TWENTY-FOUR
SACHA

It may have been a little heavy-handed but, yes, Sacha had gotten Zeke's number from Mae-Lin. When Zeke had picked up with a breathless "Parker?" even though Sacha'd been calling from his own unlisted number, it had been clear the man cared and was very concerned. Good; Parker needed someone to keep him in line. Sacha hoped Zeke was the man for the job.

He'd made sure Zeke knew where Parker was going to be, and, except for the unfortunate incident with Jacobsen, everything had gone according to plan. Part two of the plan involved luring Seth away from his house for a few days to give Parker and Zeke some privacy.

As they got out of the truck in front of Seth's house, Sacha asked, "What do you think about going east of the mountains for a few days?"

"Yeah, what for?" Seth whipped around, pinning him with a surprised stare.

"We—or you, since you've done all the legwork—can research the photograph some more, maybe check out the county records. We'll go to the source."

"Ooooh, wow! Okay, lemme call my clients so they don't think I've deserted them." He slipped inside, looking delighted with Sacha's half-assed plan.

Seeing Seth's eyes light up at the thought of spending hours driving to some tiny town to do more research was worth all the sideways glances and straight-up death glares he was getting from Parker.

"Zeke," Sacha gestured toward the man waiting for them on the walkway, "came a long way to talk to you, and he deserves to be heard."

"Fine," Parker grumbled before disappearing into the house behind Seth.

Zeke hesitated by the front door, a backpack in one hand, his other hand jammed into the front pocket of his jeans.

"You think you can do this?" Sacha asked.

"Well, before I left Miami I came out to my partner, my mother, and my boss. I'm not sure there are more bridges to burn."

"How'd it go?"

Zeke sighed and shifted his stance. "My partner seemed somewhat okay. My boss can't really say anything, but I don't think I'm going get any awards soon. Pretty sure he'd like to see me gone anyway. My mother... I think she will come around. If only because my dad left her for a younger woman, and my brother died a few years ago. I'm all she's got left. I guess we'll see."

Sacha nodded his understanding. He'd been a coward, not coming out at work, but he also hadn't forced a boyfriend to hide in limbo.

"All right, then. Let's see what you can do. Seth and I are leaving as soon as we can, and we'll be gone a few days."

TWENTY-FIVE

SETH

"What is taking you so long?"

Seth startled at the sound of Sacha's gravelly voice behind him. Goddammit, he'd sworn he wouldn't let Sacha sneak up on him. Again. Sacha was supposed to be outside getting his truck ready, not scaring the ever-loving shit out of him. He grabbed some more things out of the refrigerator.

He'd called his clients, Mrs. Anderson and Greg, and let them know he would be out of town for a few days. One of the perks of being self-employed.

There had been a mention of an Owen Penn born in Twisp on one of those ancestry sites, so that was where they were headed.

"I checked online, and there are plenty of rooms available in Winthrop." He finished stashing sandwiches in the cooler alongside several bottles of water, the rest of the beer, and some fruit. "I'm excited. I've read that the drive is beautiful. Supposedly there is a lake —okay, there *is* a lake—that looks incredible. We could stop there for the night, or we could go straight to Twisp." Seth was afraid he was babbling, but he couldn't believe Sacha had suggested the trip. "I know you're as interested these guys as I am, or I wouldn't have busted you trying to read those letters the other night." He'd come

home a few days earlier after finishing up a tiny job for Ms. Can I Get
It For Free to find Sacha on the couch with the postcards and letters
spread around him. "There's no use pretending you're not."

"I'm driving. That Jeep of yours is a death trap."

Before leaving, Seth watered the plants in the front and back,
packed a small bag with necessities, then tucked the cooler behind the
passenger seat. Sacha watched him, an unreadable expression on his
face, before grabbing his duffel bag and tossing it in the truck.

"I hope this works," Sacha muttered. "I do not want to come back
to a broken Parker."

Seth peeked around Sacha to peer in the living room window. Zeke
had moved over to sit on the couch. It didn't look like he was going
anywhere.

"He came this far; I think he's serious. And we're going on a field
trip!"

"Field trip, my ass." Seth loved it when Sacha pretended to be all
grouchy.

"No field trips for you as a kid?"

"Closest I ever got to a field trip was a tour of the local jail when I
was seventeen as part of a Scared Straight program. The only thing it
taught me was to be more careful."

IT WAS MIDWEEK, but there was plenty of summer traffic on the
cross-state scenic byway. Part of the Cascade Loop, Seth learned from
signs flashing past. The first few miles were standard: flat farmland
studded with immoveable stumps; pastures planted with corn or
possibly feed hay. Pretty farm houses in silhouette with the imposing
mountains behind them. Several tiny wineries. Every corner with a
cluster of homes and businesses offered drive-thru espresso—they
took their coffee very seriously along Highway 20.

About forty-five minutes in, after being stuck behind several slow-
moving RVs—which had Sacha muttering dangerously under his
breath—the truck rounded a blind corner and the damn mountains
were *right there*. Right in front of their faces, sheer cliffs rising mere

feet from the shoulders of the road. The highway went from flat to a steadily increasing climb. As they passed through a little town called Concrete, the road became even steeper and was reduced to two lanes for the most part.

They were both quiet. Seth, because he couldn't quite take in the majestic beauty of the Cascade range. Sacha was busy manhandling the truck into submission, his strong forearms flexing while guiding the vehicle around the sharp curves and steep inclines. Seth didn't know if he was seeing the scenery at all.

He'd seen pictures, looked at the mountains from afar for the past six months, but up close they were fucking incredible. In Scottsdale the biggest piece of rock sticking out of the ground was Camelback Mountain; compared to the Cascades, it was a pebble.

Again, they got stuck behind a flotilla of RVs. Even though the road was clearly marked with spots for slower vehicles to pull aside when there was room, none of them did. Sacha's muttering increased in volume and creativity.

After passing through the tiny towns of Rockport and Marble-mount, where one of the postcards had been sent from, the fierce, jagged peaks became impossibly dominating. Seth could see where waterfalls had worn paths in the granite over the millennia. Regardless of the warm spring and hot summer, snow still covered the highest peaks.

The Sauk River had abandoned the road miles back, but the Skagit still rolled and tumbled over fallen trees and boulders to their right. Mossy rocks peeked out of the glittering water, tempting the unsuspecting in at their own peril.

Finally, they came around a corner and Seth saw signs for Diablo Lake. "Pull over here," he directed, wondering if the photographs he'd seen did it justice.

Sacha grumbled but did as asked, parking in the Diablo Lake view point. Seth chuckled, he knew that much of Sacha's grumbling was a knee-jerk reaction to life in general. He'd secretly made it his new mission to discover what made Sacha laugh. Or, at least, what stopped the grumble.

The lake was a good start. They stood elbow to elbow, staring down at the magnificent malachite-green lake. No photograph Seth had seen was worthy. It was... verdant. Incredible, almost offending to the eye with its otherworldly beauty. Seth only had his cell phone, but he took several pictures anyway. Wondering if he could risk asking for one of them together.

"The color comes from mineral runoff from the glaciers that feed it," he told Sacha. "The dam was finished in 1930; I wonder if Owen or Theodore came up here? One of the postcards is from Marblemount, so I bet they did. Or at least Theodore did."

"Why do you care so much about these guys?" Sacha asked.

Seth pondered the question for a few moments, staring out over the lush lake and daunting peaks. "At first, I guess, it was because I'm a curious person. I like knowing about people, and that box of books and letters is about as close as I will ever get to actual treasure. Now, I dunno. We're on the same road at least one of these guys was on. What happened and why was that box hidden away? Those tools and scraps may have been because some worker was lazy, but that box was hidden on purpose, why?"

"You're a menace." But the accusation was halfhearted.

"Adam says that all the time. I'm trying to be more of a menace; it riles him up."

Sacha shocked him, taking Seth's phone and fiddling with the screen before turning them both so Diablo Lake spread out majestically behind them, and then snapping a picture. He handed the phone back to Seth before heading to his truck. Stunned, Seth stood there with his mouth open for a second before following.

Back at the truck, Seth dragged the little cooler out and handed Sacha a sandwich. They ate companionably, watching other tourists have their first glimpse of the lake and get their pictures taken, much like Owen Penn and Theodore Garrison could have. Like the two of them just had.

"Hey, you know..." He looked over at Sacha, who had already finished his sandwich.

"What."

"After Twisp, we could drive to Lake Chelan and see if we can find where that picture was taken."

Sacha rolled his eyes and shook his head, but he half smiled. *Yes.*

Seth also had Sacha pull over at the Washington Pass overlook. First of all, the bottle of water he'd had with his sandwich had gone right through him, and he needed to use the restroom. Secondly, the view was, again, stunning. Sacha didn't say much except to comment on the RV drivers and the view.

TWENTY-SIX
SACHA

Except for senior citizens maneuvering RVs the size of small cities, the drive along Highway 20 had been fine. Nice, even. Seth was a good passenger; he didn't talk too much, and he didn't cringe or grab the door handle when Sacha got impatient and gunned his truck past the behemoth vehicles.

Late that afternoon, he found himself angle parking in front of a verifiably creepy roadside hotel outside of Winthrop, Washington. Seth *had* to stay there, as some famous writer from over a hundred years ago had been in town and then gone back east to write *The Virginian*. A book Sacha had never heard of.

Anyway, the hotel was named after it, although in Sacha's mind it was closer to being a retreat for serial killers. He watched a middle-aged woman exit the office with a skeptical expression on her face. She got into her car and moved it a few spots down, where she promptly got back out, an enormous yellow lab leapt out from the back. Together the two of them disappeared up the stairs of one of the "lodges." He saw a curtain twitch on the second floor, and soon the dog was standing on the miniscule deck, panting and watching the goings-on below.

Seth came back out to the car. They were assigned to the lodge across from the woman with the dog. The room was entirely... not quaint. The walls, including the ceiling, were covered with dark wood paneling, creating a cave-like space. The ambiance was not welcoming; it ran more along the lines of "where to hide the body." Two double beds were covered with tired grey comforters that matched the tired grey carpet. A tiny coffee pot sat next to a basket of bagged ground coffee. The coffee looked like it had been there so long the cleaners dusted it on a regular basis. Sacha ran a finger along the small table next to the sliding door; make that an *irregular* basis.

"Well, it's not pretty, but it is cheap, so that's a plus. A little too close to the hotel décor in *The Shining*," Seth remarked, stowing his backpack under the coat hooks by the door. "I don't care which bed is mine; take whichever one. Or we can share." He waggled his eyebrows before disappearing into the tiny bathroom. Sacha heard the sound of urine hitting the water in the toilet bowl. Great, walls made of tissue paper, fucking wonderful.

Neither bed being ideal, Sacha chose the one closest to the door. By the time Seth emerged, he had his gear stowed away and was staring out at the river running behind the hotel property. It was flowing lazily in the summer heat; as he watched, several tourists floated by on inner tubes.

"I checked; the library is closed already, and so is the courthouse." Seth told him that all the early records, any before 1959, were stored in the county archives located in the courthouse basement. The town of Twisp wasn't large enough for such a structure, even to this day.

Sacha wasn't going to admit to Seth he wasn't focused on the reason for their trip. He was thinking about skin, scent, and the spot above Seth's ass where it sloped into the small of his back. He found himself touching Seth with intent; he wanted to have his hands on him all the time. He'd caught himself absently doing it too, any excuse to run fingers along Seth's back, touch his arm, lean in close enough to smell him. Back the Booking Room, the first thing he had done after immobilizing Jacobsen was check and make certain that Seth was safe. He often knew where Seth was without having to look, like Seth exerted a gravitational pull on his psyche.

"Wanna go for a walk?" Seth's voice jolted him out of his thoughts.

They, meaning Seth, insisted on a walking tour from the motel, across the river via the foot bridge, then along the main street to check out the town. Outdoors was still sweltering; heat waves radiated from the pavement, making the buildings and figures ahead wavy and indistinct. The town was cute, Sacha supposed, although never in his life had he been a tourist. Town planners played up the Old West feel, maintaining wooden boardwalks and storefronts that looked like they'd been stolen from a Hollywood set.

And, fuck it all, the same pain-in-the-ass dumb-wits driving massive RVs seemed to have stopped to spend their disposable income in high-priced shops the locals probably couldn't afford. Seth dragged him into a couple outdoor supply stores, a tiny bookstore, and a funky antique shop along their walk.

Sacha found himself smiling at the random conversations Seth struck up with shopkeepers and other wanderers. He was a natural at making people feel comfortable, drawing out their stories, while Sacha was an expert at avoiding that kind of thing. During the hour-or-so-long walk, Seth flitted from shop to shop, and Sacha followed along learning more about the man than he had in the previous weeks.

For all his curiosity and questions to Sacha, Seth was quiet about his own personal history. Sacha wondered if it was on purpose, or if it was his nature. He suspected that somewhere along the way Seth had learned to be careful about what he shared. Not the same as Sacha; he was reserved anyway, and a career in law enforcement had encouraged him to keep personal information out of the public sphere.

Seth, when he wasn't cheerful or questioning, seemed... wary. It had taken Sacha a little while before he became aware of it. Seth was a natural at deflecting conversation away from himself so it didn't seem strange that he never fully answered questions, or used one question to ask another.

Today was a gold mine of information. Seth had a weightlessness to him that Sacha hadn't experienced before. Getting out of town had been a great idea. Seth had never had a pet—Sacha learned this when Seth scratched the head of an indeterminate, scruffy mutt that trotted out from behind the counter of an outdoor equipment shop—but he would like one. The dog's tongue lolled out of its mouth as if the head scratch was the best thing he'd ever experienced. Sacha may or may not have had to squash a twinge of jealousy.

"The heat doesn't bother me," Seth answered a sales clerk. "I recently moved from Arizona." Right, spring training. And yet their baseball conversation had mentioned nothing about Seth's youth.

A very specific shade of blue was his favorite; Seth spotted it on a set of outdoor furniture that cost more than Sacha made in a month— if he were employed. They both stepped back like they might be fined for merely looking at it.

"Are you kidding me? I'd have to charge rent to my friends for sitting on this stuff!" Sacha thought his outrage was pretty funny.

Seth had a natural affinity for children, animals, senior citizens; even a fucking butterfly fluttering along in the breeze tried landing in his hair while they stood at the apex of another foot bridge on the far side of town.

Apparently he also drew reluctant, asshole, ex-law-enforcement types who should know better than to let their guard down. But Sacha knew it was already too late, and he was remarkably okay with that. Seth had slipped down the ladder into his life, and Sacha was going to do his best to keep him there.

The intoxicating hint of... something different, better, inviting, all vaguely Seth-like, crept into his consciousness—getting stronger each day. Laughter, quirky thoughts, the dark scent of earth and sweat from working in his yard or someone else's. "Seth-ness" loitered on the edge of Sacha's awareness, dragging him further and further out of his comfort zone.

Admittedly, that comfort-zone was entirely unrecognizable these days. The habits that had supported him for the first thirty-eight years of his life were changing fast. He couldn't fail at this, fail Seth. Provided, of course, that Seth was interested in something more than Sacha crashing on his couch.

At first it had been almost physically painful to change a habit of hiding his true self that had literally kept him alive until now... and he had a lot of work to do still. There was a pounding in his chest that increased when he even looked sideways at Seth; sometimes it made him dizzy, and he'd break out in a cold sweat. But with his eyes wide open, he welcomed Seth into his life. He'd been given a chance at happiness, finally, and fuck everything if he was going to waste it.

He suspected that, given what he did know about Seth's history, things weren't going to be simple. Oh, Seth played a good game with the lighthearted banter. Sacha knew better. Seth had a dark edge that he thought he hid. The few times they had spent the night together there had been nightmares Seth didn't remember, or mention, in the morning. He talked in his sleep too; some was nonsense, but there had been a few instances where the words were loud and clear.

"Hey." Seth put a hand to his shoulder. "You okay?"

And, yeah, Seth had that thing survivors had, where they were extremely attuned to others' emotions.

"Let's get some dinner."

THEY HEADED BACK toward the motel, where a quaint log building housed a pizza place they'd passed by on their walk. Everybody in town must have had the same idea; the two of them barely managed to squeeze around a tiny table tucked along a wall of the patio. At first they tried sitting across from each other, but it soon became apparent that Sacha was going to need to move. The scrawny kid running pizzas and beer barely fit between the tightly packed tables.

Sitting crammed next to Seth was its own kind of hell. The heat, proximity, a crazy, fucked-up head; he craved the sensation of Seth's body against his. Seth ordered them pints of a local IPA from the waiter. Sacha took a hefty gulp and focused on the bitter beverage instead of the heady desire fluttering in his stomach.

The restaurant was mostly young families on vacation, though there were a few couples like themselves with no children. The no-kid couples were all huddled as far away as possible from the families, who couldn't seem to keep their kids at their own tables. Dogs were even allowed to sit under the outside tables, which Sacha thought was kind of crazy, but he wasn't the one running around with food in his hands.

Two guys sitting at the table next to them were volunteer firefighters. He spent a few minutes eavesdropping on their conversation about the fire season—as well as watching them fend off what were clearly fireman groupies; two barely legal (if that) girls pounced as soon as they spotted them. The guys were good-natured about the attention, but it was obvious they were there for food not for picking up girls on the prowl.

Another pair of men occupied the table to the left of Seth. They looked a little out of place amongst the rough-and-tumble of family vacationers; they radiated more of a businessman-type vibe, but he supposed even a town as small as this one had a population of folks who wore chinos and button-downs.

"So, I was thinking." Seth interrupted his thoughts.

"Save me now."

Seth laughed. "I was thinking we should go for a hike while we're up here."

"Aren't there bears and other wildlife out there?"

"I can't imagine a few bears would scare you off."

"A few bears," Sacha repeated.

"Okay, so maybe not a wilderness hike. How about we take a lazy river inner-tube trip? I saw a sign in the lobby."

"I'll think about it." Who was he kidding? They both knew he would go on some goddamned float trip if that was what Seth wanted.

A kid dashed by, followed by a dad. The guy was laughing, trying to grab the toddler before it reached the end of the decking and face-planted in the gravel parking area.

"It's always weird watching that." Seth pointed his chin toward them.

"What? Why?"

"Well, theoretically I had a dad, but I didn't know who he was until recently. I don't think my aunt ever knew."

The young father scooped up the toddler, waiting while the—Sacha and Seth both did a double take —other dad caught up to them, holding a little girl's hand.

"Roland," she stomped a tiny foot, "Daddy says we are supposed to wait!" Roland garbled some laughing nonsense back, causing the little girl to frown further.

Seth was quiet while the dads grabbed their kids in tandem and put them up on their shoulders before striding down the dusty roadside bumping their kids up and down, maniacal laughter following in their wake.

"And I sure as hell never had that."

"What, two dads?"

"Family."

Sacha was sure the beer Seth had downed had caused him to cross a boundary in his head. He'd never before talked about family or how he'd grown up. Sure, he talked about his clients. Sacha knew all about Mrs. Anderson and the cute guy (Greg?) who Sacha now wanted to murder, out in the county. But he knew nothing about how Seth had grown up.

"I mean, my aunt tried—and she was awesome—but there are some things a spinster aunt can't substitute for."

"Oh yeah?"

"Yeah. Don't get me wrong, she was light-years better than my mom. I mean, at least Marnie didn't try and sell me for drugs. Or, you know, have her 'boyfriends' over while I played trucks in a closet." He chuckled, a bitter sound. "At Marnie's I had my own room for the first time ever, and, well, I couldn't believe it was mine at first. I slept in the closet for months before she could convince me that it was my own and we wouldn't be moving anytime soon. Poor woman. I was a mess of a kid."

Cold fury washed through Sacha, leaving him momentarily speechless. If at that moment Seth's bio-mother had walked into the restaurant, Sacha didn't think he would be able to keep his hands from wrapping around her throat. She'd been given a gift and treated it like trash.

"What happened to your mother?"

"Oh, Jackie?" Seth looked up at him, eyes unfocused, or rather focused on the past. "Prison. As far as I know, she served her time and got out a while back. It's not like I ever want to see her again... Why were we talking about this?"

Sacha nodded in the direction of the two dads and the laughing kids, now far up the road, the heat waves radiating upward making them soft and indistinct.

"Oh, right." Seth finished his beer in one long gulp.

The waiter stopped by, interrupting the moment. Sacha felt the tendrils of Seth's curiosity and knew he'd been about to ask a question, probably about Sacha's own childhood.

The pizza arrived after they'd each had a second beer. It was perfect for the hot weather, the tangy IPA soothing his dry throat and helping him relax, tension receding under the onslaught of alcohol and general relaxation. Good thing Seth was left-handed, or the seating arrangement would never have worked. The waiter plopped their pie down, and the aroma of cheese, green peppers, onions, and sausage had them both moaning with anticipation. Seth winked roguishly at him before taking a huge bite. It was all Sacha could do to focus on his own slice.

"So, what else do you do, besides rehab old buildings?" Seth licked his fingers after finishing his first slice of pizza, his eyes twinkling with mischief. Yes, the alcohol had released Seth's hold on his barely restrained curiosity.

"Oh, this and that." Seth's frustrated expression made him grin.

"Come on, throw a guy a bone."

"I read, a bit. In fact, I'm pretty sure I went into law enforcement because of a Jack Reacher novel I read as an impressionable sixteen-year-old. Didn't keep me from getting into trouble until I was old enough to enlist, though."

"Yeah? What else?"

Sacha rolled his eyes, trying to come up with something that would satisfy Seth. Truthfully, he'd been pretty much married to the Marshals. "Honestly, I lived and breathed my job, which is one of the reasons I retired."

"What were the other reasons?"

Beer loosened his tongue and weakened his hesitation over admitting the stark truth. "I realized I could die, probably sooner rather than later, and I would never get to live *out*. Never have a real boyfriend. I hate that word, by the way."

The waiter interrupted again, bringing Seth a ruby-colored beer Sacha didn't remember him ordering. He raised a questioning eyebrow. Seth responded, "A raspberry sour with local fruit." He took a long sip, and Sacha's gaze was drawn to the movement of his throat as he swallowed. "Mmmmm, delicious."

Seth leaned closer so they were touching from shoulder to ankle; he smelled like spicy pizza and beer, the heat of the day emanating from his skin. Sacha sighed and admitted he was rapidly losing control of the situation, and maybe that was how it was supposed to be.

As if he'd had control in the first place.

A warm hand landed on his left thigh, first rubbing and then gripping his quad tightly, sending a throb of *need* directly to his groin. He gently moved it further from his crotch. Seth didn't seem to notice where his hand had been straying; he was still rambling about fruit beers, sours versus ales, and the amazing variety of hops available in the Pacific Northwest. Far from any discussion of family or how, apparently, they had both had messed-up childhoods.

Sacha shook his head at himself, he was absolutely fucked. And... Seth was well on his way to being toasted. He was talking with his hands again, his irrepressible sparkle lighting the way for something equal inside Sacha.

They'd almost reached the stairs to their room when Seth jerked to a stop, pointing up into the night sky. "I love seeing all the different constellations here. I mean, they're not that different, but enough..." He giggled. With a strength and determination Sacha was ill-prepared to resist, Seth grabbed his arm, and instead of taking the stairs they ended up behind the little lodge, swathed in almost-complete darkness. Below them the river was burbling. The temperature had dropped significantly, reminding Sacha they were at quite an elevation. The chill was a relief. Seth tugged him a little closer to the edge. The wide expanse of night sky draped above them was dusted with stars bright and dim. A blinking satellite drifted sedately across the starscape before it disappeared behind cloud cover, or it could have been the Milky Way. Sacha had no idea about stars.

Sacha was done waiting and wanting, needed more from this crazy person who'd fallen into his life. He leaned against Seth's back putting his arms around his waist, resting his chin on Seth's shoulder and looking up at the swath of stars spread out over them like a blanket.

Sacha pressed harder against Seth, soaking in his warmth. A rough thigh brushed against his; hips bumped against his own. Seth turned and wrapped his arms around Sacha's waist. Sacha moved his head the smallest amount so his lips would touch Seth's.

Sliding his hand under the fall of messy hair around to the back of Seth's neck, Sacha pulled him closer still, barely allowing them room to breathe, plundering (fucking plundering) Seth's mouth with his tongue. Sucking that lower lip into his mouth, nipping it gently, going back for more. Licking through Seth's hot, hot mouth. Fuck.

It was an equality he'd yearned for. A hard, muscled body, slightly hairy, close to his own height, strong under his hands. Seth's erection pressed against Sacha's, and he shivered.

"We should get upstairs." He stepped away from Seth's warm body and roaming hands, missing them instantly.

"Yeah, okay. Good idea." Seth ran his hand through his hair, which was longer than when Sacha had first laid eyes on him. "I think those beers were stronger than I realized."

"No shit, Sherlock." Motioning for Seth to go first up the stairs, Sacha followed, enjoying the sight of Seth's tight ass and athletic legs as he stumbled up the stairs ahead of him. He was there in case Seth tripped. And he would catch him if he fell.

"G'NITE," Seth said blearily before crawling onto the bed he had claimed and lying facedown, his head mashed into the pillow. Seth was asleep in moments; he hadn't bothered to take off more than his footwear and the shorts he'd been wearing. Soon enough light, rhythmic breathing drifted across the room. Sacha chuckled. Seth was a cheap date. After brushing his teeth and undressing, Sacha lay thinking in his lumpy bed for what felt like hours.

What Seth saw in Sacha was beyond Sacha's ability to imagine. He ticked off the reasons why Seth shouldn't want him as he lay listening to the chug of the ancient AC unit. His best days, such as they had been, were behind him. His body was scarred, dinged, battered—not attractive. He was an orphan mutt, didn't have family to speak for him. He didn't even have a job, an idea. On a good day... Sacha tried to make a list of positives, coming up with nothing. Christ, he was going silver, and it was happening fast. Made him look like fifty was his next birthday, not forty. He was short-tempered and impatient. Not partner material.

A soft snuffle followed by a quiet mutter drifted from the other bed. "Why're you over there?"

Why was he?

Flipping the covers back, he got up and crawled in next to Seth's warm body.

"Much better." Seth turned so he could sling an arm across Sacha's chest, and promptly fell back to sleep. Sacha stayed awake a few more minutes before following him.

TWENTY-SEVEN

SETH

The basement of the courthouse was a cool haven from the heat stalled over Washington and specifically in the Methow Valley. Seth would never admit it to Sacha, but he had a slight headache from the evening before. Note to self: eat pizza first, drink beer second, especially when they are strong local IPAs.

He chugged from the bottle of water Sacha had kindly left with him. A droplet escaped, rolling down his chin before he swiped at it. Had he tried to grope Sacha in public last night? Things were blurry; he'd been too hot, hungry, and dehydrated for three strong beers.

"Jesus Christ, what was I thinking?" he groaned, covering his burning face with his hands, recalling leaning close and, yes, running his hand along Sacha's thigh. Probably would have done more if Sacha hadn't gently put a stop to it. His face grew even hotter, and Seth wondered if it was possible to burst into flames from embarrassment. Sacha hadn't said anything this morning, but Seth owed him an apology.

He was carefully leafing through the enormous handwritten census ledgers used to record births and deaths in the county through 1960. He dragged his finger down the pages and pages of delicate handwriting, stopping when Owen Penn finally made his appearance.

December 7, 1919. There was little doubt in Seth's mind that he'd found the right one. There were two older sisters, Erin and Alice. Reading farther, the records for 1930 indicated that ten years after Owen's birth, Pearl had made her appearance in the world.

It was difficult not to get caught up in the genealogical history of the entire county. He found himself emotional reading the death records of babies who only lived a few days and the mothers who died not long after, or along with, them. Or it could have been the hangover. He chugged more water.

Owen did not appear in the local census records for 1940 or 1950, but his death wasn't reported either. Seth did learn that Erin and Alice both married and moved into different households in the 1930s. Alice's death was recorded in 1938. Erin Penn became Erin Addison, passing away in 1973.

Caving, he signed up for a thirty-day free trial of the online ancestry site. His cranky laptop was taking forever to load, but eventually he would be able to look ahead and backfill the information not found at the courthouse. Erin Addison had one child, a boy, Charles Mason Addison, born in 1936.

Owen was alive as late as 1942, because the postcards were postmarked through March of that year. He would have been twenty-seven. Had he left the country to serve on the battlefields of WWII? Possibly. Seth hated that the smiling young men in the picture might have died far away from home and each other. He knew it was ridiculous, but he'd created a little story to go along with the photograph, and either of them dying in WWII kind of ruined the ending. A search of military records found nothing. No Theodore Garrison or Owen Penn. There were lots of Garrisons from southern states, and even a few pictures, but none of the images seemed close to the one he already had.

That left Pearl. Pearl could still be alive.

By the time he finished with the 1960 ledger, Seth had found no record of Pearl's marriage or death. She continued to be recorded living at the same address she'd been born into. In another, larger, town, it would have been ridiculous for Seth to consider the possibility that Pearl Penn still lived in her family home. In a small town like Twisp, with the right support, it was entirely possible. She would be eighty-seven, if she was still alive.

"You done yet?"

"Jesus fucking Christ!" Seth's heart about exploded out of his chest. "Could you at least warn a guy, mutter or squeak or maybe breathe like a normal person?" He'd made Sacha leave earlier because he was pacing around like a caged animal, creeping Seth out every time he looped around the room to come up behind him without making any sound—like right now. Sacha was as interested as Seth in the photograph, but he couldn't sit still to save his life. Seth wondered what it had been like for his partners to be on stakeouts with him... if he'd had to do that sort of thing... and decided it had probably been torture for everyone involved.

"Maybe if you paid attention to your surroundings you would be aware when there were strangers around," Sacha snarked.

"One, you're not a stranger. Two, what crawled up your butt?" Seth turned to see Sacha holding a giant to-go cup of coffee. His irritation fled. "Is that for me?"

Sacha grinned, and Seth blinked. "I thought you might need it."

"Yessss." Seth gulped the coffee, even though it was hot enough to scald. It didn't matter; the caffeine was a blessing.

"You find anything?"

"It's what I haven't found. I think Pearl, the youngest sister, may still be alive and living at the same address. I was going to look it up in the local phone book."

"I'll do it." Sacha strode over the desk where the volunteer librarian was lingering, to request a phone book, Seth supposed. Soon he was deep in conversation. The librarian was nodding and speaking in hushed tones before pulling out a phone book and flipping through the pages, clearly searching for something specific.

Sacha leaned on the counter chatting casually while she searched. Her face lit up, and she turned the book so Sacha could see what she was pointing at. He nodded and grinned back at her, jotting down the information before returning to Seth. The librarian was left at the counter basking in the remnant of Sacha's attention.

In-charge Sacha was as hot as building-remodeler Sacha, as driving Sacha, as relaxing-in-the-backyard Sacha. As kissing-under-the-stars Sacha. Seth shut his eyes against the images pummeling his brain. At this point, everything Sacha did was hot, sexy, and compelling. Seth had to remind himself not to get attached. No doubt there was also a leaving-now Sacha, and he wasn't up for that kind of heartache.

"Up for a drive? Janice," Sacha indicated the librarian watching from behind the counter, "says that Pearl is still alive. Her nephew moved her to an assisted living home in Wenatchee a few years ago."

Seth called ahead before they hit the road. Pearl would be happy to see them, but she had a social that afternoon and an appointment in the morning.

"Let's drive partway today and the rest tomorrow?" Sacha suggested.

Sacha seemed particularly amenable today. Seth wasn't sure what had brought about the change, but he liked it.

They'd checked out of the motel earlier. Seth couldn't handle that room another night. One night in their own private remake of *The Shining* was enough. Leavenworth or bust. Although waking up wrapped around Sacha's big body hadn't been a hardship.

Sacha's truck rumbled down the highway. They stopped at a little grocery and picked up some water and sandwiches to eat along the way.

"Look up somewhere to stay in Leavenworth. The cashier told me it's a nice place."

Seth narrowed his eyes. Who was this Sacha? The grumbly one he knew how to handle. Sacha being pleasant and planning ahead where to stay put Seth off balance. Nevertheless, he did as asked, quietly researching places to stay on his phone.

"How about the Bavarian Ritz? It's downtown and doesn't look like a getaway for meth cookers." Ha, no, it looked like someone's German granny had been in charge of room decorations. "They offer free parking and Wi-Fi."

Leavenworth was originally a fall and winter retreat, but town planners had managed to parlay the quaint Bavarian-style town into year-round tourism. Seth's personal favorite was the nutcracker museum. Because... nutcracker. The more he thought about it, the harder he laughed. Sacha looked at him, shaking his head.

They'd arrived a little early for check-in, and the hotel staff directed them along Front Street for a walking tour. Of course, they stopped and had a couple beers at the closest beer garden.

Something hummed between them. Their shoulders bumped together, as if Sacha was walking closer than normal. Their hands occasionally brushed against each other while they meandered along. Seth's body felt hot and tight with awareness of Sacha, of where he was, of his... everything. He had to keep reminding himself he couldn't walk around with semi-erection, but Sacha was making it...difficult.

In fact, Sacha was making a lot of things difficult. It was harder and harder keeping things light between them. Seth was so lost in thought he hadn't realized they'd made their way back to the hotel. Trailing after Sacha through the lobby, he wondered what the hell was going on, and if he would survive it.

Something like the ominous pressure of the calm before a storm crowded against his thoughts. He wasn't sure if what he was feeling was good or bad. Sacha wasn't like anyone Seth had ever been attracted to before. He had a lethal innocence. Sacha made Seth nervous, he was somehow exposing parts of Seth he wasn't certain should see the light of day. There was a reason he preferred casual.

Sacha opened the door to their room. "Jesus Christ. This makes me wish I was color blind," he muttered.

Seth peered over Sacha's shoulder. "Well, we can always go back out for drinks. I'm sure we can reach a stage where even this," he waved a hand toward the four-poster bed covered with a vomit-inducing canopy, "can be ignored."

There was one bed. He knew he'd selected a double room. "I'll call down about the room; they must have made a mistake."

"Nope." Sacha dropped his duffel to the floor. "I've had enough beer for now. Enough to take the edge off, but not enough to make me forget how much I want to have sex with you."

Seth felt his eyes widen. "Oh?" he barely managed to squeak out, his throat inexplicably dry even after two beers. Completely unprepared for this... onslaught. His body was ready, though; the semi-erection he'd been quelling all afternoon throbbed against the zipper of his cargo shorts. Fucking hell.

"Yeah," Sacha confirmed. "Is that okay?" Not really a question. Sacha did that thing when stalking into the middle of the hotel room, a large feline, his prey in sight and unsuspecting. Or suspecting and mesmerized. Holy fuck.

Seth opened his mouth to reply, but nothing came out. He nodded instead.

"Take your clothes off."

Apparently when Sacha wanted something, it was full on, one hundred percent. If there had been air in Seth's lungs, it was gone now. Shit, he'd never been nervous before; he wasn't going to let nerves stop him now. With thick, stumbling fingers, he loosened his laces and tugged off his boots. The shorts and T-shirt followed, landing somewhere on the floor. They could've landed on the moon for all Seth cared.

When he looked up from his task, Sacha was naked. Naked and waiting impatiently. Seth swallowed. Sacha was a big man, and he seemed somehow larger with his clothes off. His broad chest tapered to a waist no one would call narrow, but he was fit. Solid. Perfectly proportioned. Thick thighs brushed with dark hair, unh. Sacha's cock, semi-erect and uncut, hung heavily against his inner thigh as he waited for Seth to finish his perusal.

"Come closer. I need to touch you." Jesus Christ, if Sacha *didn't* touch him he was going to explode. Or implode. One of the two. Both.

Sacha ran his hands from Seth's shoulders to the top of his ass, kneading his cheeks. Seth shuddered in Sacha's arms.

"I dreamt about you last night. About this. Touching you." Sacha demonstrated by skimming his hands back up, cupping Seth's nape and lowering his lips against Seth's. "I've been dreaming about you a lot."

Holy fucking fuck. Seth's cock pulsed again; he knew without looking that precome had dribbled out the tip, leaving a wet streak along the top of Sacha's thigh. Sacha's tongue licked at the seam of his lips, and Seth opened. They stood together, simply kissing. Learning each other. Sacha sucked on Seth's tongue before licking the roof of his mouth and nipping his lower lip. He licked Seth's lip again before returning to the business of sucking Seth's brains out through his mouth. He heard a groan and wasn't sure if it was his own or Sacha's.

Seth shuffled closer, putting a hand on Sacha's chest, right where his tattoo marked him.

Sacha grabbed his face for another almost-punishing kiss. It was excruciating, the possessive, gentle touch with steel behind it.

They tumbled onto the bed, all arms and legs and caresses. Frantic, because Seth felt like he could come from merely this, but also limitless, a bliss they could both ride on for an eternity. Sacha was disconcertingly gentle. Seth half expected to be ravaged, but instead he was being handled like something precious. Cupping Seth's face with his large warm palms, Sacha kissed him and held him. Sacha's weight kept him from floating away.

Sacha sat up, his knees straddling Seth's hips, holding him a willing prisoner. He was divine and decadent, his massive chest covered with a mat of intermingled silver and black hair. His nipples were dark, and Seth wanted to lick and suck.

As Sacha leaned down so he could whisper into Seth's ear, their cocks brushed against each other again, making Seth's hips jerk upward. Sacha grinned evilly.

"You like that? I hope so, because I want more." Even his whisper was decadent.

He nodded. Mute was, apparently, the new thing.

"I hope this isn't presumptuous; I bought supplies while I was walking around today. Because all I could think of was fucking you, being inside you, feeling you come around me again." Funny, he didn't sound apologetic, and, no, Seth didn't care.

"Please, yes... that." Seth knew he was begging. Didn't. Fucking. Care.

The assault was gentle and overwhelming. Seth laughed at himself for, weeks earlier, imagining he would be the one to teach Sacha the finer nuances of sex. He groaned when Sacha tweaked his nipple before continuing downward to caress his cock, a soft touch that sent him almost into orbit.

Sacha's hand lingered there for a few minutes, stroking him, keeping him begging for more, harder, for Sacha to fuck him into the mattress.

"What do I need to do to shut you up?" Sacha muttered as he scooted down the bed. Green eyes blazed up through soot-colored lashes, and all Seth could do was moan because Sacha chose that moment to suck him into his hot, wet mouth with no warning.

"Fuck!"

"I must be doing it wrong if you can still speak." Sacha sucked harder, opening his throat, and Seth felt his cock bumping against the back of it. The sensation was close to too much and close to making him come. It couldn't be over yet.

"Stop, please—I mean, don't stop. Fuck me already." Seth was barely able to rasp out the demand.

Sacha released him with a wet pop. Seth's painfully hard cock dripped onto his stomach, spit and precome together forming a small pool.

"I'll fuck you when I am good and ready."

Next thing Seth knew, Sacha's thick finger was tapping at his hole. Seth shamelessly let his legs fall farther apart, begging for more, pushing against the finger. Sacha pushed in, Seth gasping at the slightly dry burn. It was good; it made him yearn for more and gave him a chance to gather his wits.

"Hurry up."

"You're talking again." Sacha pushed his finger further inside, seeking Seth's prostate. "Save the talking for later." Sacha emphasized his point by pressing a little further and starting to add another finger. Seth writhed and pushed down, forcing the fingers farther into his ass, loving the sensation of being full. Of being thoroughly fucked.

"Could you come from this?"

Seth focused on the words instead of his ass. "Uh, fuck, yeah, but..."

"Don't worry. I wondered for next time." Oh, fucking hell, that nasty grin.

He whined when Sacha took his fingers away. Soon enough he found himself on his stomach with his ass in the air. Cool gel slipped between his cheeks, and he arched his back as far as he could, shamelessly needy.

Two of Sacha's fingers were nothing like his cock. Seth breathed out and relaxing as much as he could while Sacha slowly pushed his condom-covered dick into Seth's ass.

"Move already; you're not going to break me," Seth huffed.

"Patience is a virtue."

One Seth didn't have when it came to sex. Before Sacha he'd been more of an "If it feels good, why slow down" kind of guy.

Semi-reluctantly, he gave himself over to Sacha. The pace started slow, a torturous drag against his prostate every... fucking... time. Seth was panting, and his dick was leaking copious amounts of precome onto the hideous bedspread. Soon, though, Sacha was pounding into him, pulling his hips back to meet his own. Seth had been hovering on the edge of orgasm for what felt like hours, and a more insistent tingle began at the base of his spine. He tried to shove a hand under his body so he could jack himself, but Sacha swatted it out of the way.

"Fuck, please, I need—need to touch myself."

"Don't worry, I've got you. I promise."

Sacha sat back on his haunches, dragging Seth with him so he was quite literally impaled on his lap. The pressure was intense and immediate. All Sacha did was reach around with a hard stroke along his pulsing, engorged cock, and Seth was coming. Coming so hard it fucking hurt. He could feel Sacha inside, through the condom, pulsing against his inner walls. A little more come dribbled out of his spent penis. Seth fell forward onto his elbows. Sacha ran his hands along his ass, massaging him, tickling his lower back.

"Me, inside you, fucking beautiful," Sacha whispered so quietly Seth almost didn't hear it.

Seth couldn't bring himself to care when he collapsed in the wet spot; he had nothing left. Sacha had fucked him into a coma.

Later, when he could use his lungs for breathing and his mouth for verbalizing, Seth rolled over. Sacha lay on his stomach along the edge of the bed, watching Seth with an unreadable expression.

"That was…"

"Yeah, it was." Sacha turned his head, his smile crooked and endearing.

"I don't think I can move, or feel my legs."

"Heh."

Seth shut his eyes.

He must have drifted for a while. The next thing he was aware of, Sacha was coming back into their room loaded with bags of food that smelled delicious. He'd even brought a growler of something to wash down the sausages and buns.

"Oh my god, I'm starving," Seth said around a mouthful of bratwurst.

"The front desk said these were the best in town."

Seth watched in fascination as Sacha ate a sausage in three bites, then reached for another.

"How do you do that?"

"What, eat? It takes a lot to maintain this manly physique." Sacha crumpled the paper plate and tossed it into the small trash can before heading to the bathroom.

Fuck coma, food coma. Whatever. Once Sacha was back, Seth took a quick shower and dug out a clean T-shirt to wear. Sacha sat watching him from the uncomfortable-looking settee, his ankle crossed over one knee, while flipping through channels on the TV.

"G'night," Seth offered, before crawling under the covers and pulling a pillow over his head. He was drifting along a lazy river of sex and a full stomach when the other side of the mattress dipped from Sacha's weight.

The bed shifted, and a heavy arm draped across Seth's waist. Sacha dragged him close, tucking Seth's head under his chin. His heart leapt with wanting so badly, wanting what Sacha seemed to be offering. But Seth knew, if there was one lesson he had learned in this life, what the cosmos gave with one hand it took away with the other. Sacha would leave, because one way or another everyone did. It was inevitable, so inevitable that Seth had quit fighting it.

It took Seth a long time to go to sleep. At some point he was going to have to tell Sacha whatever they were doing couldn't continue. Sooner rather than later.

TWENTY-EIGHT
SETH

"He was handsome and kind. I was so much younger than my sisters, and Owen too, of course, but he paid attention to me. My sisters were courting and learning to be proper wives. Owen was my prince and my protector." Pale blue eyes watered at the memory of her older brother. They were visiting Pearl at an independent living facility in Wenatchee, about miles from Twisp.

Pearl Penn was, at eighty-seven, about five feet tall and weighed no more than a hundred pounds. A strong wind would blow her away. She was setting a good pace as they walked the grounds of the facility. A pathway stretched out in front of the three of them, winding amongst rose bushes and well-cared-for hedges that offered shade to those who ventured out in the summer heat.

"Erin's great-grandson looks after me. She married an Addison." Seth nodded, having no idea who an Addison was, but Pearl, as she insisted they call her, thought them important. "There's only one of them left now. Owen won't have any children, and I never married, so that's the end of the line for us."

"Owen is named after your brother?" Sacha asked, trying to get the conversation back on track. Seth didn't mind the wandering focus.

Pearl was clearly enjoying having visitors and remembering her long-dead family.

"Yes. By the time little Owen was born, much of the stigma of being like he is... well, my father called my brother a fancy boy. Little Owen doesn't have to hear that kind of nonsense." She chuckled. "He hates being called little Owen." The sparkle in her eyes faded a bit. "My Owen wasn't really fancy. He was beautiful, though. Too beautiful for this earth." They approached a little seating area, and the three of them crowded around a metal café table. "May I see the photograph again?" Pearl asked. Seth pulled out the envelope with the postcards and photograph, handing it to Pearl.

Removing the photo, she held it like a treasure, staring at it for several minutes. "Theodore Garrison changed everything. When he came to town, Owen stopped pretending. Stopped pretending to court the Carroll girl, like Daddy asked. Stopped listening to Daddy." She trailed off. Seth could see that she was trying to control her emotions, but her eyes teared up again. "This picture, it's how I remember him. How he would want to be remembered. Owen is the one on the left." Her slim finger traced along the face of the taller man in the photo.

"Would you like to tell us what happened?" Sacha prompted. Seth was enamored with this side of Sacha. He knew, of course, that under the grim exterior Sacha was a gentle man, but Seth thought maybe he was the only one.

Pearl stared out over the green lawn and late-blooming roses before answering. "Well, of course Daddy found out and there was a terrible fight. I ran upstairs and hid in my room; my sisters were already married by then and had their own houses. Mother stood by and wrung her hands. My biggest regret is that I did not stand with Owen."

She looked so distraught Seth reached out and took her hand where it lay on the table. "You were young; no one would have listened. You don't need to tell us. We didn't come here to upset you."

"You misunderstand, young man... Seth?" He nodded. "In a way you have brought him back for me. Let me remember him when he was happy, when he lived." She squeezed his hand. "Owen left town, of course. Daddy allowed him back in the house for a few moments to take what he could in a small satchel, and then he was gone. I remember the house fell silent after he left. All the life had been sucked out of it. We were never the same again.

"This picture must have been taken soon after he left. I don't know how Owen met Theodore; he appeared one day and, as I said, our family was never the same. What our father suspected before was confirmed." She sighed. "I learned later some local boys had followed them and spied on what they were doing, then came running here to tell Daddy." It was disturbing how much hatred a tiny old woman could pack into the word "Daddy."

"I don't really know much. What I do know I had to sneak around and pry like that girl detective, Nancy Drew. Owen and Theodore left and traveled around; who knows what young men could get up to back in those days. Theodore eventually returned to the east coast, leaving Owen behind. Owen ended up in Skagit working for a bank, then a paper mill, but he was let go from both places for drinking. Then he worked at a bakery; Daddy called in a favor, and Owen was allowed to work there as long as he stayed away from liquor and men. But he couldn't do either. I remember the day Daddy got the notice from his friend who owned the bakery saying they had let him go. He was so angry." She stopped for a moment, and Sacha offered her a bottle of water from his pack. "Thank you, young man." Seth smiled at Sacha being called "young man." Pearl took a long drink of water before restarting her story.

"Daddy traveled all the way to Skagit. Back then it was quite a trip. He was gone for over ten days, and he brought Owen back with him. My brother had been gone from town for years by that time. He looked so much older, broken. You know how people say 'a shadow of his former self'?" Seth nodded.

"Owen wasn't even a shadow. There was nothing left of him. Daddy thought that under his watchful eye Owen would repent, behave himself, but he got into even worse trouble—he didn't care at all anymore. Owen didn't care what anyone thought of him. Sometimes he would talk to me, when he was sober enough. He would tell me about Theodore and remember that he'd been happy once.

"His drinking got worse, and his carousing, and Daddy put him in a sanatorium here in Wenatchee. Owen was in his early thirties. I never saw him again; he died not long after. I think it was of a broken heart. Because I spied on him too, and those men he spent time with —he didn't care about them. I think he did it to get back at Daddy.

"Daddy paid Theodore to leave Owen. There was a letter in his things after he died. In Daddy's things," she clarified. "I don't know which one of them is worse for such a sin. Daddy for taking away Owen's love or Theodore for agreeing. I've thought about it a long time. I think it was my daddy, but on bad days I'm still not sure."

They all sat quietly once Pearl finished her story. Birds were chirping recklessly, as were crickets and other loud bugs. A breeze blew, strong enough to ruffle the tips of the grass. A few other residents were out and about, enjoying the pleasant day. Seth had hoped there would be a happy ending for Owen and Theodore, or, at least, a happier ending.

Pearl interrupted his thoughts. "There's Owen now. I wondered how long it would take the front desk to tell him I had strangers visiting."

The afternoon light was behind the man walking toward them. Until he reached their table, he was a black outline against the glare of the sun. Up close, the resemblance to his great-great-uncle was uncanny. He was lanky with short dark hair, somewhere between late twenties and early thirties. Because the photo was black-and-white, Seth didn't know the color of Owen senior's eyes. Young Owen had striking amber eyes. Seth stared, caught by the golden intensity of his gaze. Simply exquisite.

"Hey, Auntie P." Owen stopped by her chair, crouching so she wouldn't have to crane her head. "Jennifer told me you had guests."

"That girl has better things to do than gossip about my male visitors. She wouldn't call if it had been someone from the seniors group," Pearl huffed.

Owen chuckled and stood. "Owen Addison, Pearl's nephew and

partner in crime. May I join you?" He proceeded to sit without waiting for an answer.

"These boys came here asking after big Owen. Sacha Bolic and Seth Culver, meet my rude, several times great, nephew." They all laughed and shook hands before Pearl finished telling her nephew what the strange men were doing visiting her. "Sacha and Seth found some of Owen's belongings, can you believe that?"

Owen looked at them for confirmation, eyebrows raised. "Yes," Sacha answered, "in a building I'm remodeling in Skagit."

"Oh yeah? Weird. What were they?"

"A book of poetry, some mysteries—the kind with colorful covers and ridiculous plotlines—"

Seth interrupted, "Says the ex-US Marshal."

Narrowing his eyes at Seth, Sacha continued, "A pair of glasses, a stack of postcards—from Theodore Garrison. That was about it." He shrugged. "I'm sorry we didn't bring everything with us. We weren't sure Ms. Penn would be able to see us."

"Please call me Pearl," Pearl admonished.

Owen gave her a stern look. "Auntie, you should have had me check them out first. You didn't know who they were."

"For crying out loud, Owen, I live here." She waved at the grounds and facilities. "No one is going to do anything here, and not to an old bat."

"Quit fishing for compliments; you are beautiful and you know it." Pearl beamed at him, and Seth saw the young woman she'd been shine through. She looked much like both Owens, although her eyes were a faded blue-grey instead of amber.

"So, you found this stuff and, what, decided to be detectives and figure out who the owner was?"

"Well," Sacha reminded him, "as Seth said, I was a US Marshal until recently. But you have Seth to blame for most of this. He was determined to find out who the men in the photograph were."

"Can I see?"

Pearl handed the photograph to Owen. He stared at it for a long time, everyone silent while he looked at the man he was named after.

There was a lull in the hum of crickets and chatter of birds that made the moment stand out. "He looks so happy here. I'm glad he got to be happy, even for a little while."

The men were afraid of tiring her, but Pearl insisted they all visit the small cemetery where Owen had been laid to rest. He'd died in Wenatchee and her father had buried him here away from home, forever exiled. She said he hadn't allowed a funeral. Owen was buried and forgotten.

If there was such a thing as a typical small-town cemetery, the Lower Wenatchee River Cemetery was it, situated amongst rolling hills above the lazy river with a panoramic view of the valley. The grass in the cemetery was green, of course, but the surrounding parcels of land were golden under the heat of the eastern Washington sun. From the top of the hill, Seth could see the stubble of wheat fields as well as rows of corn waiting for harvest. Wenatchee was known for apples; orchards lined the valley floor, alongside the river, expansive netting covering many of the trees in an attempt to thwart thieving birds and other pests.

Owen's grave was set away from the family plots. Instead of a large standing stone, he merely had a flat piece of granite laid even with the ground.

OWEN LEE PENN
B. DECEMBER 7, 1919
D. AUGUST 12, 1954

It was painful to imagine the hurt and betrayal Owen must have lived with. Standing over Owen's grave, the world still turning more than sixty years after his death, Seth felt emotion well up for this man he'd never known, who had loved, lost, and never regained his sense of balance. He'd taken a risk, and the world had crushed him. Sacha ran a hand down the back of Seth's arm.

Nothing was wrong with Pearl's eyesight; she caught the movement and smiled. "Are you two young men together?"

Owen turned beet red. "Auntie P, you don't ask people that!"

Seth gaped, his mouth opening and shutting as he tried to come up with an appropriate answer. He had no idea what he and Sacha were doing, so finding a way to answer Pearl was impossible. After being awake half the night panicking about how to tell Sacha they couldn't be anything other than friends with benefits, he had no response.

Sacha looked slightly embarrassed by the question, but managed to direct a not-so-scary smile at Pearl. "Seth and I met early this summer." Seth tried not to look freaked out by the answer, one that implied they *could* be together.

"You two make a handsome couple. Do you know any other single young men? Owen is never going to meet someone in this little town."

"Auntie P! You do not, just, just—" Owen sputtered to a stop.

"Out your nephew to complete strangers?" Seth prompted, glad to turn the attention away from Sacha and himself.

"Yes, that."

This time Pearl rolled her eyes. Seth had no idea eighty-year-old women could look that skeptical. "Owen, my heart, you were never 'in.'"

Owen groaned, covering his face with his hands, muttering to himself about boundaries and old women.

"This is going to sound crazy," Sacha said.

"Nothing is crazier than my aunt outing me while standing over my uncle's grave," Owen said in a disgusted tone.

"A good friend of mine is getting married in the spring. Would the two of you like to come? You could pick up the box of Owen's things and maybe make some new friends?"

"Um, aside from how you don't know us, your friend *definitely* doesn't know us. Why would he invite strangers to his wedding?"

Seth laughed. "Joey and Buck are throwing the biggest, gayest wedding Skagit has ever witnessed. Pretty sure they won't care about a couple crashers, and Joey would probably be offended if you don't come now that you've been invited."

Owen glanced at his aunt, who had an expectant, hopeful look on her beautiful face. He sighed. "When is it?"

They stayed a little longer at the gravesite. Pearl told some stories from childhood and had Owen pull a few weeds that were too close to the granite marker. When she was obviously tired, she allowed Owen to take her elbow while they walked back to their respective cars.

"We should head back to Skagit. Parker and Zeke should have had time to sort things out – we need our privacy back." Sacha smirked. "And I got a phone call from the electricians, I'm hoping for good news but they didn't leave a message."

TWENTY-NINE

SETH

We.

How had "we" snuck in? When had it happened? When Sacha said it, it sounded so good, so normal, except Seth knew it wasn't... and it wouldn't last.

The drive back to Skagit was torture, at least for Seth. He couldn't think of any topic of conversation that didn't begin with a panicked, "What the fuck is happening?" As much as he was trying to deny it, to avoid it, something *was* happening. Something Seth was terrified of. The silence grew until it felt like a living thing trying to suffocate him.

If trees and mountains flashed by along the highway, Seth didn't see them. If anyone asked, he wouldn't have been able to say what route they took or if there had been traffic. Instead, a heavy mass of anxiety centered in his chest, pressing in and making him feel sick to his stomach. He stared unseeing out the truck's window.

Truthfully, the knot had been forming for weeks, but he had ignored it. Pushed it aside in favor of the effortlessness enjoyment of Sacha's company. Parker *had* warned him, though, and the conversation came back to haunt him at the most inopportune times. Like now, as Sacha masterfully guided his truck along the scenic highway back to Skagit.

It wasn't casual.

Nothing about what they were doing was casual.

"What are you thinking about over there?" Sacha's voice surprised him over the rumble of the truck's engine.

"Uh, nothing." Everything.

"Sure doesn't seem like nothing. I don't think you've been this quiet since we met."

"I, uh, don't think we should do this anymore." The words vomited out of his mouth. Seth hadn't known they were there.

"All right... do what?" Sacha asked carefully.

"This." He waved a hand back and forth between them, hoping Sacha would understand.

The truck slowed as Sacha pulled off onto the shoulder. "You're going to have to be more specific than 'this.'"

Seth's face heated. It was tempting to escape Sacha's curious gaze by walking the last few miles back to Skagit. He breathed in a lungful of air. "Um, this... what we're doing. It can't be more than sex." He couldn't look at Sacha. "It's me. I, ah, don't do anything more than casual. And I, uh, have probably led you on a bit... okay, a lot, but it has to stop."

The truck engine rumbled again. Seth dared a glance over at Sacha. He checked traffic before pulling back out onto the highway. "Okay." And yeah, this was a level of uncomfortable silence Seth had never experienced.

It wasn't until they got to his house that he realized Zeke and Parker were probably still holed up inside.

Sacha stopped him as he moved to get out of the truck. "You do what you need to do. I'll round up the boys. We'll stay somewhere else, give you some space."

Parker was going to kill him.

He couldn't... It was safer by himself. In his excitement over meeting someone new, the thrill of a little historical sleuthing, Seth had let his guard down. He had done exactly what Parker said he would: hurt Sacha. And it was worse than that, because once they had left, Seth was sitting in his quiet, empty living room wishing they were back. Well, Sacha, at least.

THIRTY

SACHA

"He what?!" Parker moved as if he was going to get in the truck and go give Seth a piece of his mind. "I warned him not to fuck with you."

"Excuse me? What did you say to him?"

Before Sacha could interrogate him, Zeke chimed in. He and Parker had come to some sort of understanding, which involved coming home to find them all wrapped up in each other, watching some show about teenaged werewolves. "Let them sort it out. Don't you think we have enough drama of our own?"

"Look, Parker, Seth and I are both adults," Sacha said. "We'll figure it out, or we won't. But the last thing I need is you sticking your disaster-magnet self into the equation."

"I am not a disaster magnet!"

"You so are," Zeke affirmed.

"I told Seth that he better not break you, that he needed to take you seriously."

Oh, for fuck's sake. "You know what, Parker, stay out of it. You and Zeke go somewhere and have hot monkey sex, watch a movie, go on a roller coaster—but stay the fuck out of my love life."

"Love life?" Parker arched his eyebrows at Sacha. Zeke, the smarter of the two, grabbed his boyfriend and dragged him out of the room.

They'd temporarily checked into a bed and breakfast. It wasn't ideal or cheap, but it would do for a few days.

Sacha should have done this before, realized that Seth was feeling overwhelmed and found somewhere neutral to stay. The signs had been there, if Sacha had been paying attention. Not so much in how Seth acted or what he said, but what he didn't say.

Sacha wasn't too worried; they had a real connection. Maybe Seth was going to try to deny it, play it off as nothing, but Sacha wasn't. He was going to fight for what he wanted.

In the meantime he had a meeting to attend in the morning.

WITH WHAT HE hoped was a polite smile pasted on his face, Sacha hesitated outside room 103 before entering. A sign taped to the door indicated the Skagit Chamber of Commerce meeting was from 8 to 10 a.m. Jesus fucking Christ, what had his life come to? From the startled glances he received, he wasn't sure how successful he was with the smile. Maybe he had something on his shirt? He brushed his chest, surreptitiously glancing down at himself. Nope, his black T-shirt and the half-buttoned short-sleeved plaid shirt covering it were clean. Thanks to Seth's washer and dryer.

The Skagit Nordic Center, where the Chamber of Commerce held monthly meetings, dated from the 1920s, as did the cooling system. The large conference room was stiflingly warm. Tables were arranged in a U shape. A flimsy-looking credenza sat to one side, laboring under the weight of two huge ancient coffee urns and several trays of doughnuts provided by a local bakery. The pastries were visibly wilting while members loitered, waiting for the meeting to begin.

While standing in the line for coffee and thinking about a doughnut, Sacha tried to decide if coming to the meeting had been a good choice or not. Parker and Zeke seemed to think something positive could come of it. He'd finally reached the front of the line and was pouring coffee into a paper to-go cup when a familiar voice cut across his thoughts. A hand clasped his shoulder, "Sacha Bolic, great to see you. Skip the coffee; you'll thank me later."

He stepped away, forcing the overly friendly Christopher Meyer to drop his hand. Sacha gritted his teeth. He was here to see if they had contacts for electrical contractors, not make friends, but he needed to be nice. So said Parker.

As Sacha was on the way out the door, Parker had flung a last piece of advice at him. "Remember, you are there to network, not intimidate. Don't get the two confused. One means you meet some people who may be able to help you. The other means even cold-call salespeople will avoid you," Sacha'd perked up a bit, "which may sound great but is not good for your future business." Tricky fucker.

"Meyer," Sacha ground out. Parker's advice to try to relax bounced around in his head. He took a breath and tried again. "Meyer, nice to see you."

"Glad you decided to join." Meyer's deep voice carried across the room. Sacha almost turned and walked back out the door. "Come on." Meyer deftly maneuvered Sacha away from the coffee before he could grab it. "Sit with me."

Was this guy for real? Chris (as he corrected Sacha again) dragged him over to a set of seats at the corner of the U. "Best seats, not in Halsey's direct line of sight. Let me warn you, these things can get really boring, but they're great for networking," he whispered, scooting his chair a little closer to Sacha's.

Networking. A circle of hell Sacha had never considered before.

A tall older woman with straight, iron-gray hair dropping past her shoulders strode to the podium. The scattered whispered conversations quieted as she looked around at her audience.

"Good morning, lovelies." Oh, fuck. Sacha tried not to groan out loud.

It *was* boring. Mind-numbingly boring. Sacha regretted not grabbing coffee, regardless of the warning. He could feel his brain cells atrophying.

There was roll call (Sacha declined to raise his hand). Minutes from the previous meeting were read aloud. Finally, members motioned to add new items. Sacha's eyes began to roll back in his head, and Meyer nudged his shoulder, chuckling quietly.

After a motion to add something about "nuisance noise" after eleven at night, the chairperson, Halsey, stood at the podium and began an excruciating speech about regressive taxation and why the Skagit City Council was hurting the economy with its current bid to tax something that Sacha should probably care about. Sweat trickled down his spine, and he shifted in his chair. He would rather have been back in Kansas City listening to a basic procedures refresh than this... dreck.

Chris pushed a business card toward him, flipping it so Sacha could see something written on the back, Halsey was *good*; she saw the movement and narrowed her eyes at the both of them before continuing to drone on about Q3 tourism numbers and the possibility of a neighborhood gardens tour. Sacha suspected she'd been in law enforcement at some point.

What kind of adult male passes notes? Sacha swiped the card up and shoved in his pocket, but not before seeing a phone number scrawled on it with "Call me." Fuck his life. It had never occurred to him that Chris Meyers was *interested*. He scooted his chair a little further away.

When the droning ended, Sacha left his seat, avoiding Chris, and began shaking hands with other members and introducing himself as the new owner of the Warrick. He fielded a number of questions about what he was going to do with the building before he finally met someone with connections to the city permitting office. Of course, it was Halsey.

"Darling," she gushed, "I know *just* who you need to reach out to." Sacha ground his teeth, refusing to look in Chris's direction, as Halsey (Valkyrie came to mind) led him to a group huddled by the podium. It was obvious they were waiting to talk with her, and with no effort Sacha had cut to the front of the line.

Twenty grueling minutes later, Sacha had two more phone numbers and a scary promise that Halsey would follow up with him in a few days about the permitting process. Did she have a last name? He was scared to ask.

"Hey what are you doing here?" A soft voice, not Chris Meyer's, came from behind him. Sacha turned to see Buck Swanfeldt looking a little nervous.

"Buck." It was like having a lifeline thrown to him. He didn't think he could shake another stranger's hand or field one more question about what he was doing in Skagit. "Thank fu—god, do you wanna to grab a coffee or something?"

Buck took in Sacha's frazzled state before eyeing the empty paper cup he was holding. "I'm not sure either one of us needs coffee. But yeah, let's see if we can escape."

Outside the Nordic Hall, Sacha stopped. He didn't have a clue where to go. "Is there a coffee place around?"

"I, uh, can't be gone from the shop much longer. I left Miguel in charge—he's going to need a break soon."

"How about I follow you?"

After parking his truck outside the chain-link fence, he followed Buck toward his auto shop. The bay doors were wide open. Sacha could see Buck's partner, Miguel, bent over the open hood of a sedan, a younger mechanic standing on the other side listening to him. His hand gestures spoke louder than his actual voice. A second, younger kid stood off to one side, laughing.

"Jeez, I hope Miguel isn't using sex as a metaphor again," Buck commented. "Every time he does, Dom nearly dies of embarrassment. Although I have to say it is effective; he hasn't forgotten a lesson yet."

"Thanks for rescuing me from that hell."

"The Chamber? Yeah, they mostly have good intentions, but Halsey, she's new at being chairperson and has taken the role seriously." Buck snorted as he led Sacha through the shop to his little office. "What brought you there?"

The office was dimly lit and sparsely furnished. Buck motioned toward an uncomfortable-looking chair before he sat behind a big metal desk.

"Electrical wiring permits," Sacha said. "And I need a new box, and a bunch of other things I can't do myself." He went on to tell Buck about the Warrick and fill him in on his plans, which he was going to have to thank Micah for, because the longer he was in Skagit the more he believed an artistic office space was needed and might actually turn a profit. Sacha Bolic, businessman extraordinaire.

"Wow. Uh, that's crazy, I thought I was imagining things when I saw you there." He looked a little sheepish and a lot shy. "So you're really not here in some kind of official capacity?"

"Nope, I'm retired. I promise, I'm done with my life of crime."

Buck grinned. He was handsome, huge and Nordic. "I can't wait to tell Joey I saw you again. He's going to be jealous. He's been talking about you since that day at the Loft. You need to come over for dinner or something. I know he would love to see you." He pulled his cell phone out of his pocket where it must have started vibrating. "Hey, yeah, guess what? You'll never guess. Sacha is here in the office. I ran into him at the Chamber meeting today." Leaning over the desk, Buck shoved his phone toward Sacha. "He wants to say hi."

THE NEXT MORNING, Sacha tracked Joey down at Buck's house. It wasn't until they'd hung up the day before that Sacha realized he needed honest advice and Joey was the sole person he could ask. He'd given Seth two days of 'space' it was time for action.

"You do know, people who work night shift need their sleep. As do hot US Marshals who looked like they stayed up all night," Joey said when he opened the door. The kid's shit car was parked in front, so Sacha had known Joey was there.

Joey opened the door wide enough for him to slip inside. His fiancé was sprawled on the couch with a cup of coffee, flipping through the morning news channels.

"Morning," Buck offered.

Sacha came further into the room, motioning for Buck to stay where he was. "Morning," he replied before flopping onto the smaller couch.

"By all means, make yourself at home," Joey snarked. There was no heat behind his words, though. Sacha had a soft spot for both young men.

"Coffee?" Buck asked, waving his cup around like it would magically refill.

Sacha opened his mouth to answer when Miguel from Buck's shop appeared in the living room, shirtless, only a towel wrapped around his waist. He was medium height, falling somewhere between Sacha, who was 6'4", and Joey, who insisted he was 5'7". Dark, almost-black hair, mocha skin, an aristocratic face—sharp cheekbones and a straight nose, although it looked to have been broken at least once. Vibrant green eyes were his most striking feature, Sacha had never seen that color before. He didn't have words to describe the shade, but they reminded him of the lake he and Seth had stopped at.

The room fell noticeably silent. All three men were watching him, and Sacha realized, much to his embarrassment, he'd been staring. He cleared his throat, not knowing what to say. Joey sniggered.

"Don't mind Miguel, he's kind of an exhibitionist."

Buck laughed. "Kind of? Go put some clothes on, Romeo. Sacha can't handle you."

"Most of the boys can't. It's a shame, really." Instead of leaving, he walked over to Sacha and stuck out his hand. The other kept a precarious hold on the towel Sacha was ignoring. "Miguel Ramirez, pleasure meeting you."

"Miguel," Buck growled, "he's a cop. I thought you had an allergy."

"Retired. I, uh, retired a few months ago."

"See, he's retired, so I don't have to be allergic."

"Go. Put. Some. Clothes. On." Buck again.

"Don't mind Miguel, he's a tomcat," Joey said. "Acts all friendly and flirty until you get too close, then he bites—rawrr." Miguel flipped Joey off and left the room.

Buck stood, swallowing the last of his coffee. "Sorry 'bout that. Miguel is good people, a handful for sure I don't envy the who ends up with him. I gotta go open the shop. Nice to see you again. Don't stay too long, Joey had a night shift last night, I like it better when he gets the sleep he needs." Joey shot Buck a nauseatingly sweet smile, following him to the door for a scorching kiss. Sacha had to avert his eyes.

After Joey closed the door behind Buck, he turned back to Sacha. "So, why'd you stop by? Wait, before you start, let's get some coffee going."

"Will you be able to sleep after coffee?" He didn't want to piss Buck off.

"Honey, I haven't survived in the medical world this long without learning how to fall asleep almost on command, coffee or no coffee."

Joey reminded Sacha of Parker. A little irreverent and a tendency to get into trouble. Although, as far as Sacha knew, Joey had only been in trouble the one time; he hadn't made a career out of it like his brother.

Miguel came back in the room—dressed, thank fuck, in coveralls with a Swanfeldt's logo stitched on the left pocket. He waved again but kept heading toward the front door. "We've got a lot of tickets today. Not sure when your man will call it quits." With that he was gone, and the house was noticeably quieter.

"Hard to believe," Joey muttered, handing Sacha a steaming mug.

"What?" There were so many ways this conversation could go.

"Buck told me that when he first met Miguel, he came asking for a job—any job Buck would be willing to offer. He was," Joey paused, searching for the right words, "dispirited, downtrodden, a shell of the man we saw today. That was three years ago. Whatever he'd been through, it took a while to recover from." His gaze narrowed, and Sacha felt his stomach clench. Joey might act airy, but he was not a stupid man. "What brought you here this fine summer morning?"

The story came out about falling off the ladder. About going to get coffee and coming back with a new friend who'd pretty much swarmed his defenses without him realizing. He even told Joey about finding the postcards and books stashed in the wall.

Nodding and, thankfully, not interrupting, Joey listened and sipped his coffee. When Sacha was done with his tale, Joey grinned. "That is an awesome story. Did he find out anything about the people in the pictures?"

"Yeah. I hope you don't mind; I invited them to your wedding. I figured the entire city is going to be there, you wouldn't notice one little old lady and her nephew."

"The more the merrier!"

Sacha rolled his eyes. The way he figured it, city officials were going to have to create a special holiday so all the people Joey invited would be able to attend.

"All right. So, Seth freaked out. And you think it's because he's afraid?"

"I *know* it's because he's afraid. From what little he's said about his history… well, I don't think there has ever been anyone permanent in his life except an aunt who died when he was at college."

"And you want to be permanent?"

"Yeah." Sacha did. Maybe it was quick after a lifetime of denying himself, but he wanted whatever was happening between them to continue.

"So you gotta prove you're not going anywhere."

"Yeah."

Joey looked him right in the eyes. "There's one obvious way to do that."

Sacha stared back. "I don't think he would say yes. Frankly, I don't think he's the type to get married."

Joey nodded. "There are a lot of ways to prove your intentions without a wedding ring. You could make a promise."

A promise. A promise to Seth to be there, to stay. To the best of his ability, be as sure as the stars, the moon, and the sun. Sacha could do that. He leaned back against the couch, trying to think of the best way to lure Seth back out into the open.

"Okay, big guy, here's what we're going to do."

Sacha narrowed his eyes. "We?" Joey had a way of taking control of a situation.

"I'm going to take a nap. I'll set my alarm for a couple hours, and then we can work on your grand gesture."

"Grand gesture?" A nap?

"Yeah, to tell Seth that, you know…" his voice dropped to a whisper, "you l-o-v-e him."

Jesus fucking Christ, he did. "You're killing me here."

"Well, obviously, you need help. That's what I'm here for."

He found himself agreeing to a nap, since he hadn't actually slept the night before, and to mulling over a "grand gesture." It was Joey, after all, and some of his schemes were suspect, but this could actually be a good one. Leaning back against the arm of the couch, he allowed himself to drift to sleep. And consider what a grand gesture would look like.

THIRTY-ONE

SETH

Seth slept like crap. When he woke, Parker, Zeke, and most especially Sacha were still gone. He called Adam, but his phone went straight to voicemail.

He needed his aunt. It was stupid, a grown man wanting to be comforted. She was dead, and thinking about her merely made the hollowness he was feeling all the more vast and unmanageable.

Even though he hadn't run in months, Seth dug around for his running shoes and track pants. Ten minutes later he was out the door. What he was running *from*, he didn't know.

He ended up at Adam and Micah's house. Because he had nowhere else to go.

Micah must have seen him, because the front door opened. "Why're you standing out there?"

"I'm an idiot. I'm broken, and I don't know how to fix myself." The run had helped somewhat. At least now he had aches and pains to focus on, not solely the panic from his brain.

"Okaaaaay." Micah looked at Seth standing on the sidewalk, panting and sweating from running. "Why don't you come in? At least have some water?" He held the door open, stepping back from it like

Seth might consider running away if Micah got too close. Funny, he was considering it.

Correctly interpreting Seth's expression, Micah sighed. "Do. Not. Leave." In a moment he was back with his car keys and cell phone. "Let's go for a drive, okay?" He led the way to his car, Seth trailing pathetically after him.

The drive was silent. Seth didn't know, or care, where they were headed. Micah was pretty quiet, Seth had learned, but if he had something to say he wasn't afraid to speak his mind. Aaannd cue…

"Tell me what happened. Is it something to do with that US Marshal you've been hanging out with?"

It helped that Micah kept his eyes on the road.

"I don't know how much you know about how I grew up." Adam must know some, but whether he would've said anything to Micah, Seth wasn't sure. "I've never been in a relationship. Saying the word practically gives me hives. My, uh, mother was a terrible person. Broken, anyway. We lived on the streets and on other people's couches; sometimes she'd get a place from—" From god knew where; Seth had been too young to question, but he did have vague memories of waiting outside in dark hallways while Jackie "took care of business."

Deep blue sparkled from his right, glittering under the summer sunshine—the ocean, a deep that could handle anything. Micah directed his car toward Old Charter along Skagit Bay. Taking a deep breath, Seth continued, "Anyway, we were in and out of housing, shelters, anyplace with a roof. Sometimes she would leave me with 'friends.' A lot I don't remember. I do remember being alone a lot; being hungry, cold. Sometimes too hot. She tried to make it an adventure, like it was perfectly natural for a little boy to be a spy or something. As I got older, she trained me to help her steal from her marks." Out of the corner of his eye he saw Micah's hands flex on the steering wheel.

"Long sob story short, she tried to sell me for drugs and got busted by an undercover cop. That guy saved my life." It made Seth's skin break out in goosebumps thinking of what might have happened if Jackie hadn't been caught.

"Jesus, Seth," Micah breathed.

"Yeah, crazy, huh? So, uh, after a short stint in foster care I went to live with my aunt. Why some hippie lady would take in a little boy with every issue under the sun, I have no idea. But she did. Marnie died while I was away at school, and I gotta tell you that almost finished me off. So, yeah, I'm kind of used to me against the world. It's much easier."

They drove in silence for a few minutes before Micah pulled over at one of several viewpoints. Thankfully, only a few other cars and a single RV shared the parking area. Micah rolled the windows down—the breeze was a relief—but made no move to get out of the car. "What happened with Sacha?"

"Nothing. Everything. He said 'we,' meaning us, together, and I panicked and told him something like we couldn't be a thing. Actually, that is exactly what I said. Then he left, saying he was giving me space, and I want him back, but it scares the ever-loving shit out of me. I literally get shaky thinking about it."

"Okay. I am going to paraphrase what I think you told me. You grew up in an unsafe environment where the one person expected to protect you, didn't." Seth nodded. "Where there was a lot of uncertainty about your basic needs being met. I'm going to assume you learned not to get attached to things or people, because nothing ever stayed the same?" Seth nodded again. "And now, Sacha scared you when he essentially laid claim?"

Well, when Micah put it like that...Claim. The word was solid.

Growing up, Seth had hoped to belong to...someone. He remembered feeling like the pathetic kid in a Christmas movie looking at shop-window reflections of happy families walking by: he could look but not touch. Being claimed? That had happened once, when Marnie rescued him.

He was reminded of what Parker had said about Sacha being feral when he'd come to live with them. Because there was the distinct possibility that this epiphany was him recognizing the same thing in himself. Keeping people at arm's length, never entertaining the idea of a romantic relationship. Yeah, it was kind of confused and backward, but human brains were often pretty fucked-up.

The Gerald Klay painting he'd discovered when he was packing up Marnie's belongings had brought him to Skagit in search of blood relatives. He hadn't thought his search through, he was merely curious to know if there was anyone out there related to him.

Seth didn't think Marnie had known she had the watercolor. Jaqueline had probably stashed it there on one of her rare visits before incarceration. It was an early Klay, most likely painted in the 1950s. Three islands hovered in mist, swathed by verdant evergreens. Was the cloud of mist and trees, or the three islands the focus? Seth didn't know; his eye was drawn to either depending on his mood or even which angle he approached the piece from. Regardless, the painting had changed his life.

"Look," Micah said softly, "I get you. I get the both of you. Fuck—" Wow, Micah never swore; that was Adam's specialty. "—from what Adam has told me about his childhood and what you've said, both of you grew up in vacuums. Devoid of casual affection, acceptance… human touch, probably. Adam, anyway. He raised himself, pretty much acting as an adult since he was a little boy." He stopped, running a hand through his unruly hair.

A quiet voice, the one he thought of as Marnie, nudged Seth to speak. "Do you mind if we drive again? I can't sit here and talk."

Micah nodded and restarted the engine.

Seth loved Charter. The old road stretched along Skagit Bay and seemed like it traversed the very edge of the known world. When the weather was bad, clouds crowded in blocking the water view but you could hear the waves thundering below, making Seth feel like he was floating. A day like today, cloudless and hot, the view stretched for miles, the San Juans sprawling across the horizon, eagles, osprey, seagulls careening on the winds.

"Can I ask a question?"

Seth waved a hand in a bring-it-on gesture.

"What did you expect when you started searching for Adam?"

A question he had asked himself more than once, with no answer. When he'd searched Gerald Klay's name and seen the eerie resemblance to himself, Seth had known in his heart Gerald was his biological father. The father's name on his birth certificate may have been left blank, but Klay's genetic signature lived on in Seth's face, his height and coloring. He hadn't known about Adam until later. Adam had remarked that Seth looked more like Gerald than he did.

"I didn't expect…" Ugh, how to say this without sounding like a complete tool. He hadn't expected to find anything worth staying for. A case of morbid curiosity had led him to Skagit, and he'd expected it to be cured by meeting his relative. "I guess I didn't expect *anything*. I mean, in my experience family is not always a good thing. But I was curious."

"But you're still here."

Micah was crafty. Yes, Seth had stayed. Had gone back to Scottsdale for a short time before returning, permanently, to Skagit. "I'm still here." He was still wondering how that had happened.

"No offense, Seth. But I think, for Adam's sake and maybe Sacha's, you need to decide: are you staying or leaving?"

Trust Micah to cut right to the heart of the matter. Seth still didn't know if he was coming or going. He was, as Sacha would put it, a fucking mess. Oh, he'd *thought* he had everything figured out. That he knew how to live, free of entanglement and true responsibility.

He scoffed at himself. At his naïveté.

"I don't know Sacha at all, but he strikes me as similar to Adam," Micah continued. "When he gives his heart, it's the whole thing, not simply little parts of it. And I've seen how he looks at you."

Seth wanted to ask Micah what he'd seen. He was uncomfortably certain, however Sacha had been looking at him, he'd been looking back the same way.

They, he and Sacha, were both broken, but differently. Sacha was brave enough to pull back the layers he used to protect himself against the world. Sacha had claimed him and Seth had been too much a coward to own it, instead continuing to hide behind his lackadaisical exterior. He had all the answers and mocked people who thought love was the answer to anything.

Well, they had the last laugh now, didn't they. All those men he'd fucked and then left without a goodbye or acknowledgment, not making any sort of effort at a connection. If they knew the state he was in now they would be breathless with laughter. And he would deserve it.

He'd tricked himself, thinking he was getting to know Sacha, when it was Seth exposing little bits of himself to Sacha. Seth whose soul yearned for the safety and comfort of a relationship and until this moment hadn't known it. What a fool.

No, he didn't suddenly crave marriage and a passel of kids, but he did hope to come home to the same person every night.

Not *any* person - Sacha.

"I'm a mess." He thunked his temple against the car window.

"For what it's worth, I don't think you have a corner on that market. It's kinda part of being human. If you want my opinion, and you are getting it regardless, you've been alone long enough. You don't have to keep proving you can do it by yourself. Let us help. Let Adam be a part of your life. If Sacha wants in on the action, let him. Are you opening yourself up for hurt? Yeah, and that's part of the human condition too." He sighed, glancing quickly at Seth, looking for his reaction. Seth tried to hide it, but Micah had gone one further than Parker. He'd discovered the soft underbelly of Seth's personal defenses: he *did* want to be part of something, belong to someone. He hungered for it.

He thunked his head against the window again. What was he supposed to do now?

A cellphone buzzed. It was Seth's, and the caller was Sacha.

"Where are you?" Sacha's voice crackled over the phone's tiny microphone.

"With Micah." He stared out the open window toward the San

Juan Islands, glimmering in the heat of the day. "We're out on Charter."

"I came by to talk." There was a small silence. "I thought maybe you'd left."

THIRTY-TWO

SACHA

Sacha was calm. Parker had been relatively quiet since they'd moved their things from Seth's house to the bed and breakfast. Maybe Zeke had said something; maybe Parker had realized that Sacha could fight his own battles.

This wasn't a battle, though. No, nothing like one. This was Sacha being patient, waiting for the right moment, attempting not to panic. Hoping he had it right. Seth had gotten scared, maybe even terrified. Sacha should have realized he had been scared almost since they had met, but he'd hidden it well. It was entirely possible Seth didn't realize he was scared until the moment when Pearl had commented on their relationship.

Regardless, Sacha was moving forward. What Seth couldn't admit with words he said with his body. With the way Sacha had seen Seth looking at him unawares, like he was stunned by Sacha's existence. Like he couldn't believe Sacha was with him.

Once he'd heard the story about Seth's mom, Sacha should have known Seth would try to push him away. Seth's early life lessons had been similar to Sacha's own, which made it easier for Sacha to understand what Seth was going through. But Sacha had always been surrounded by band of cohorts. Whether on the streets of Sarajevo or Kansas City, in the military, or as a law enforcement officer.

Driving over from Joey's and finding Seth's house empty had scared the shit out of Sacha. The nap at Joey's, drifting in and out, thinking about grand gestures, had left him more pensive than rested. God damn Joey. Sacha needed, more than anything, for Seth to understand that everything Sacha was saying with his body, with kisses and caresses, was his way of accepting the both of them together—and he was playing for keeps.

In the real world, words needed to be said out loud, Sacha just needed to figure out the right ones. The ones that would help Seth understand that this wasn't some sort of fling for him. That by outing himself, even to people who didn't care, like Pearl and Owen, Sacha was making a commitment. He needed words to express himself, words that wouldn't make Seth run away.

Pulling out his cell phone to call and find out where—*how far*—Seth had run was one of the harder things Sacha had ever made himself do. His relief when Seth said he was with Micah left him dizzy.

He arrived at Micah and Adam's before Micah and Seth returned. By the time they pulled to a stop in front of the house, Sacha was a mess but determined. Micah said a quick hello before disappearing inside.

"Hey." Seth walked over to where Sacha was waiting.

"Hey."

"Micah took me for a drive; I needed a good talking to, I guess."

Sacha quirked an eyebrow, and Seth grimaced. "My messed-up head."

"I don't think you're the only one."

They got in Sacha's truck, and he headed toward downtown. Soon enough Seth would figure out where they were going. He had no idea what day of the week it was; traffic was light. It could have been the weekend, or there could have been an evacuation warning, either one. Today would be the day he wooed Seth.

Stretching his hand across the console without looking, he laid it, palm up, in Seth's lap. A few seconds passed, ones where he dared not glance over to the passenger seat. Finally, Seth took Sacha's hand in his own, squeezing it slightly. He let out a little sigh, and Sacha risked a look. Seth's eyes were shut, his head lying against the headrest.

When they arrived at the Warrick, Seth's eyes were still closed. Sacha thought he saw him shudder.

"Are you okay?"

Seth turned his head and opened his eyes. His open gaze slayed Sacha. Seth was letting Sacha see inside. See where he was vulnerable, where hurt lurked, where a little boy had been abandoned and never quite gotten a foothold on life again.

"Um, were you crying?" A dried tear track was clearly visible near the corner of one eye.

"A little, I guess. I feel stupid."

"Why?"

"I outsmarted myself." He laughed grimly. "I thought I was so smart, had everything figured out. Turns out I am a hot mess."

"As long as you're *my* hot mess."

"What?" Seth's eyes opened comically wide.

"You heard me."

Seth responded with an inarticulate sputter that Sacha chose to translate into "Yes," because he didn't argue, and when Sacha came around to meet him on the sidewalk Seth waited for him instead of running off... though Sacha thought it was probably a close thing.

The electrical work was starting soon. Luckily for Sacha's plan, contractors would be starting upstairs. Sacha unlocked the front door and ushered Seth in with a hand at his back, hoping there had been enough time.

Seth released a quiet gasp. Because, yeah, Joey had come through. Lacking any other grand gesture, Sacha had decided to treat Seth like he was something special. Because he was. Seth had barreled into Sacha's world changing it for the better, forever.

Even if—which he fucking hoped wasn't the case—he and Seth couldn't make it as a couple, Seth had turned Sacha's world upside down. There was no going back for him now.

In the late afternoon light, the plants Joey (and most likely Buck) had brought in looked incredible. It looked like someone had robbed an entire nursery. There were blooms in all shades: purple, blue, yellow, orange. Sacha had no idea what most of them were; he was extraordinarily pleased Joey had been able to create a secret garden inside the Warrick. They'd even gone so far as to find a little metal café table and two chairs in the shade of blue Seth had pointed out a few days earlier in Winthrop.

"How did you... wha—? How?" Seth choked out.

"Friends in high places."

Seth made a strangled sound, twisting around and hiding his face against Sacha's neck. Great sobs escaped him. Sacha would have been worried except for how tight he was holding on. As if Sacha alone was keeping him tethered to the earth. Sacha would to be that man, the one Seth used to hold on. Seth had to understand that he would do everything in his power to be there for him forever.

He nudged Seth, pushing him a little away so he could see him. Taking Seth's face between his hands, he tilted it so he could see clearly into the depths of his eyes. "Look, maybe it's the wrong fucking time for this. And too soon. But I guess... I guess, there'd no point in waiting anymore. Neither one of us is fooling anybody but ourselves. And I don't want to wait until it's too late. There's no reason to." He took a deep breath through his nose, feeling like he was about to jump off a high dive, or, worse, from a perfectly good airplane. Seth's eyes widened. "I care for you, Seth. A lot. It's probably more than that, but—" It felt like liquid cement was being poured down his throat, trying to force out what he *needed* to say. "I need you." He started to drop his hands, but Seth lifted his own hands to hold Sacha's wrists in place, staring at him.

"I need you too. I never thought I would need anyone. I never wanted to need anyone, and I kind of resent it. But I *need* you. It scares me."

THIRTY-THREE

SETH

The quad on the university campus was majestic. The atmosphere was cool and verdant under the broad canopy of the cherry trees planted in an intricate pattern along the walkways. The school website raved about the cherry trees, which usually bloomed in March. Seth made a note to try and visit next year.

Students streamed in and out of various buildings. Summer school was in session. The steps up to Miller Hall were deeply grooved from years of students and professors climbing them, as Seth was doing today. Many also looking for answers, he supposed.

The secretary for the English department was housed on the third floor in a cramped office barely large enough fit a large desk, a chair, and the person sitting in it. Across from which lurked an uncomfortable-looking couch. The walls were covered with notifications and reminders of both past and upcoming events. A youngish woman looked up from her typing when he peeked in the doorway.

"May I help you?" He was clearly interrupting her work, and she was not pleased, one red eyebrow raised impatiently. There was a paper taped to the back of the computer monitor: "Disturb the dragon at your own risk."

"Seth Culver. I'm here to visit Professor Garrison? It's a long story, but during some construction work I found some items that I think may belong to him." Seth turned on his charm; it wasn't often he was refused things when he really turned it on.

She looked skeptical; who wouldn't? "I'm Jane, the one you talked to. Professor Garrison is quite elderly, but still sharp as a tack. When he found out someone had been asking about him, he was adamant I reach out."

Seth pulled the envelope with the photo and postcards out of his bag. "I know this is a long shot," he said, handing her the picture, "but do you think the shorter man could be him?"

Jane looked at the picture, tapping it with a multicolored fingernail. "It's possible. He spent a lot of his youth traveling around the area. He talks about it quite a bit, and I know it informed his poetry. What else do you have?"

Seth felt protective of the postcards; after being hidden for so long, they deserved a little privacy. "Some letters, but they're personal. I would rather give them directly to him."

Jane scrutinized him, obviously trying to make some sort of decision. She sighed, then picked up the phone and dialed a number. With her hand covering the receiver, she asked, "Do you mind stepping into the hall for a moment?"

From the hallway he could hear her talking quietly. Instead of eavesdropping Seth wandered the length of the hallway examining various billboards, awards, and notifications. Class must ended, because soon a flood of humanity jammed the hallways, chattering and shuffling papers, heading toward more classes or out for the day. Sunlight streamed in through large windows lining the outer wall. The clouds had given way to afternoon sunshine, and everything—flowers, trees, even the lawn—seemed to glow in the aftereffects of the earlier rain.

"Are you ready?"

Seth started; he hadn't heard Jane come up next to him. "Uh, yeah. Where am I going?"

Jane went with him. She was Theodore Garrison's self-appointed watchdog, and she wasn't letting him face Seth alone.

But, she said, he'd been insistent that he meet Seth and see the documents.

Theodore lived in a pleasant retirement community near Green Lake, about twenty minutes from campus. He used a walker to get around, but was by no means slow. He led Seth and Jane to a little courtyard shaded by Japanese maple and tall potted bamboo. It was pleasant. Seth wondered that an old English professor could afford such a nice retirement.

"May I see the photograph Jane told me about?" Theodore asked without preamble. "No point in pussyfooting around with small talk; I'm too old for that nonsense." Jane snorted and rolled her eyes at his manners.

They sat along two benches that were positioned beside a small pond filled with koi and lilies. The colorful fish swam hopefully to the top of the water. Seth handed the entire envelope over, watching as the old man tenderly opened it, his hands trembling, and took out the contents. He thumbed gently through the postcards before stopping to stare at the photograph for a long time, tracing a thumb along Owen Penn's face. If Seth had any doubts, they were gone. This was the Theodore they had been looking for. And not so far away from Skagit, either. He wished he'd waited for Sacha.

"He saved these?" Theodore asked no one in particular. "I stopped writing when my letters were returned with no forwarding address. Tell me how you found them?"

Seth found himself relating the story of meeting Sacha and kind of inviting himself to help with the Warrick renovations. How Sacha had found the boxes in the wall and they had both gone to Winthrop and then Wenatchee, following the trail of Owen Penn. He told him about Pearl, that she was still alive. About Owen Addison, who, it seemed, was more than a namesake to his great-uncle.

Hardest was relating what Pearl believed, that Theodore had been paid to leave Owen. That Owen had died miserable and alone. Tears rolled unchecked down the old man's face, dripping into the intricate pattern of wrinkles formed from a long life. Jane went to his side, putting an arm around him for comfort.

When Seth finished, the three of them sat in silence for a long time. Birds chirped, bamboo rustled with the breeze, a dog barked and someone shushed it, the fish continued swimming around hoping for a treat. Seth didn't know what to do. He sat listening to the sounds of the neighborhood and waited for Theodore to compose himself.

"I was a young fool. Pearl, bless her, isn't far from wrong. Their father did give me money to leave Owen alone. To leave. I was so young, both in body and spirit. When I met Owen I was merely fifteen, but I told Owen I was twenty. He was so beautiful."

His eyes were either still teary or watery; Seth was betting teary at this point. "His father accused me of seducing Owen away from God and his family. I did. At least from his family. I'd never seen anyone like him before. He was magical in form and thought. Kind beyond words. It was both soothing and the crackle of an electric storm when we were together. We finished each other's sentences, had similar dreams. He would read poetry to me; his voice alone..." He trailed off.

"I'd forgotten about this photo. Someone from one of the Forest Service camps took it with my camera. I had worked my way west cooking and doing odd jobs in the camps. Or being a hobo. It was quite a romantic adventure for a young man."

He waved a hand. "None of it matters now. I took the money Father Penn gave me and went back to the east coast. I'd run away, you see, and the money meant I could go home with my head held high. Why this was important, I don't remember. Owen begged me not to go. Begged me to stay. Promised we would find a way to be together, but in the end, it was me who didn't believe."

The unadulterated anguish flowing from Theodore was almost too much for Seth to bear. The sorrow he felt for two men who clearly had been happy together but were torn apart by fear and expectation.

"May I keep this?" Theodore's voice surprised Seth from his gloomy thoughts. "I don't have much time left on this earth; it would be nice to be able to look at Owen's face again." He snorted, finally wiping his face. "I really have no business being upset after all these years. But I put him out of my mind, assuming that he'd married and gone on to live the life his father wanted." Jane hugged him tightly again. Seth shrugged. There was no good reply.

"You can keep it all. There are books as well, old mysteries and a book of poetry," Seth told him.

Because the gods hated him, or were feeling particularly mischievous, traffic was complete hell heading north that evening. Between an RV fire and several multicar collisions, traffic was backed up for miles. Seth briefly debated between sitting in traffic or stopping and having dinner. Sitting in traffic or eating first, then driving, would still get him home at the same, much later hour than he'd intended.

Plus, he didn't feel like driving yet. All he could think about was Owen slowly killing himself with alcohol while he grieved for the boy who had left him. By the time Theodore moved back to the west coast, Owen had been dead for twenty years, and Theodore had been afraid to look for him anyway. Afraid he would find him married to a woman, surrounded by a happy family. Theodore himself never married, using his students instead as proxy family, Jane the most recent and the last.

She'd tearfully embraced Seth when he dropped her back at campus. He left her one of his brochures with his phone number and email before leaving.

THIRTY-FOUR

SETH

The two of them lay on their backs with sleeping bags as a cushion, under the starry June night sky. They'd driven Sacha's huge truck off the highway onto a Forest Service road to make their own campground. Seth was planning some outdoor man-sex; they did not need an audience.

Sacha didn't need an audience; Seth wasn't opposed.

Seth couldn't believe Sacha had never been camping for fun before. Sure, he'd slept in the rough when he was in basic training, but had never built a campfire for s'mores or spent hours making the perfect tarp enclosure. There really had been no need for tarps, as the chance of rain was zero, but Seth crafted one anyway, getting a lot of unsolicited advice from Sacha. If it did rain, they were prepared.

"This is nice," Sacha said, making it clear he was surprised.

Seth chuckled, rolling so he could put his head on Sacha's chest. "It *is* nice. Thank you for coming."

There was a quiet snort. "Somebody needs to keep their eye on you. I nominate myself."

Seth didn't bother pretending to be put off. "I think my days of picking up strange men and bringing them home are over."

"Damn right."

"Speaking of change, you didn't swear once around Pearl."

The wedding had been the day before, and true to his word, Owen Penn had escorted his great-aunt.

"I can actually control myself. Besides, I like her."

"Me too." Seth took a deep breath. "I wish it had turned out differently for Owen and Theodore."

"Yeah. It turned out differently for us, though."

"Mmm."

"I never thought I could be happy. I certainly never thought I'd meet... some weirdo who would end up being everything I didn't think I could have."

Seth reached up to pinch Sacha's nipple. "Nice."

"Gimme a fucking break," Sacha groused, wrapping his arms around Seth and holding him tight, "I've lived my whole life with my head down." Seth started to protest. Sacha squeezed him hard enough to make him squeak. "Then you showed up. You didn't let me scare you off or intimidate you or—" He broke off, considering his words. "You found a part of me that I'd hidden for so long I'd forgotten it existed. You reminded me I didn't simply have to survive; I could live." He felt a kiss on the top of his head. "I'm saddened life didn't end better for Owen and Theodore too, but... but maybe we can work together on living a better life out of respect for theirs? Does that make sense? Being free to lie here holding you in my arms, it's a gift. Fuck, I am shit with words."

"I think we're doing pretty good."

They were. In April they had officially moved in together. The caveat being Sacha had wanted to move into a new place. Luck shone on them, and they found a little bungalow not far from Adam and Micah's. They'd signed the rental papers and moved in a week later. Seth didn't care about the house; the yard was a canvas waiting for him to build it into a masterpiece. And he would.

Sacha had opened the Warrick Studios to much acclaim and already had a waiting list of small business owners, artists, and other creative types who needed only a small amount of office space. Or only needed it a few times a month.

The Warrick was gorgeous now that it was finished. Sparkling white granite façade; floor-to-ceiling windows on the main floor that flooded the interior with natural light, making the hardwoods shine. Sacha had found an antique bannister and retrofitted it for the staircase. Seth surprised him with an ancient safe they placed under the stairs. Sacha took the door off and used the two shelves to display the dime-store novels they'd found in the wall so many months before.

"Our memorial to Owen," Sacha commented. Jane had emailed Seth in March, informing him that Theodore Garrison had passed away in his sleep. Seth hoped Theodore found Owen waiting for him; they deserved some kind of cosmic happiness. She returned the book of poetry, saying Theodore had wanted Seth to have it. With reverence and sadness, Seth placed the small volume in the safe along with the garish penny-dreadfuls Owen had collected. A final resting place of sorts.

THIRTY-FIVE
SACHA

Sacha stared up at the brilliant night sky, Seth quiet in his arms. A shooting star flashed across, followed by a second a moment later. He smiled. Wrapping a hand around the back of Seth's neck, he pulled him in for a possessive kiss. Seth met him equally, lips open, wet and hot against each other, tongues tangling.

Touching like this under the stars was fucking amazing. Pushing harder, he rolled on top of Seth, reveling in the responsiveness of Seth's strong body beneath his own, still unable to believe it was his to touch, caress, love.

Grinding his hips down, he thrust his erection against Seth. Both of them were wet, their cocks sliding easily against each other. Seth set everything off inside him, skin against skin, more than he'd ever dreamed of.

Because he couldn't wait, Sacha reached between their bodies, grasping both of their cocks in his hand. Seth moaned against his mouth, rutting harder, fucking into Sacha's hand and against his cock. He bit, mostly gently, at the base of Seth's neck, having quickly learned that spot was a landmine of sensation for his lover. Sure enough, Seth's hands, which had been at Sacha's shoulders, moved down to grip Sacha's ass, while his legs splayed wide, allowing Sacha more freedom to move his hips and his hand.

"Fucking fuck," Seth moaned as he came, the warm liquid spilling into Sacha's hand, onto Seth's abdomen. Slick and heat had Sacha losing what restraint he harbored. Quietly, he came too, groaning against Seth's ear, shaking to his core with the intensity of his orgasm.

"I love you, Seth Culver." If there was one thing in his life he was sure of, as sure as the sun rose every morning, he was sure of his love for Seth. It buoyed him up and carried him through each day.

He rolled onto his back, lumpy ground and rocks be damned. Seth followed, twining around him like a vine. The stars shone down, their brilliance breathtaking.

"I love you too," Seth whispered back.

* * *

BE SURE TO KEEP READING, Miguel and Nate are up next in River Home. When Miguel's past comes back to haunt him will FBI Nate Richardson be able to protect him and will he lose his heart in the process?

* * *

DID you jump in at the middle? Storm Season is the first Accidental Roots novel, read it now.

* * *

DON'T MISS another first in series, Conspiracy Theory. Detective Niall Hamarsson remembers Mat Dempsey, but he'd prefer to avoid him. Too bad Mat is one piece of his past Niall can't escape...will Mat be able to coax Niall in from the cold?

AFTERWORD

Post-Script dedication:

As Sure As The Sun is dedicated in part to my Great-Uncle Owen. While he did not live exactly the life described here, he lived a great deal of it. Upon my grandmother's death in 2001 (she would have been Pearl's age) I found letters between her grandfather (Big Daddy) and her husband about Owen. Big Daddy was at wits end with his son by the end of the 1920's. He forced Owen to marry, one son was born during this time but eventually the marriage fell apart after he continually lost jobs due to 'drink and carousing' and Big Daddy committed Owen into a sanitarium. Owen died alone, sometime in the 1940's. My grandmother loved him dearly and always referred to him with great affection, a woman before her time, she didn't care that he was gay she only remembered that he was a kind and generous soul. I want Owen to have had a better/happier life, since I couldn't make that happen *As Sure As The Sun* was born.

EK

MIGUEL EXTRA

EXTRA CONTENT

Spoiler/Content alert: This extra scene begins after Spring Break and ends during Buck and Joey's wedding. I debated including this but in the end decided readers would like to know Miguel a little better and, we've all made choices we regret....

Miguel wondered where he had gone wrong. He'd been waiting three years for the other shoe to drop and only recently had managed to force the underlying worry out of his mind. Looking back over the past few days, even weeks, he couldn't think of anything specific that Buck would need to talk to him about. What had he fucked up now?

Nervously rubbing the scar along his palm, he paced the tiny office where Buck kept the shop records and gently informed customers that their beloved vehicle was bound for the scrap heap. Kevin peeked in. "You want lunch? Dom's ordering from that new Thai place." His cheeks held a faint blush. Miguel mentally rolled his eyes; the kid was cute, but even he had some standards, and taking advantage of a little crush was, well, against them. Kevin looked over his shoulder. "Oh, hey, Buck, sorry." Kevin moved out of the doorway to be replaced by Buck.

Buck was Miguel's best friend. There was nothing he wouldn't do for him. Buck had, quite literally, saved Miguel's life. He owed Buck everything. Shutting his eyes, he took a deep breath. Maybe he could explain.

If he knew what it was.

"Walk with me?" Buck was a quirky guy. When he wanted to talk, he always asked Miguel to walk with him. Maybe he'd been imagining things? Fuck, he hoped everything was okay with Joey. Joey was the light of Buck's life; if he had done something... but they lived in the same house, and Miguel hadn't heard any fighting or raised voices when Joey was over.

Taking a right out of the small graveled parking lot, they headed toward a tiny city park tucked in between an industrial complex and a couple fast-food joints. The park was as old as the city, and aside from the rose garden on Old Charter it had the biggest display of specialty roses in the area. Miguel thought it was funny that the park had been surrounded by a small industrial neighborhood. It was kind of a secret that locals knew about.

Buck broke the silence as they stepped from the hot dirty sidewalk to the grounds of the park. "You know you are my best friend?" Buck looked sideways at Miguel, so he nodded. "Okay, I, uh," Buck's voice broke and he stopped speaking.

Miguel took a good long look at his friend. Buck's skin had a weird pallor to it; he was also sweating. "Are you feeling okay? I think maybe you need to sit down." Grabbing Buck's enormous biceps, he tried steering him to a nearby bench. Buck resisted the attempt.

"I'mgonnaskjoeytomarryme."

"What? Slow down and say *what* again?" Miguel was pretty sure he had understood but needed to be perfectly clear.

Buck took a deep breath and wavered a little. This time Miguel made him sit down on a little bench and put his head between his knees. Then, because sometimes when Buck was in a state he needed touch, Miguel wrapped himself around the larger man. Miguel figured Buck had been starved for any kind of touch as a kid, and now his body (and psyche) needed it sometimes the way a diabetic needed insulin. And, frankly, it wasn't any hardship to touch all that muscle. Miguel benefitted from this too; he missed the feeling of touching a strong man, even though what he felt for Buck wasn't sexual.

A few more deep breaths and Buck had himself back under control. "I'm going to ask Joey to marry me."

Something inside Miguel swelled; pride, he suspected. Buck had come so far since they'd met, especially in the past few months. Once excessively shy and unsure of himself, Buck was now part of a healthy and loving relationship, spreading his wings. A stupid metaphor, but it had been a little like witnessing the birth of a butterfly—not that Miguel had personally witnessed anything of the sort. Where he grew up, the kids were more likely to pull the wings off of them.

No longer did Buck shrink from random physical contact, hide in his office for days, or spending the weekends with the cars he was refurbishing. He hadn't been a complete hermit, but he hadn't gone out of his way to interact with anyone but Miguel until Joey burst into his life.

"You know he's going to say yes, right? The man adores you; as far as he's concerned you get up extra early every morning in order to make sure the sun is coming up for him."

"Will you be my best man?"

Sound ceased. Miguel's heart stopped beating for a moment. He returned to the living and blinked. "What did you say?"

"I want you to be my best man."

Sagging against the back of the bench, Miguel contemplated his life choices. It was Buck's turn to peer at him.

Buck reached over and brushed something from Miguel's cheek. "What's the matter?"

Miguel's heart squeezed so hard it physically hurt. He looked away from Buck's questioning gaze. The long moment's quiet faded, and now everything was loud. Miguel was raw and exposed under the overly warm June sunshine.

When he could speak without fear of breaking down, he managed to get the words out. "Why me? I'm nobody."

Buck looked angry. "I'm asking you because you're my best friend and I want you, and no one else, to stand with me."

Damn. When he put it like that. "Who is standing with Joey?"

"Why, you have a preference? What's wrong with you?" Buck was still scowling.

"I'm not good enough," Miguel forced out, trying to make his friend understand. "I'm a no-good drifter you took in out of pity. I'm pretty good with cars..." The look on Buck's face said he didn't believe him. Refused to understand.

Passersby would probably have thought the two of them were lovers, the way Buck took Miguel's face between his large warm palms, looking him in the eye. "If I wanted someone else to be my best man I would have asked someone else. But I don't. So I didn't. Am I making myself clear?" Miguel nodded. "Let's try this again; Miguel, will you please be my best man?" Miguel found himself nodding again. Buck dropped his hands, and Miguel missed their warmth.

"I still want to know who you think Joey's going to ask."

Buck rolled his eyes, "I have no idea. But Kon will be the ring bearer." Miguel smiled because that kid was cute. Miguel felt a sense of comradeship with him, even though the Russian foster child had no idea that Miguel had grown up in the system as well—although Miguel had been nowhere near as lucky as Kon. Not even close.

Of course Joey said yes.

Pandemonium reigned at the engagement barbeque. Joey leapt into Buck's arms, accidentally letting go of Xena's leash. Kon panicked at the sight of his beloved dog dashing off and heading directly to the closest table laden with chips, salads, burger buns, and assorted snacks.

Racing after the dog in a desperate attempt to catch the end of Xena's leash, Kon tripped over his own feet and fell flat on his face. Sterling Bailey tried to help him, but Kon wouldn't be comforted until Ira, from the Booking Room, came over and started consoling him in Russian. Letting go of Joey after a passionate kiss, Buck stood and went to the boy. Kneeling next to him, he quietly asked Kon if he would be willing to carry the rings for them. *Everyone* started crying then.

Meanwhile, the dog, obeying an unheard command, dropped and sat, still as a statue, waiting next to the cake Maureen James had placed on the table. Written on the top in beautiful curlicue writing was "Buck and Joey, Together Forever." Gah, it was so sweet Miguel's teeth hurt.

If he was going to be honest with himself, and Miguel prided himself on honesty, most especially self-honesty, he was jealous of the men around him finding happiness. If he were happy, the sweetness wouldn't bother him.

Leaning against a picnic table, he watched the interactions of the partygoers, feeling extremely single. Joey and Buck of course were holding hands, tearfully accepting congratulations. Sterling was being fed potato chips by the hot young FBI agent, laughing when Weir leaned in and whispered a secret in his ear. Even Adam Klay, who Miguel knew slightly, was smiling and leaning against his boyfriend.

He couldn't shake the oppressive feeling of loneliness and was glad Sara was in Seattle. If she had been at Ed's party they would have ended up in bed again. Miguel did love Sara and, obviously, found her attractive, but it wasn't right. They weren't right together, and they both knew it. Sighing, Miguel dug up a happy face for his friends before rejoining the celebration.

The Following Spring:

Miguel eyed himself in the mirror. A stranger stared warily back at him. Joey and Buck had, thankfully, gone for fairly casual when it came to wedding attire, but since Miguel mostly wore coveralls from the shop or one of a few pairs of worn jeans and a couple T-shirts he'd had for years, he felt out of place. He'd never had a need to dress up. When he did go out— which hadn't happened for a while—he would end up undressed anyway.

The khaki shorts and white linen shirt looked good, but he felt like a stranger. He rolled up the sleeves of the shirt and half-heartedly tucked the shirttails into his shorts. Dressing up only changed the outside. No matter how much he loved Joey and Buck, nice clothes couldn't change who he was or wasn't.

At the window he stared down into Maureen James's backyard. It was huge. From their guest list it appeared the grooms had invited the entire town to witness the blessed event. After spending the entire summer making the yard into an oasis for their guests, the big day was finally here, and so was everyone Miguel knew and many he didn't. Joey was the youngest of six kids, and his brother's and sisters' families alone were taking up half the guest space. Sisters', anyway; Miguel had seen no sign of family for the older brother. Mark, he thought.

A knock on the door startled him, and Buck stuck his head in before Miguel answered. "You okay? You've been up here for a while."

They'd talked more since Buck asked him to stand with him when he married Joey, but Miguel still felt unworthy. He literally was *no one*, a broken man, one who hid it well. Everything he had in his life, he owed to Buck. He would be nothing if Buck hadn't taken pity on him over three years ago; he'd probably be dead.

All the belongings he'd had left had been crammed in an old army-surplus duffel. He was soaked from the near-constant drizzle and hungry because he was quite literally penniless. Miguel had spotted Swanfeldt's Auto Body and Repair and decided to try one last time. He would cross the street, ask for the owner or manager, and hope they needed someone. If not, he would be forced to contact his ex. He almost preferred death from exposure to asking Justin for help.

His lifeline had come in the form of Buck, who didn't hesitate. He'd tugged Miguel inside the shop, handed him a spare pair of coveralls, showed him where the tools were, and said, "Show me what you can do." Miguel had, and three years later he was still there.

"I'm seriously nervous."

"I'm the one getting married; what have you got to be nervous about?" Buck was teasing. He knew Miguel was two seconds away from running screaming out the front door. "Come on, let's get this over with so I can make an honest man out of Joey."

Miguel snorted. "I think it's far too late for that." Buck crossed to where he was looking out the window, fixed Miguel's collar, and tucked the shirt in a little more. "Knock it off. I've been dressing myself for years."

"Yeah, I think that's part of the problem." What did Buck mean by that? Before Miguel could ask, Buck dropped his hand from Miguel's collar and turned to head back downstairs. "Come on, we're on in ten minutes."

Twenty minutes later, standing under the perfect September sunshine while his best friend got married, his gaze traveled across the crowd. It *was* a crowd; every seat was full. There were even people standing at the back. Buck had managed to rein Joey in, and they had gone for a simple theme. The decorations consisted of two white arches covered in flowers and tulle. Fairy lights had been strung along the back porch and around the fruit trees along the fence line. As it got dark they would begin to light up. Someone, Miguel wasn't sure who, had made a song list that would start as the grooms walked together from the ceremony.

Insects were humming and buzzing in the shimmering heat, and a trickle of sweat snuck down his spine. He twitched, trying to stay focused on the ceremony. A movement caught his eye. At the back of the crowd, set aside from most of the back-row stragglers, was someone he had never seen before. Miguel knew he hadn't, because there was no way he would ever have forgotten.

Inappropriately, Miguel felt a stir of attraction for the stranger that distracted him from the heat of the afternoon. From his viewpoint the man looked taller than average; he had short dark hair with bangs that fell adorably across his forehead into his left eye. His shoulders were slightly hunched, as if he was trying to hide or felt out of place.

"Psst. Dude." Miguel snapped back to attention, embarrassed to have been caught staring. He refocused on Joey's vows. The rest of the ceremony dragged by; no offense to Buck and Joey, but if Miguel ever tied the knot he was eloping on a beach after a five-minute service. When he looked back out into the audience, the stranger had disappeared. Damn.

Finally Miguel was watching the newlyweds walk down the center aisle hand in hand with Kon leading the way. The audience stood, clapping and throwing rose petals along their path. Once they had started the receiving line (a tradition which had to be explained to him), Miguel headed straight for the liquor. He needed a head start.

Deciding to forgo the punch bowl, Miguel instead went straight for the bar and proceeded to get quietly and thoroughly drunk. All the time chatting with people who, if they really knew him, wouldn't stop to scrape him off the street. There were FBI agents, professors from the university, and a bunch of Joey's family, all of whom seemed to be doctors or lawyers. And him. Car mechanic. Foster kid. Whitewashed Mexican. Maybe Mexican. Didn't really know.

He tried to keep his eye out for the man at the back of the crowd, but between chatting and drinking he didn't see him. Too bad; considering the kind of wedding this was, there was a high chance that the man was gay. Or bi, like him, although many people seemed oddly unwilling to admit to being bi these days. Like it was cheating or something. Well, fuck that.

Oh, and fuck *that*. Miguel saw a tall figure slide sideways through the French doors leading to Maureen's kitchen. The stranger caught Miguel's gaze before disappearing.

"Excuse me, restroom." Miguel gestured with his champagne glass. When had he started on champagne? At this point he couldn't bring himself to care about the consequences—of the champagne or anonymous sex. Putting the glass down on one of the many decorated tables dotting the yard, he headed inside.

The older guests were seated in the living room out of the heat, and there was no sign of his quarry. Miguel hazarded a wave and continued on his quest. His plan, such as is was, entailed pretending he didn't know someone was in the bathroom and going from there. The bathroom off the kitchen had a line, so he passed it by. There was another down the hallway near Kon's room and a third up the first flight of stairs. Upstairs it was.

The crystal knob turned easily under his hand.

"Oh, hey, I didn't realize anyone was in here."

Startled amber eyes were the first thing Miguel saw. Champagne, sweet white wine, and several shots of tequila kept him moving forward. The stranger was tall and elegantly formed. Even his eyebrows were elegant slashes drawn above those incredible eyes. Miguel stared for a dangerously long time into their depths.

"Uh, what are you doing in here?"

"Following you." Miguel moved closer, catching the waistband of the other man's shorts. "You are the most beautiful person I have ever seen. Can I kiss you?"

Miguel's drunken mind translated the sputtering that followed to *Please, yes*. So he did. A quiet instinct warned him to take care. He stood on his toes, using his other hand to pull the man's face closer to his own, lightly rubbing his nose under his earlobe. God, he smelled good. Miguel breathed in the scent along the man's face and back toward his ear before lightly dragging his lips along the man's cheek as he returned to his mouth.

There was no further protest from... "What's your name?" His question startled the man, but he answered without pulling away. "Owen."

"Owen, I'm going to kiss you and then fuck you." Owen's long body shivered against his, generating a visceral reaction from Miguel. Jesus. If it was like this when they didn't know each other, hadn't done more than touch for thirty seconds, what was sex going to be like? He couldn't wait to find out.

Strong hands, warm and solid, dropped to his shoulders before skimming down his back to land on Miguel's ass, pulling him close enough to feel a hefty erection pressing against his hip. Miguel had no problem showing affection with his body. He loved the feel of skin against his own, of heat and breath, the wet of tongues and slide of precome from cocks. He loved it all. Owen shuddered against him again, and Miguel almost lost it right there.

"Come on." Grabbing Owen's hand, he opened the bathroom door. The hallway was clear; none of the other wedding guests had ventured upstairs. The faint sound of music floated up from the backyard where Buck and Joey were probably having a first dance. Praying that they wouldn't be missed, he dragged Owen up to the third floor, to

Joey's room where he'd changed earlier. He would ask forgiveness later.

Miguel pushed Owen through the door and shut it firmly behind them. The air in the small room was stifling, the covers on Joey's bed rumpled, and Miguel nearly tripped over a discarded dress shoe. Desperate for more touch, Miguel pressed his lips against Owen's again, bringing their chests together. Owen moaned, nearly snapping Miguel's resolve to last longer than three minutes. It had been a dry spell since Sara.

Miguel licked at Owen's mouth, drawing a succulent lower lip into his own mouth, nipping it, chasing his tongue. Miguel tried unbuttoning Owen's shorts, but his fingers wouldn't cooperate. Their panting filled the small room. Miguel tasted coffee and liquor on Owen's tongue. Owen pushed Miguel's hands away impatiently, unbuttoning and pushing his shorts down over his hips, dragging his underwear along with them. Miguel was momentarily mesmerized by the sight of Owen's cock, erect, slick from precome. His mouth watered.

Lips crashed down on his, demanding entrance. This wasn't lazy kissing any longer; this was crass, hard, passionate. Spit coated their lips. Miguel was going to have beard burn, he thought; wondered if he cared. Whatever Miguel was feeling, Owen felt it too. Everything was a haze of touch, feel, press, lick, nose pressed into the crook of Owen's neck while Owen licked the shell of his ear. They were both slick with sweat from the heat of the attic room. His spine buzzed with sexual awareness, the promise of orgasm, of dizzying completion.

Miguel fell backward onto the bed, and Owen followed, his hard, rough, taut body creating a havoc in Miguel he hadn't felt in too long. Sex was one of Miguel's favorite things—okay, *the* favorite thing. Skin against skin, soft touch or rough, the scent of arousal—which in this moment was heady; he was drunk on it. Sounds too, like the ones they were both making as they rubbed frantically against each other. His balls tightened. Miguel fought it; he wanted this to last.

"I don't, I can't—" Owen whispered into the ear he was mauling. "Wha-what do you want?"

"I want you to fuck me." Miguel rolled onto his stomach and realized he was still mostly dressed. Struggling to sit up, he pulled off the damp linen shirt, probably losing a few buttons in the process. Owen grabbed his hips from behind, pressing himself against Miguel. His fingers failed him again. Owen pulled Miguel against his bare chest and stuck his free hand down the front of the offending shorts to grab his cock. Miguel's entire self shorted out; he thrust mindlessly into Owen's grip, loving the slick of his precome as Owen held him, pumping him.

He was helpless against the onslaught. When Owen slid his fingers behind Miguel's balls, the world exploded. Miguel came, ribbons of come shooting across his chest and Owen's fist, the bed. His body shuddered, cresting, then came to rest. He felt like he'd been in a car wreck. But a good one. Or he was a piece of driftwood adrift in a storm, then washed ashore and...

"Can I, still?" Owen's deep voice filtered through the haze of the best orgasm he'd had, maybe ever.

"Yeah, fuck me." He would be sensitive, it could hurt, but he wanted it anyway.

Owen pulled his shorts down around his knees. Miguel leaned forward, barely able to support himself on his elbows, ass in the air, forehead pressed against Joey's comforter cover. Joey was going to kill him if he ever found out.

A soft whisper from behind him. "I don't, uh, have any protection."

"Bedside table." There was no way Joey didn't have stuff, three floors up from his mother and Kon forbidden from the upstairs. Shutting his eyes against reality, he heard the drawer open, a quiet rustle, and then the wrinkling sound of a condom wrapper being opened. Thank fuck.

There was little finesse with the rest of the encounter. Owen parted his ass cheeks and pushed into him, gently enough at first, but his groans killed Miguel and he pushed back against Owen, needing him inside. Owen moaned and cursed. He grabbed Miguel's hips, yanking them against his own, and began to pound into him in earnest. His balls—Miguel hadn't seen them, but they must be damn big—slapped against the back of Miguel's ass, sending a tingle shooting up his spine.

He lay there, face in the mattress, and took it. Because that's what he craved: to be taken, to be completely gone from himself. Owen muttered and cursed; he swept his hands up and down Miguel's back before grabbing his shoulders, pulling him upright, and ramming his cock in as far as he could. It was heaven. Miguel wanted it all. Wanted more. Wanted. Owen grunted and shook. He held Miguel down hard on his pulsing cock before sighing and letting him sink back onto the bed.

When Miguel woke, he was alone in the room and Joey James-Swanfeldt was standing at the side of the bed, hands on his hips, an undefinable expression on his face. At least the covers had been pulled over him. Because if he felt like a loser most of the time, right then he felt like nothing but a fuck.

END.

Don't fret Miguel will get his HEA, maybe with Owen, maybe not.....<3
Spring 2018....

A THANK YOU FROM ELLE

If you enjoyed As Sure as the Sun, I would greatly appreciate if you would let your friends know so they can experience Sacha, Seth, and the rest of the gang as well. As with all of my books, I have enabled lending on all platforms in which it is allowed to make it easy to share with a friend. If you leave a review for As Sure as the Sun, or any of my books. on the site from which you purchased the book, Goodreads or your own blog, I would love to read it! Email me the link at elle@ellekeaton.com

* * *

Keep up-to-date with new releases and sales, *The Highway to Elle* hits your in-box approximately every two weeks, sometimes more sometimes less. I include deals, freebies and new releases as well as a sort of rambling running commentary on what *this* author's life is like. I'd love to have you aboard! I also have a reader group called the Highway to Elle, come say hi!

ABOUT ELLE

Elle hails from the northwest corner of the US known for, rain, rain, and more rain. She pens the Accidental Roots series, the Hamarsson and Dempsey series, and Home in Hollyridge all set in the Pacific Northwest. Elle is chief cook and bottle washer, the one always asking 'where are my keys and/or wallet' and 'why are there cats?' (This question not yet answered).

Elle *loves* both cats and dogs, Star Wars and Star Trek, pineapple on pizza, and is known to start crossword puzzles with ballpoint pen.

Thank you for supporting this Indie Author,

Elle

Made in the USA
Monee, IL
11 March 2021